THE PALACE

CHATEAU #4

PENELOPE SKY

HARTWICK PUBLISHING

ONE
FORGIVENESS

Melanie

We fell back into our old lives.

Laundry. Dishes. Cooking. Getting coffee at the café down the street.

But we barely talked to each other.

It seemed like neither one of us was ready to share the details of our separation. She had been a slave at the camp, witnessing unspeakable things, and I had been in a palace, living a life of luxury with expensive clothes and a butler.

My old clothes didn't quite fit me the way they used to because Gilbert was right. I'd gained some weight. My old clothes were also cheap, so they didn't fit me the way the custom designer clothing did. The guest bedroom was uncomfortable because the sheets were low quality—and there wasn't a man next to me.

A few days later, we had breakfast together. I sat on the stool at the kitchen island while she stood across from me. Now that Raven was no longer at the camp, she ate whatever she wanted. Right now, she whipped up fluffy pancakes and fries.

I ate across from her and sipped my coffee, which had tones of pumpkin, nutmeg, and cinnamon. It was February now, but it still felt like December, the month when we were taken. My thoughts drifted to Fender often, wondering if he was sitting at his desk in his office, shouting at someone in French or just sitting there staring at the fire.

Or was he thinking about me?

Raven cut into her pancakes but didn't take a bite. "You can talk to me...if you want to talk about it."

I kept my eyes on my coffee, the dollop of cream sitting on top. "I don't want to talk about it." Those dark eyes were in my dreams. Sometimes, I felt big hands grip me around the waist, but it was just my imagination. There were times I smelled him, but I wondered if a bit of scent was still on me, even though I'd showered a couple times.

Raven dropped it.

"Are you okay?"

"I'm fine."

I knew she wasn't, but I let that go. "Are you going to see Magnus again?" He hadn't returned to the apartment. They seemed to say farewell, and that was it.

"No." She continued to eat.

"He helped you so many times...and that's just it?"

"What else should happen?"

"It just seemed like there was something there...between you."

She dipped her pancake into her pool of syrup and brought it to her mouth.

"Did you sleep with him?"

She sighed at the question but answered anyway. "Yeah, a couple times."

"And you seem sad that he's gone..."

She lowered her fork to the plate. "I'm forever grateful that he saved us both. He's a good man in a bad situation. But what kind of future could I have with someone like that? How could I ever want to be with someone who participates in something that's so morally wrong...?" She shook her head and bowed toward her food. "Never going to happen."

I dropped my gaze and looked at my own plate, feeling a flood of guilt for the complicated feelings I had for the boss —the man responsible for it all. As much as it hurt to leave him, I knew I made the right decision. I would miss him for a long time. Maybe I would always miss him. But Raven already hated so much about me, if I ever confided those feelings to her, she would hate me even more.

"Are you going to go back home?"

My eyes lifted to hers, the question striking a chord within me. This apartment didn't feel like home, and my old apartment in America definitely didn't feel like home. Home was in a palace outside Paris, with a man who marched around the house in nothing but sweatpants. "I'm not leaving you." I shook my head. "I'm not leaving Paris. This is my home now." I understood Raven had come here just to get away from me, but now I would never let her go, not after I'd lost her so many times.

Raven stared at me, her eyes studying my face.

The emotion bubbled up inside me, all the regret and remorse. I'd spent my time reflecting on the person I was, and once I realized how terrible I had been, I never wanted to be the same again. I wanted to be better. I wanted to be like my sister. Before I could beg for forgiveness, she provided it.

"I forgive you."

I inhaled a deep breath, the weight floating away like birds off a branch, a closure to this horrible chapter in our lives. "I know I've been so terrible to you since Mom died. I'm so sorry, Raven." Tears started to drip like a leaky faucet. "But I'm a different person now. I'll get a job, get my own apartment, be independent—"

"Melanie, it's okay."

"It's not okay. All I've been doing since we were captured is thinking about how I treated you. You know the reason I came here in the first place?" The knob of the faucet turned, and more tears fell. "Because I knew you moved here to get away from me, and I resented you for it. I was so angry that you moved all the way across the world to get away from me...because I'm so horrible. But I am a horrible person—was a horrible person—and that's not me anymore. I'll be more like you."

"Melanie." Her voice stayed soft despite what I'd just confessed—as if she already knew. "I don't want you to be like me. I want you to be like you. Some growth is fine. It's appreciated. But don't be somebody else. Be the best version of yourself."

Tears still streaked down my face as I gave a nod. "Thank you...for forgiving me." I needed it like air, and all this time, I'd been holding my breath, waiting for that gulp of air that would release the tension on my lungs. "Thank you..."

I SPENT the day looking for a job, searching for something in a touristy spot where they'd want to hire someone who barely spoke French. I knew a bit from Gilbert and my time with Fender, but being able to say I had a perfect cunt wouldn't land me a job anywhere.

The manager at a café a few blocks away agreed to give me a job, even though I'd never made a cup of coffee in my life, and I was grateful that someone took a chance on a dumb American girl.

When I came home, Raven was there. "I got a job."

She was on the couch in front of the TV, and she immediately turned to give me a puzzled look. "What? Where?"

"Café Rome. It's a block over." I sat on the other couch.

"But you don't speak French."

"I know a little bit, and it's a tourist spot, so most people speak English anyway."

"Or the guy just thought you were pretty." She turned back to the TV.

The manager couldn't stop staring at me, but it wasn't the way Fender looked at me. It was more sleazy than romantic. It was more pathetic than strong. Another man would never look at me that way as long as I lived. "I start next week, so I'll be able to pay half the rent."

Raven turned back to me, wearing a serious expression, like my new job was the last thing on her mind. "I'm going to go to the police."

I gave her a blank stare. "Why?"

"You know why. Are we just supposed to live our lives like we don't know what's going on out there?"

I didn't want to talk about Fender, so I didn't tell her that he had everyone in his pocket, that he dined with the president, that he owned this city and everyone in it. "Magnus really stuck out his neck for you."

She sighed. "It's not about him."

"I just don't think that's going to do anything."

"I think the police would be very interested to know that there's a labor camp out in the wilderness, Melanie."

I couldn't say his name. "Look, the boss is really powerful—"

"I don't care. I'm not going to sit here and sip my coffee like it's over. Bethany is still there. Innocent people are still there."

I knew there was no way to convince Raven otherwise, so I just let it go. "Alright."

WHEN RAVEN CAME HOME, she told me exactly what I'd expected to hear. "They acted like I was the crazy one." She threw her purse down. "Like I was making it up to get attention. But they totally know about it. It's so obvious." She immediately grabbed a bottle of wine and filled a glass.

Told you so.

"I just can't believe how fucking corrupt the police are. The fucking police." She tilted her head back and took a deep drink.

I left the couch and stood on the other side of the kitchen island. "I'm sorry."

She grabbed another glass and filled it for me.

I was used to the finest wine money could buy, so it made everything else taste like piss. It was hard to drink it, but I forced it down so I wouldn't seem snooty.

She stood with her hands on the edge of the counter, looking past me at the window behind me. She was like that for a long time, her eyes glazed over, deep in thought.

A part of me expected Fender to show up at the door and drag me back to his palace, but he never did. Magnus had asked him to let me go, and he did. He'd probably only agreed because he believed I would stay, that there was nowhere else in the world I'd rather be.

Then I chose my sister over him.

I felt guilty when I shouldn't.

She took a deep breath. "I have to go back..."

"Go back where?" I brought the glass to my lips and forced a sip.

Her only answer was a stare.

I pictured the cabins and the snow, the fire in the fireplace, the coke down the line, the faceless guards, the blood stained on the snow under the noose. I heard the howling wind against the windows, felt the ache in my legs as I walked through several feet of snow every single day to the clearing.

"And I'm not going alone."

TWO
BOTTOM OF THE BOTTLE

FENDER

The fire died down in my office. The flames were absent, and only a red smolder remained. The bottle on my desk was empty, and so was my glass. It was late into the night, and work no longer required my attention because I'd been spending all my time working—and nothing else.

Gilbert entered the study, hands behind his back, his posture upright even though it was well in the evening and he should retire to bed so he could wake up early and repeat this shit all over again. "Shall I add another log, sir?"

I gave a slight nod.

He added more firewood, got the fire going again, and then approached my desk.

I pushed the empty bottle toward him, silently asking him to bring another.

He didn't lift it off the desk. "We're out, sir. First thing tomorrow, I'll fetch more."

My eyes narrowed on his face. "Don't lie to me."

He stilled at my accusation.

My eyes shifted back to the fire. "I have enough people lying to me as it is."

Gilbert lingered, as if he expected different orders. "Sir, I think it's in your best interest to take a break. You've been hitting that bottle pretty hard the last few days..."

My eyes shifted to him. "You're disobeying my order."

He didn't flinch at the heat in my expression. "Yes. To save your life."

It was an outlandish claim. Nothing could kill me—especially not a bottle of booze. But I let it go, too drunk to argue.

Gilbert glanced at one of the armchairs that faced my desk. "Mind if I take a seat for a moment?"

He'd never asked anything like that before. My eyes studied his face, unsure if I actually heard that or imagined it in my stupor. When I realized he was serious, I gave a nod.

He lowered himself to the chair and rested his hands on his thighs, joining me as an equal for the first time. "I want you to know I'm here...even if it's just to listen." He regarded me with a concerned expression, a subtle eagerness, an innate affection that was almost familial.

I straightened at my desk and rested my arms on the surface. My forearm slid the empty bottle and glass to the side, a subtle rim of amber around the ridges at the bottom of the scotch bottle. "My brother betrayed me. My woman betrayed me. Are you next?"

He held my gaze without blinking. "Never."

"You say that now..." I shifted my gaze to the fire and watched it brighten the room once more. "But anything can change...once your interests change."

"My only interest is to serve you, sir. That will never change."

I kept my eyes on the fire and ignored him. "Goodnight, Gilbert." It was harder to sleep now than before, even with the booze in my system.

He dropped his chin for a moment but didn't rise from the chair. After a moment, he regarded me once more. "Broken bones heal. Scar tissue repairs itself. Physical pain can be masked with pills. But a broken heart...doesn't heal, doesn't repair itself, and can't be masked with pills. Sometimes, time is all that works. But even then, not always."

I turned my gaze back to him.

"I'm sorry that you have to go through this, sir. Truly."

THREE
WITH KNIVES AND FIRE

MELANIE

Our horse was tied to a branch.

It was dark with the exception of our light, and we made our way down the snow-covered path, seeing the torches gleaming in the darkness of the camp.

My heart had never pounded this hard.

I'd never been so terrified.

It was unlikely that we would save the girls and escape with no repercussions. Raven could be killed, and I wasn't certain that Fender would give me any protection, not after the way I'd left.

But it was the right thing to do.

We inched our way into the camp, and I took a torch from one of the holders on a cabin. The fire was hot against my face, making me extend it farther outward to protect my skin from the burn.

We stood together in the snow, our torches held above us, looking at the clearing and the blood that stained the snow underneath the rope. Raven stared at it for a long time, the fire illuminating her face, showing a cacophony of emotions she could never express with words.

She switched the torch to her other hand when her arm grew tired before she looked at me. "This is for freedom—for all." She turned away and headed in the direction she'd claimed.

I watched her go, knowing I had to go alone on my own path and do my part. I had to be brave for once in my life. I had to do the right thing. I gripped the wooden torch and turned into the darkness, making my way past the cabins and lighting them on fire, moving quickly, torching everything I could get access to, doing as much damage as possible before the guards realized what was going on.

It didn't take long.

The girls broke through the windows and fell onto the snow, pulling others out to safety, screaming into the night. Pandemonium took over, the fire rising from all the buildings, bringing a brightness to the camp. It didn't feel like winter anymore—but blazing summer.

When my work was done, I threw the torch into the snow.

It went out with an audible sizzle. Wisps of smoke started to rise. The snow that had surrounded it immediately melted away from the heat, and now it sank deeper into the powder.

The girls screamed as they ran from the cabins.

"This way!" I ran to the first group and guided them away from the burning cabins and to the main road, which was lit by torches to guide the way. "Follow it to the road!" I continued to run back into the camp, collect more girls, and organize the exodus.

Sometimes, I passed Raven doing the same, directing the women to safety.

When most of the girls were gone, I searched for Raven, knowing we had to run before we got caught.

But she was nowhere in sight. "Raven!" I shouted into the night, over the clamor and screams of the guards, over the loud crackle of the fire because it made a cabin collapse into burning rubble. The smoke was starting to get too thick, making it harder to breathe. "Raven!" We had to get out of there before we were caught or suffocated.

Then I found her.

The executioner had her by the throat, ready to choke her to death right there in the snow. "Raven!" I sprinted to her and noticed another girl coming from a different direction. She jumped onto his back and slammed her fist into the back of his head.

I ran faster, pulled out the knife Raven gave me, and did the bravest thing I'd ever done.

I jumped on him too—and killed him.

I killed someone.

There was no hesitation as I slammed the knife into his back, into his legs, any piece of flesh I could find. All I cared about was my sister, and I would kill anyone who got in between us.

He collapsed, his blood spilling out into the snow.

I dropped the knife, looked at my red hands, and felt disoriented from all the blood. "Raven, are you okay?"

She was already on her feet, sprinting to a collapsed cabin. "Help me!" She stuck her bare hands into the fire and tried to lift the burning wood. Her palms immediately pulled away at the heat, but she tried again anyway.

If she was willing to burn her own hands, someone important was underneath. I rushed to her aid and did the same, grinding my teeth as we lifted the heavy piece of wood a little higher, revealing Magnus underneath.

But the two of us weren't strong enough.

"Bethany, please." Raven turned to the blonde who had helped me take down the executioner.

She took one look at Magnus, not showing an ounce of pity.

Raven's hands were nearly on fire, but she didn't drop the wood.

I had to pull my hands away because it was too much. I could smell my own burning flesh.

But Raven held her position without me. "Please, Bethany. Please...not him."

Bethany still looked uncooperative, but she did it anyway.

The three of us lifted the wood off Magnus and pushed it aside.

Bethany and I immediately shoved our hands into the snow to cool the burns to our flesh.

Raven ignored the agony and hooked her arms underneath Magnus and dragged him away from the building, across the snow, and to safety.

Bethany pulled her hands out of the snow, rubbed them together, and then turned to me. "We've got to run now. They're coming."

I nodded.

She ran for it.

I lingered behind, watching Magnus rise to his feet and scream at Raven. "I fucking saved you!"

I ran to Raven on the ground and pulled her up by the hand. "Come on! We gotta go."

Magnus was livid, his anger brighter than the flames destroying the cabins that had once surrounded us. "Run... before I kill you."

She finally ran with me, her hand in mine, and didn't look back.

WE MADE it back to Paris.

Bethany was with us, packed in the car with a couple other girls we could fit. Everyone else had run, waved down cars on the road, took different routes through the countryside so the guards couldn't hunt them down.

That part of the exodus wasn't organized because we didn't have the resources of the police, so we'd just hoped for the best.

We returned to the apartment, Bethany with us, and it was strange to be back in the living room after everything that had just happened. The burning cabins were still in my eyes. My hands still ached as if they were on fire. The fear and anxiety were just as paramount.

I wondered if Fender knew yet.

Would Magnus tell him the truth...that it was Raven?

Would he tell him I was there?

When Bethany stepped into the apartment, she had a breakdown. She fell to her knees and sobbed, touching the rug under her fingertips to make sure it was real, her tears making stains on the cream color.

Raven kneeled beside her and rubbed her back. "I know...I know." She got choked up too.

It was impossible not to.

AFTER BETHANY TOOK the day to get back on her feet, we helped her reunite with her mother and daughter. They lived outside Paris, in a little town in a small cottage. Raven used the last bit of her savings to rent a car and take her there.

We walked with her to the door, watched it open, and then saw the way her mother looked at her.

It was the same way my mother used to look at me.

The way Raven had looked at me when she saw me at the top of the stairs.

They hugged, cried, and then the sweetest little girl came down the hallway. "Mommy?"

Bethany fell to her knees and cried harder than she had in our living room. "Oh, baby..."

IT'D BEEN days since we burned the camp to the ground.

Raven and I didn't talk much about it.

Like we were waiting for the repercussions.

We didn't run because we had no money and nowhere to go.

And Raven was convinced the guards hadn't seen our faces, that Magnus was the only one who knew. "He wouldn't say anything." She sat on the couch, her eyes out the window more than on the TV.

I was in the corner of the other couch, my knees pulled to my chest, watching the rain pelt the windows. "He looked pretty pissed off, Raven."

"I know...but he wouldn't." Her face was permanently somber now, the high of liberation gone the second we'd left Bethany behind. Once the action and excitement were over, she was filled with sadness. Maybe even a little guilt. "He...wouldn't."

"Even if you're right, there's only one person who could have done it." Fender would figure it out even if Magnus lied. I was the only other free person who had escaped the camp, and I certainly wouldn't have done that alone.

She stared at the TV with a blank face. "The camp doesn't exist. The girls are free. The drug enterprise doesn't exist. There's nothing for them anymore. They'll move on."

I knew Fender better than anyone. "He'll want revenge."
And I wouldn't be able to protect her this time.

"Then he can come and get it," she whispered. "I have no
regrets—and I never will."

FOUR
DISLOYAL TO LOYALTY

FENDER

In the center of the bed, I lay still.

The fire had died out, my bedroom engulfed in shadow.

My eyes were on the ceiling, the chandelier that was twenty feet above me, the crystal having a faint shine from the lights coming in from the property outside. Sleep was a luxury I didn't enjoy anymore, no matter how hard I worked, how hard I drank.

My phone rang on the nightstand.

I almost didn't answer it because this cloud of indifference hit me right in the heart. But I reached for it and answered in silence.

Chaos was loud over the line. Screams. Orders being barked out. "Stop them!"

I sat up. "What the fuck is going on?"

It was Karl, not Magnus. "We've been hit. Camp is on fire. The girls are loose." He was out of breath, like he was running from something that very moment. "We can't save the cabins. They're all torched."

I jumped out of bed and grabbed my clothes. "Where's Magnus?"

"No one's seen him..."

My heart fell into my stomach, picturing him burned alive in his cabin that he couldn't escape because he was trapped. "Who...the fuck...did this?" I'd take my men and hit them now. Kill them, their entire family, and destroy any legacy they could have had. My jacket was thrown on, and I was out the door and marching to war.

He hesitated, as if he didn't want to say. "The girl..."

I halted at the second landing and looked down at the foyer, where she'd stood just weeks ago, twisting an invisible knife into my brother's back to get what she wanted. Gilbert ran into the foyer because he must have heard me, his hair messy, dressed in his pajamas.

"Sir?" he asked, half asleep. "What's happening? I'll get the car..." He sprinted outside and shouted to one of the men.

The blood that pounded in my head began to pound everywhere, a headache for my entire body. My heart pumped as hard as it could, giving me every ounce of blood I would need for what I was about to do. My fingers squeezed so tightly that I nearly crushed the phone. "I'm on my way."

I GOT there in record time, but it didn't make a difference.

Every single cabin had been destroyed.

There was hardly any snow because it had melted from the heat of the fires. The piles of wood still burned gently because there was still more destruction to be had. The drugs had been destroyed. The clearing was unrecognizable. The camp had once been an organized congregation of cabins and civilization.

Now it was just a pile of garbage.

The only building that was spared was the stable.

Horses were fine.

The men grabbed what women they could and sent them off to our headquarters to hold in the meantime. But we'd lost over half of our labor. We'd lost a quarter of the guards in the fire.

And we lost every single ounce of the drugs.

I walked through the rubble, passed the men who'd stayed and waited for my arrival. Some of them rummaged in the cabins to see if anything could be salvaged. Others were being treated by the doctor, their broken arms wrapped in casts. Soot was all over their faces, burns on their skin.

They all looked at me as I made my entrance to the camp, aware of my presence the second I left my horse.

But my eyes were on only one man. Like the aim of a sniper, my eyes pierced his skin like fucking bullets. My gait quickened the closer I came, rage taking over my body, my mind fading because reason lost all control.

He watched me approach, his eyes strong but his posture weak, like he knew what was coming and accepted it. He had a few scratches and marks on his face, but other than that, he looked perfectly fine.

He shouldn't be fine.

When I made it to him, I stopped and stared. My jaw trembled uncontrollably because I was just so angry, so angry that there wasn't enough room inside my body to contain it all. I felt the headache pounding in my temples because the fury hadn't calmed once since I'd gotten that goddamn phone call. Tendons stretched in my hands, my flexed muscles pulled on all my bones, and I resisted the very real temptation to kill him. "Everything I built is ash—because of you."

His face tinted red because of his own anger, his eyes penetrating with rage, just as angry as I was that she did this.

"The cabins. The drugs. The men. Because of you." I got in his face. "Because you helped her. You didn't just humiliate yourself. You humiliated me." I inhaled a deep breath and kept my hands to myself even though I actually wanted to kill the only family I had left. "You lied to me—for someone who turned around and stabbed you in the back the second she had the opportunity.

His breathing intensified, like my speech angered him even more.

"She will pay for this—"

"Kill her." He said it with such conviction, spit flying from his mouth.

Nothing would give me greater pleasure than killing her, but that wasn't an option. "You will rebuild this camp, with your own money, and it will be better than it was before. You will pay me for everything I lost. I will bring that cunt back here to work for the rest of her life...since she loves it so much."

The vein in his forehead popped, like her servitude wasn't enough for what she'd done.

Even in my rage, I pitied him. Because I knew exactly how it felt to trust a woman—and have her turn on you the second the opportunity presented itself. To lie beside her every night and believe it meant something, and then for her to turn around and bite you like a fucking snake. His humiliation and pain seemed like enough punishment. His hatred was enough to make him forget about this woman who didn't deserve his obsession in the first place.

But I had to punish him. "The only reason I will spare your life is because you're my brother—and I haven't forgotten what that means to us. You've been disloyal to me, but my loyalty to you continues. I hope this moment has taught you a lesson that you'd obviously forgotten."

He dropped his gaze for the first time—ashamed.

"But I have to punish you. I wouldn't respect myself if I didn't."

He looked at me again, facing it head on.

I pulled out my knife then nodded to my guards. "Hold him down."

The guards were eager to force him into the chair, one of the few things that had survived the fire, and restrained his hands.

Magnus didn't fight. A calm defeat was in his gaze.

I held my knife at the ready. "Drop his pants."

Surprise and fear moved into his gaze when he realized what was about to happen, the punishment we reserved for the worst betrayals. But he still didn't fight. He breathed harder and let them reveal his nudity.

I stepped forward, and with a straight face, I held the knife to the flesh.

He breathed harder and harder, but he refused to look weak.

I looked at him before I sliced through the skin. "You can thank her for this next time you see her."

FIVE

A PROMISE KEPT

MELANIE

As the months passed, life became more normal.

I worked as a barista in a coffee shop, and even though I was bad at my job, the manager didn't fire me. My salary wasn't much, but it was enough to cover half the rent, along with food and utilities.

I never officially asked if I could be her roommate. It was just unspoken. After being apart from each other for so long, I couldn't imagine us wanting to be apart ever again. Raven went on a few dates, but I didn't.

It just...didn't feel right.

I thought about him often, wondering if someone had replaced me in his bed, if he was back to his French whores.

I wondered if he still thought about me. Often. Occasionally. Or not at all.

I expected retribution for what we'd done, but as the weeks trickled by, I started to wonder if it was really over. The camp was destroyed. The girls were free. It was too much work to start the business up again, so they must have chosen to retire.

I couldn't picture a man like Fender retiring.

Raven walked through the door after work, carrying a bag of takeout. "Hungry?"

No. "Sure." I left the couch and joined her at the kitchen island. We grabbed utensils and napkins then ate across from each other. "So, how'd your date go the other night?" We lived together, but there were times when we didn't see each other because of our work schedules.

She shrugged. "Eh."

"Eh doesn't sound good."

"There was just no chemistry." She sliced her fork into the lasagna and scooped it into her mouth.

I pushed my food around with my fork, still missing the food from the palace even though I'd left months ago. Food never tasted as good. Wine was never strong enough. My bed was never warm. Arousal was never the same either. Attractive men hit on me at the café all the time, but their numbers were always tossed into the wastebin.

"You haven't dated at all." She took a bite then watched me as she chewed.

Like a deer in the headlights, I froze. Accusation blanketed me, like she was trying to make a point. My eyes moved down to my food, and I sliced my fork through the layers of pasta, sauce, and cheese. "Yeah, I..." My voice drifted away when I heard the sound of heavy footfall against the hardwood in the hallway.

Raven turned at the sound, the noise immediately triggering the same memories that jumped into my mind. Even though we had been in different cabins, we'd experienced the same terror, the sound of those heavy boots approaching the front door.

I held my breath and waited for the boots to move past our door.

But they stopped right outside, the shadow of the feet visible in the crack underneath the door.

Raven immediately spun and pulled out two knives from the drawer. One was slid across the surface of the counter to me. "Just like you did with the executioner, alright?"

I gripped the knife and nodded, but I was terrified, just like I had been on that cold night.

Raven grabbed my hand and pulled me behind the kitchen island so they wouldn't see us.

They tried the knob discreetly, and then the knob turned slightly and shifted, like they were picking it the way Raven had done in the camp.

My heart pounded. The anxiety hit. But I gripped the knife tighter because I knew it would be either them or us—and it wouldn't be us.

The door opened, and their boots stepped inside. There were three of them, as far as I could tell. One gave orders in French before the other two scattered, searching for us throughout the apartment.

I peeked around the corner at the door, hoping we could sneak out of the apartment. But the guy remained in place, blocking our exit. Raven moved around me then inched around the kitchen island, getting closer and closer to him so she could lunge out and catch him off guard.

I held my knife at the ready.

She went for it and slammed her blade into his stomach.

"Ahh! Bitch!"

I sprinted around the island and jumped on him, stabbing him just the way I did with the executioner. He collapsed to the floor in a bloody mess while the other two ran to us.

"Go!" Raven shoved me out the door.

I fell but quickly got to my feet, leaving the blade behind. But then I stopped.

Two men were stationed at each end of the hallway.

Raven knocked into me and grabbed my hand to prepare to run. But when she saw what we were up against, she stilled.

The two men stepped over their dead comrade and walked into the apartment, yelling in French.

We shouldn't have gone back to the camp.

It was a mistake—a big fucking mistake.

Raven held on to me, protecting me even though there was nothing she could do.

The men marched toward us and grabbed Raven first. "Fucking cunt." They shook her by the arms then threw her down. "You thought we wouldn't come for you?" He pressed a boot to her back. "Tie up this bitch."

Ropes were bound around her wrists, right there in the middle of the hallway, like they didn't care if they were seen by anybody.

I lowered myself to the floor and lay beside her, knowing a fight was pointless so I should just cooperate.

They lifted Raven to her feet then marched her away.

No one touched me.

"Wait...what about me?" I pushed to my feet and ran after them. "Take me with you!" I wouldn't be left behind, not when she would be dragged to her fate alone. I didn't want to live without her, so I'd rather share her gruesome death. "Please!" I grabbed one of the guys and yanked him back.

He gave me a hard shove. "Bitch."

The other guard turned on him. "We don't touch her. We don't look at her. You know what the boss said." He slammed his gun into the other man's face, making his nose bleed immediately. "Leave her." They continued down the hallway and to the stairs until they were out of sight.

I fell to my knees on the floor—and cried.

I SAT on the couch in the living room, arms wrapped around my body, broken down in tears. It was dark now because I didn't turn on any lights. Raven's knife was still on the floor where she'd left it. Without my sister in that apartment, it didn't feel like home anymore. The only thing that remained was her ghost.

The dead man lay in the kitchen, his blood everywhere.

Eventually, some of Fender's men returned and took the body and cleaned up the mess. They didn't look at me. Didn't acknowledge my existence. The door was shut like nothing happened.

Now what?

I knew the location of the camp, so I could drive out there, take the long road on foot, and find her.

But there was no camp anymore.

I didn't have a clue where they'd taken her.

She might be dead right now.

Or she might be alive...and I was just wasting time.

It didn't matter how pointless it was. It didn't matter if he hurt me. He was the only option I had—so I took a cab and headed to the palace.

THE SECOND I stepped out of the cab, the driver took off. Armed men stood on the other side of the iron gate, carrying assault rifles like this was a war zone rather than the entrance of a historic mansion.

Couldn't blame him for being scared.

I was scared too.

The palace looked different in spring. The lights on his lawn showed the lively flowers and bushes. The lights were on in his bedroom on the top floor, so he was probably in bed right now or watching TV on the couch.

I was in jeans and a blouse, the attire I'd worn to work earlier that day. The clothes were cheap material with faded colors. My makeup was still on but it wasn't fresh anymore, and it wasn't perfect like it used to be. Without the luxuries he'd given me, I was ordinary.

I took a breath to steel my nerves and approached the gate. "I...I'm here to see Fender." There were half a dozen of them, all dressed in black with bulletproof vests over their clothes. They hadn't seemed so scary from my bedroom window, but up close, they were terrifying.

The men spoke to one another in French before the one in charge stepped toward the gates to speak to me. "Who are you?"

"Melanie."

"Is he expecting you?"

I shook my head. "But please, tell him it's important." Now that I was nobody, I couldn't get to him anymore. He could deny me, and that would be the end of it. I'd have to go back to that apartment alone, accepting that I would never see my sister again.

He spoke into his intercom in French. "Une femme est là pour voir le patron."

A voice spoke back. "Je n'attends personne. Son nom?"

He pressed his finger into his ear. "Melanie." Then he listened over the line, waiting for orders.

Please let me in.

He motioned to his men, and then the gate opened.

Oh, thank god.

A guy in a golf cart pulled up then nodded for me to sit beside him.

I got into the passenger seat, and we began the long drive toward the palace, around the fountain, the winding road through the gardens and brush, and approached the entrance to his mansion.

I'd been scared every moment since those men had come to the apartment. But I was far more scared now.

Because he was there.

Standing out front.

Waiting for me.

On the very bottom step, where his valet would bring his car.

Shirtless. Black sweatpants. Barefoot.

It'd been a long time since I'd last seen his face, and his expression made me breathless, because instead of just being scared...I was sad. I was sad because I'd missed his face every day that we were apart. He'd literally just taken my sister out of our apartment...and I missed him.

What the fuck was wrong with me?

His gaze was dark and intense.

But it was more than that.

It was fierce.

Angry.

Terrifying.

The golf cart came to a stop in front of him. The driver didn't look at Fender, keeping his eyes forward as he waited for me to get out so he could drive away. My breath was shaky and I was suddenly weak, but I forced myself to rise.

The driver took off the second my ass left the seat.

When the noise of the small motor faded, the only sound was the fountain behind me, the constant splash as the drops struck the surface and the lily pads that floated there. I stood in the driveway while he remained on the step, thicker and bulkier than he used to be, the cords in his arms and neck so tight they would snap.

His arms hung by his sides, one foot planted slightly in front of the other, but the fury in his heart was palpable. The energy around him burned brighter, hotter, as if he was his own sun. His chin was tilted down so he could look at me, spraying with me bullets from the barrels in his eyes.

All I could do was breathe, frozen to the spot by that menacing look.

A minute passed and he didn't speak. He didn't blink. His fury had endless fuel because he continued to stare at me like he might snap my neck.

"Please...please don't kill my sister." Every word came out shaky, without the confidence required in a negotiation. But this wasn't a negotiation. This was a plea. And if I had to get on my knees and beg, I would. "Please..." My eyes watered because the fear overwhelmed me. Life was too hard right now, and my mind wanted to regress and take me elsewhere. It wanted to put me under because this was all too much. All I'd had to do was listen to Raven that night, and none of this would have happened.

His fingers tightened until his hands were fists, and he released a loud sigh that sounded like a growl from a bear.

"I know I have no right to ask you for anything—"

"Were you there?" His voice was deep like the deepest chasm in the ocean, full of terrifying sharks and monsters that lurked beyond our sight. It was deep like a cave in the mountainside. It was deep like the lowest note on the spectrum.

My hands came together at my waist, using one to stop the shake of the other.

"Answer the question."

"I don't know what you're asking—"

"Did you fucking burn my camp to the ground?" His voice came out as a shout, barking into the night, making the palace behind him shake.

I dropped my gaze and instantly stepped back at his ferocity. I shouldn't have come. There was no point. I wanted to lie. The men hadn't identified me. Otherwise, he wouldn't have asked. But I just couldn't lie to him. "Yes." I kept my eyes down, as if a sword would slice through my neck and sever my head from my body.

Nothing happened.

I breathed.

He breathed.

Silence.

When I got the courage, I lifted my chin and met his gaze.

As if he hadn't blinked once, his expression was exactly the same, like he was already so angry he couldn't possibly get any angrier. "I'm sorry...but we had to. What you do is wrong—"

"Leave."

"I know you know it's wrong. And I know it's not you—"

"Leave, Melanie."

My eyes filled with tears, cut deep by the name he used. It wasn't *Chérie* anymore. "You're a good man. I know you are."

He turned around, his back immense with power, and walked away.

"Please don't kill her. Please...she's all I have."

He stilled at my words, standing tall with his shoulders back, his hands tightening into fists once more, knuckles turning white.

My breath stopped, my lungs full of hope.

He turned back around, and I had been wrong before; he could look angrier. A lot angrier. "The camp has been rebuilt. She will work every day to earn back every goddamn coin that I lost." His dark eyes shifted back and forth as he looked into mine, impaling me from front to back. In the darkness, he looked as if he had stepped out of the underworld, his flames invisible because they existed beneath his flesh. "Now, leave—and don't come back."

I WENT to work because I had to.

I'd be homeless if I didn't.

But I was a worse worker than I had been before, constantly distracted.

Without Raven, the apartment was unbearable. It was inhospitable, like a haunted house filled with spirits that stared at me as I slept. If Raven was condemned to work at the camp for the rest of her life, at least she would live.

But she'd probably rather die.

My only option was to take the road to the camp and try to free her myself.

They would probably expect it and send me packing.

There was no probably, no chance that I would ever succeed.

So, what was I to do? Live here in Paris forever? Go back to America and crash with a friend until I figured out what to do? How would I ever carry this guilt for the rest of my life? How would I ever move on?

Fender's face had burned in my mind every moment of every day since I'd left.

I'd never forget the way he looked at me.

He hated me.

I did what was necessary to keep my sister and myself alive, but I still felt guilty for what I'd done.

That man loved me...and now he hated me.

My eyes drifted to the window, and I stared at the apartment across the street. My neighbor was in his usual spot, on his laptop at the dining table, living a normal life of work and home...ordinary.

Don't touch her. Don't look at her. You know what the boss said.

He already knew I'd burned down the camp with Raven, but he spared me.

When I'd left with Raven, he'd let me go. *Goodbye, chérie.*

And when Raven burned down his most prized possession...

He didn't kill her.

He...didn't kill her.

I got to my feet even though I had nowhere to go. The apartment was dark because my mind was shrouded in misery. I could make out the furniture and the kitchen from the light that had been left on in the bathroom. "He kept his promise to me..."

SIX
A BEAUTIFUL LIE

FENDER

The camp was back to its former operations.

But working double time to make up for the losses.

Magnus supplemented my salary along with those of the surviving guards out of his own pocket. My distribution partners were promised double their order for the next shipment to make up for their losses.

Magnus hadn't left the camp in months because he had too much work to do.

We barely spoke to each other.

If he was pissed that I'd emasculated him, I didn't give a damn.

He didn't leave me a fucking choice.

I sat in my office with the fire burning. Spring was here, soon to intensify into summer, but I still enjoyed the fire for company. It complemented the burn down my throat from the scotch Gilbert tried to hide from me.

Yes, I was killing myself.

And, no, I didn't care.

There was work to do, but I'd been at it all day, so I closed my laptop with the glass between my hands, my eyes on the enormous mantel that took up most of the wall on the other side of the room.

Gilbert entered the study. "Sir?"

I looked at him and lifted the glass to my lips for a drink.

He came closer, walking quicker than usual with a flare of urgency. "Sir, Melanie is here to see you."

I nearly dropped the glass onto the desk. My fingers tightened to prevent the slip. My sip was cut short, and my drink was returned to the surface of the wood. Anger rushed back like an unexpected tidal wave. She used to be the face that brought me peace. Now she was the face that brought me misery. It was still in my dreams. It was still in my thoughts. It was still in the fire that burned right this very moment. "No." I grabbed my glass again and took the full drink I wanted seconds ago.

"Deny her entry?" Gilbert asked for clarification.

"Yes." I leaned back in my chair and stared at the fire like the matter was settled.

Gilbert nodded then departed.

The last time she'd looked me in the eye on the grounds of my palace, I'd expected a very different request from the one she made. I expected her to admit that leaving me was a big fucking mistake. That I ruined her for all other men. That she didn't feel safe unless she was with me. That she missed the life I gave her. That she missed being taken care of. That she missed me.

Instead, she asked me to give her something I had already promised.

Pissed me the fuck off.

Now she was probably here to ask for something else—like her sister's freedom.

Never.

Gilbert returned to the study. "Sir...she refuses to leave."

"Then she can sleep out there. I don't give a shit."

He nodded then stepped out again.

But he was right back inside a moment later. "She's climbing the gate. What are your orders?"

"She's what?" I slammed down the empty glass, knowing she was going to slip, fall, and break something. It was dark, and that gate was fucking high. And she had no athleticism or coordination.

He listened to the radio in his ear. "She's climbing, sir."

"Jesus fucking Christ." I pushed to my feet. "Tell her to get down. Have them open the gate." I marched out of the study, through the foyer, and out the front door to the roundabout that circled the fountain. In nothing but my sweatpants, I watched the golf cart come around, drop her off, and then depart.

She stood in front of me. Unafraid.

She should be afraid. Now, she was in ordinary jeans and a cheap blouse, her makeup unremarkable. Her hair wasn't as shiny. She was thinner than she used to be. But she was just as gorgeous as I remembered—and that made me angrier. "What the fuck do you want, Melanie? I owe you nothing, and I will give you nothing. If you came here to get me to release your sister, you've wasted your time and mine."

Her hands came together at her waist, her mannerisms exactly the same. With bright eyes, she looked into my gaze, giving me a look she'd never given me before. "I want to come home..." Her eyes watered as she let those words float off her tongue on a whisper.

My eyes narrowed instinctively. It was the confession I'd wanted to hear—just at the wrong time. Months had passed, and I hadn't heard from her. The one time I did, she wanted something from me. She was an accomplice to her sister, destroying everything I'd built entirely on my own.

When I said nothing, she winced with rejection. "I'm sorry that I hurt you—"

"I'm not going to release your sister." She only wanted me for one thing. Women used me for my money and my dick, but she bled me dry for her obnoxious sister. I wouldn't bleed another drop. "Not now. Not ever. Go home."

"That's not what I'm asking you—"

"I'm not stupid, Melanie. You insult me."

She instinctively shifted back at my vile words. "I left with her because I had to. If I'd stayed, I never would have seen her again. She wouldn't have forgiven me if I'd chosen to be with you. I didn't have a choice—"

"You told me that you would stay even if you could leave."

"And that was the truth. I'd never expected Raven to get out, and when she did, it changed everything."

"That's the difference between us, Melanie. You break your promises. I don't." I stared her down hard, flooding her with hatred, before I turned back to the house. "It doesn't matter if the circumstances changed."

"Fender." She came after me and grabbed my arm.

I twisted out of her grasp as I pivoted back to her, my hand now on her wrist. All of it happened quicker than she could even blink. "Leave." I pushed her hand off me, ignoring the electrical impulse that zapped my hands and traveled all the way to my brain in a nanosecond.

With heartbroken eyes, she stayed. "You have no idea what you've done to me. You're the reason we were in that camp in the first place. You're a drug lord and a murderer. And yet, I'm absolutely lost without you..." Her eyes overflowed with tears.

I hated it when she cried, but that wasn't enough for me anymore.

"I've spent the last month dreaming about you. Missing you. Every time Raven asked about you, I didn't say anything...because she would hate me if I told her the truth. She would never look at me the same if I told her that it broke my heart to leave you." Liquid diamonds streaked down her cheeks and reflected the sconces outside my palace.

My expression hadn't changed. "I'm not going to release your sister—"

"I'm not asking you to!" Her voice rose in a scream. "I'm asking you...to let me come home. I can't live in that apartment by myself. I can't go to work every day and focus. I can't go on dates with men I'm not even interested in—"

"Melanie." I shut her up with just the slight raise of my voice. "If all of that were true, you would have come back sooner, not when you want something from me. You were here a week ago, and you didn't want me."

The tears continued to drip down her cheeks, to her chin, and then drop to the cobblestones underneath her.

"You only want me because of what I provide for you. That was fine before, but not anymore. Not after you left me. Not after you burned down my camp. Not after you betrayed me." Every day without her was more painful than the last. Every night with another woman was unsatisfying. Every breath I took without her taking the same breath beside me was wasted. While I still wanted her, even after all this time, it wasn't enough. I gave her a final look before I turned around and walked up the steps.

This time, she didn't follow me.

I made it to the front door, which was still open as I'd left it.

Her voice rang out behind me as an emotional outburst. "Je t'aime."

I'd almost crossed the threshold before her words hit me like a bullet to the bone. I stilled, replayed it in my head, and slowly turned around to regard her.

She remained where she stood, tears pouring down her cheeks. Her hands were clasped tightly together against her waist, a slight tremor to her body, the aftershock of her catharsis still making her shake.

I walked back to her, my bare feet hitting the cold stone as I approached, my eyes absorbing her appearance in a way I never had before. My hands ached for those hips. My lips yearned for her kiss. All it took was to hear the words I'd whispered to her so many times in the hope that she would say them back...and I was lost.

My hand snaked into her hair, and the instant I touched her, her face melted like that was exactly what she needed to find peace. My fingers fisted her hair tightly, and I tilted her head back to force her to look up at me. The moment I'd laid eyes on her, she was all I ever wanted, not just for the night, but my entire life. But like a shadow passing overhead, clouds promising rain, my anger approached over the horizon.

I was so angry.

Her eyes closed, as if expecting a kiss.

I never gave it.

My hand tightened in her hair and locked her in place. She'd risked her safety to march through the snow and destroy me. She'd left me without a backward glance. She'd lured me to bed and got my eyes to close, and then she stabbed me in the darkness. I gave this woman everything—and she gave me nothing.

Her eyes opened, revealing trepidation. They trembled slightly as she looked into my eyes, the fear setting in when she realized there would be no kiss, no embrace. Her words had fallen on deaf ears.

I squeezed her hair tighter, wanting to push her into the road and leave her there. My eyes burned with a hatred I couldn't sheathe. I wanted to abandon her the way she'd abandoned me, leave her out there on her own without anyone to protect her. She'd hit me where it hurt the most— and I wanted to do the same to her.

Her hand moved to my forearm, and she gripped it like a lifeline, her cold skin melting like snow at my heat. Despite my rage, she continued to cling to me, prepared to latch on when I threw her on her ass.

That was all it took to bring me back, to change my mind in a split second. "Tu m'aimes?" *You love me?*

She seemed to understand me because she gave a nod.

That wasn't enough for me. I tugged on her hair tighter. "Oui?" *Yes?*

Her answer left her lips with emotion. "Oui." *Yes.*

My eyes seared into her face, branding her as mine once again. "Then prove it."

SEVEN

COLD SHOULDER

MELANIE

I slept in the apartment alone.

I packed the few things that I had and prepared to be picked up in the morning.

Life as I knew it would be forever changed tomorrow. Once I left this place, I wouldn't be Melanie ever again.

As with every night since Raven had left, I could hardly sleep. It wasn't just the fact that she was gone. It was the fact that I was alone, footsteps from strangers audible on the other side of my doorstep, the sounds of the cars and ambulances loud from the street outside my window.

The only sound I heard at the palace was the fireplace.

The next morning, I sat on the couch with my packed bag beside me. My hands were in my lap and my shoulders slumped, waiting for whoever Fender sent to retrieve me. Footsteps came a moment later, belonging to a single man.

I inhaled a deep breath and waited for them to step inside. I'd left the door unlocked.

A knock sounded. "Melanie?"

I recognized that voice immediately, like I still listened to it every single day. "Gilbert? It's open." I rose to my feet and grabbed my bag.

He let himself inside, dressed in jeans and a shirt.

I stilled at his appearance because all I'd ever seen him in was a tuxedo or his pajamas. Sunglasses hung down the front of his shirt, and his snug jeans fit his hard body like a glove.

He took a step inside, and with his typical snootiness, he examined the apartment with obvious disapproval. He moved to the kitchen island, dragged his finger across the surface, and then turned it over to see the dark smudge of dirt there. He rubbed his fingers together to remove it. "Charming..."

I approached with my arms raised, eager to hug him even though I'd never hugged him before. I moved into his chest and wrapped my arms around his neck. "I missed you."

He didn't return the embrace. After a few seconds, he grabbed my bag off my shoulder and stepped back. "Is that everything?" He scanned the apartment with disdain, like he hoped all I would take was this single bag of items, and if he had it his way, probably not even that.

"Yeah."

He turned to the door then stopped when he spotted a small drop of blood on the wall near the baseboards. He turned to me and gave me a headshake of disapproval.

"That wasn't me—"

"Let's go." He led me out of the apartment and to the blacked-out SUV parked at the curb. There was a driver in the front who didn't say a word as we got inside. He silently pulled into traffic and drove toward the palace.

We sat in silence the whole way, Gilbert sitting against the opposite window with his elbow on the armrest. His fingers rested against his jawline as he surveyed the buildings and then the countryside.

"So, you hate me again."

He ignored me.

I realized I had to start all over—with both men.

MY OLD BEDROOM looked exactly the same.

There were fresh flowers ready for my arrival, in big vases around the quarters. My designer clothes were in the closet like they'd never been removed. The diamonds and jewelry were still in the vault. All of my makeup and hair supplies were on the bathroom counter, pristine and undisturbed.

It felt so strange to stand there.

It was as if nothing had changed.

But also, everything had changed.

"Will you take your lunch in the garden room?" He set the bag on a shelf in the closet before he reemerged, his arms behind his back like he was dressed in his formal attire.

"Sure."

He gave a slight bow then made to depart.

"Is Fender in his office?"

He stilled just before he crossed the threshold into the hallway. "Yes. But you're unwelcome."

I'd expected that, but it stung anyway. "Will he join me for lunch—"

"No."

"Then when will I see him?"

He turned back around and gave me a cold look. "Whenever he feels like it, Melanie."

I DIDN'T SEE Fender for a week.

Gilbert left my birth control on the nightstand like he expected me to resume the contraceptive, and I was taken to a doctor's office to be tested for my reproductive health— even though I hadn't been with anyone.

It was springtime, so I spent more time outside. The garden bloomed with colorful flowers, and I'd sit there for hours and watch the bees fly from one petal to the next. Whenever the sun was directly on my skin, I felt like a cat lounging in its rays.

When I took my walks, I passed the guest quarters.

If my sister hadn't run, she'd be there right now.

She'd be safe. Taken care of. Maybe even happy...

But that was gone now.

I was supposed to convince Fender to release my sister, but I wasn't sure if that was even a possibility. I couldn't ask, because if I did, he would grow suspicious. I had to earn back his trust, but I wasn't sure if that would ever happen either. His guard was up higher than it used to be. He would never lower it, and it was too high for me to climb.

He wouldn't kill Melanie, so I had all the time in the world to make this happen.

IT WAS WARM OUTSIDE NOW, so no reason to have a fire.

But I still asked Gilbert to make them because there was something comforting about it. It took me to a different time. A time when Fender would look at me like I was his one and only, when he would keep me warm with his touch, when he would give himself to me completely. It took me back in time to when life was better...in some ways.

I sat in the living room in my bedroom and stared at the fire. My old translation textbook was there, along with the notebook Gilbert had scribbled in. A pen lay there, shining in the light of the flames. The TV wasn't on because I wasn't going to bother trying to learn French at this hour. It was late, time for bed, but I had no reason to get up in the morning, so there was no point.

My bedroom door opened.

I heard it, the sound immediately flooding my memory because I'd heard it so many times in the past.

It shut again.

My heart pounded. My ears throbbed with blood. Bumps formed on my arms even though I was warm. My gaze remained on the fire as I listened to his bare feet thud against the hardwood, becoming muffled once he hit the rug, approaching slowly.

I breathed deeper, afraid.

His footsteps stopped.

I knew he was right behind me. Standing over me. Lurking.

His hands moved to the back of the couch, and he gripped the frame behind the cushion, his arms slightly in my periphery. His energy surrounded me like a cloud of humility, electrifying all the particles in the air so they burned my lungs every time I took a breath. He leaned down, his face coming closer to my ear. "Get on the bed." His hands disappeared. The energy evaporated. His footsteps announced his departure.

This was different.

He was different.

I could feel it.

I left the couch and looked at him for the first time, standing near the bed in his sweatpants and nothing else, his gaze burning into me like it possessed the heat of the sun. He watched me approach the bed, watched me strip down to nothing. His eyes combed over my naked body, but his expression still didn't change.

I crawled onto the bed and laid my head on the pillow.

He dropped his bottoms, revealing that rock-hard cock that was anxious for me. His hard body was built bigger than it used to be, an increase in mass but a tightness in inches. The veins bulged more than they did before. He moved to the bed, one knee dipping the mattress and then the other knee doing the same.

My body tightened as he came close, my sex glistening, my breaths of fear turning into breaths of arousal. I hadn't seen him in the flesh since our conversation outside his home, and now that he was mine again, my fingers were anxious to grip those muscles, my thighs were anxious to squeeze his hips. I wanted his passionate kisses. I wanted him to whisper beautiful things to me in French as he claimed me as his. I'd missed this, and I hadn't felt that quite as strongly as I did now.

On his knees, he looked down at me, but he didn't separate my thighs with his knees. His hands gripped my hips, and then he quickly flipped me over. His fingers fisted my hair and pressed my face hard into the pillow as he lifted my ass into the air. Then he gripped both of my wrists and held them together at the small of my back, like I was a prisoner. His dick slid through my tight opening then slammed in with a hard thrust.

I shifted forward and let out a moan, my hands automatically wanting to break free, but were unable to move. It was a shock to feel that size deep inside me, that thick and throbbing rod of flesh.

His hands tightened on my body like reins to his horse, and he slammed into me hard, smacking my headboard against the wall, giving quiet moans as he pounded into me like I was a whore.

I imagined his face above mine, kissing me as he rocked into me, brushing his nose against mine as he looked into my eyes and slid all the way inside before he pulled out again. I imagined it slow, with our quiet breaths floating to the high ceiling and echoing back to us.

This was carnal.

Vicious.

Animalistic.

It wasn't what I wanted—but I came anyway.

WHEN HE WAS FINISHED, he immediately released his hold then moved away.

I lay there, a crick in my neck from the way my face had been thrust into the pillow. It hadn't bothered me in the moment, but now there was a definite ache. I heard him get off the bed and grab his clothes.

I lifted myself and looked at him, naked and covered in his sweat, his come dripping out of me.

Without giving me a glance, he pulled on his clothes and left.

He took me once, got off, and then just left.

FENDER and I hadn't spoken once since I'd come here. I'd expected pillow talk after sex, but he got what he wanted then departed like there was no reason to stay. His office door was closed, and he didn't join me for lunch.

He only wanted me for one thing.

He came again the next night.

After his full week of ignoring me, I hadn't expected to see him again for a while.

I sat up in bed with a book in my hand, and the second the door opened, my eyes flicked up to watch him enter.

With that same constantly pissed-off visage, he approached my bed and dropped his bottoms, his dick hard like he was in the mood before he even looked at me. Tall and muscular, he stood there and stared me down, telling me what to do without moving his lips.

I closed the book and set it on the nightstand. "I want to talk—"

"Don't care what you want." He approached the bed. "Turn over."

My only action should be obedience, but I didn't want this version of him—even though I deserved it. "Please—"

He grabbed my body and threw me over, forcing me onto my stomach and knees. My nightgown was pushed above my hips, and he yanked my thong down with such force he could have ripped it. He moved me to the edge of the bed, ass in the air, directed his dick to my entrance so he could pound me as harshly as he had last night.

I tried to push up against his hand at my neck, but it was no use. "No."

Everything stopped.

His hand released my neck, and he pulled his dick away.

I breathed hard against the sheets before I raised myself to look at him.

He was already dressed and headed to the door.

"Wait, no."

He ignored me and walked out.

"Okay, okay..."

His footsteps halted outside the door before he returned to the doorway, his sweatpants snug because his dick bulged in the material. He stared me down, his dark eyes full of anger. But there was still desire there, subtly masked underneath the stare. He didn't move toward the bed, as if he expected something from me.

I put my head back down on the sheets, my ass up in the air, and pulled my nightgown to my hips.

He stared for a while before he came back in. He didn't take off his bottoms this time. He pushed them to his thighs, got me in the same hold as last night, and fucked me harder than he had the night before.

IT HAPPENED every night for a week.

He fucked me the exact same way. The exact same position. Not saying a word. When I tried to talk to him, he would just leave.

These were his terms—and I didn't have a choice but to accept them.

I ate lunch by myself in the garden room, my depression increasing in weight the longer my social isolation lasted. Gilbert didn't speak to me. Just dropped my tray and departed. Fender would only see me under one condition— if he was fucking me.

The tray remained in front of me, but I didn't take a single bite. I had no appetite. Raven was back at the camp, and I'd foolishly thought getting Fender to release her would be easy. He was a man who shouldn't be crossed—and I'd crossed him a couple times. It was a miracle I'd earned his trust in the first place. What were the odds I could ever do it again?

Gilbert approached the table in his tuxedo, his eyes perpetually annoyed whenever he had to be in my presence. "Is there something wrong with the meal?"

"No." I stirred my tea with the spoon, watching the steam rise.

He waited a moment longer before he turned away.

"Gilbert?"

He halted, and with a loud sigh, he turned back around and regarded me.

"What do I do about Fender?" I was desperate for a solution.

"Why are you asking me?" His tone turned icy, his eyes like rain clouds.

"Because you know him better than anyone else."

"I think you should leave and never come back, Melanie. That's what I think." His words were clipped, every syllable becoming more difficult to speak the longer he had this conversation. "You don't deserve him. I have no idea why he allowed you to come back at all."

My eyes returned to the tea. "I missed him every day I was gone—"

"Oh, you missed him?" he asked sarcastically. "Did you miss him when you burned down everything he'd built with his bare hands?"

Now I shut my mouth.

Gilbert turned away.

"I didn't realize...I'd hurt him so much."

Gilbert stayed still for a long time, took a deep breath as if deciding if he should just let this conversation drop, but then he turned back to me. "I never thought he was particularly happy when you were here. His mood and behaviors didn't change. But when you were gone...I definitely noticed the difference."

HIS OFFICE DOORS WERE CLOSED.

But I knew he was inside.

That was where he spent all of his time while he was in the house.

I turned the knob and let myself inside.

He was staring at his laptop, his fingers gliding over the touch pad as he scrolled through a page he read intently. Shirtless, with his big arms on the table, he didn't notice my entrance, or if he did, he assumed I was Gilbert to feed the fire.

I approached his desk, my feet quiet because I'd ditched my heels in my bedroom.

When I was right in front of him, he lifted his chin with a look of indifference.

I could tell that he expected Gilbert because his face changed the longer he looked at me, as if it made him physically angry to see me. His jaw tightened like screws that were twisted farther to the right even though they were already tight. His eyes darkened to coals. The veins in his arms protruded even more.

"I'm sorry to disturb you—"

"Then don't." He straightened in his chair, pulling his arms off the desk as he leaned against the back. His arms fell to the armrests, one elbow bent as his closed knuckles pressed against his cheek.

"I just want to talk—"

"I hate talking."

"You didn't hate it with me..." My fingers came together in front of my waist, interlocking to stop the fidgeting.

His eyes narrowed like that made him angrier. "I hated it then too. Trust me."

My eyes dropped to his desk, this attempt at conversation pointless. "I'm sorry...about everything."

His stare remained as cold and intense as ever.

"That probably doesn't mean anything to you—"

"It doesn't." He was still and lifeless like a winter morning. He'd once had a beating heart, but now he was made entirely of stone.

"It's been weeks, and you still won't even talk to me. If you hate me so much, why don't you just throw me out?" I didn't want to leave. I had nowhere to go. I didn't want anyone else but him. And he was the only viable option to get Raven out of that camp.

He didn't answer the question.

"How am I supposed to prove anything to you if you won't even look at me?" My eyes suddenly filled with warmth, a warning of impending tears. I'd been lost until I came here, and now I was here, but I still felt lost. I gave a quiet sniff to try to suck back the wetness, but it didn't work.

He used to soften at my tears. Now there was nothing. "If you expect my anger to thaw so quickly, then you really don't understand how deep your knife went. You fail to grasp the significance of your betrayal. I'm not a man who grants forgiveness. I'm a man who grants death. You should be grateful that I still have no desire to ever hurt you."

Tears broke free and dripped down my cheeks. "You're hurting me right now..."

EIGHT
WINTER TO SPRING

Fender

I came into her room every night and took her the same way.

It was quick, just to get off, and then I went to bed.

Words weren't exchanged.

She didn't try to talk to me. She just let me be.

I was in my office on the phone when Gilbert entered. "We aren't taking more partners right now. Period." I hung up then looked at Gilbert, annoyed that he stood in front of my desk in expectation when I was on the phone. "What?"

"Melanie just left. Wanted me to give you this." He placed a piece of paper from her notebook in front of me.

I stared at him blankly, but then I looked out the window, as if expecting to see her walk past. My hand grabbed the note and read her feminine handwriting.

I CAN'T PROVE something you won't allow me to prove.

I'm sorry for everything.

-Chérie

I GOT to my feet and tossed the note aside. "When did she leave?"

"A few minutes ago—"

"Tell the men to keep the gate closed."

Gilbert looked bewildered by the order. "Sir? I thought this was a good thing—"

"Do as I say."

"Of course." He stepped away and spoke into his intercom. "Quincy, don't open the gate."

I marched around the desk and prepared to go after her myself.

Gilbert turned back to me. "The cab just pulled away, sir."

I stared at him blankly, unable to believe she'd just taken off like that. She'd left me once and it hurt. Now that she'd left me again, it just pissed me off. "Bring the car around."

I PULLED up to the curb of her apartment building and ignored the people who stared at my car.

My boots thudded against the stone as I entered the building, up the hardwood of the stairs, and the sound of my beating heart matched the thudding. The fury was barely contained in my tight fists.

I arrived at her apartment, tried the locked handle, and then broke through the lock when I shoved my shoulder against it with a single push.

The door flew open, revealing Melanie on the couch with her bag beside her. She didn't flinch at the sound, as if unsurprised. The windows showed the lights of the city and the apartment across the way, hitting her face with the right light to show her glistening tears.

I'd come here to scream at her.

But like always, those tears made me go still.

I pushed the door shut behind me then entered her small apartment. There was a drop of blood on the wall where my man had been slain with a knife by that obnoxious bitch. There were coffee mugs on the counter beside the sink. A couple blankets were thrown over the couches. To her, it had been home. To me, it was a dump.

She didn't belong in a place like that.

I stared at her from the kitchen until she lowered her gaze to her lap and wiped her tears away.

I moved into the living room and stopped near the couch where she sat. An ambulance passed on the street below. Then a car pulled up to the intersection, playing loud and obnoxious music. There was no silence.

Silence was a luxury.

After a quick scan of the apartment, I dropped my chin to her.

And stared.

She gave a quiet sniff.

"I have more important things to do than chase you down."

"I didn't ask you to come."

"What did you expect me to do?" I stared at the side of her face, my gaze burning into her cheek, irritated that a woman so beautiful was sitting in an apartment that didn't complement her appearance. She deserved a fucking tiara and a crown.

"Let me go." She fidgeted with her hands in her lap. "You don't talk to me. You don't look at me. You don't...even like me."

I stared at her for a while before I lowered myself to the armchair, sitting at the very edge with my arms on my thighs. My hands came together as I looked at her. I waited for her to meet my eyes.

She wouldn't. "I want the man that I remember. Not this version of you." Her voice came out as a whisper. But then her voice grew louder, full of offense. "I don't want to be fucked like a whore."

Her request made the anger dump into the atrium of my heart like blood from the lungs. "You're not in a place to make demands—not after what you did. I'm entitled to my anger. I'm entitled to treat you however I damn well please."

She lifted her chin and looked at me, her eyes red because she'd cried during the entire cab ride. "Then I don't want to go back with you."

My visage didn't change, but her declaration made me feel the same bout of loss as when she'd left the first time. It hurt me—again. It hurt me, when I'd thought she couldn't hurt me anymore. "You don't expect winter to thaw into spring in a moment. It takes time, a very long time, for the snow-caps to melt and flood the rivers. I'm a man of the elements. You should manage your expectations. A mountain won't move just because you wish for it to move."

Her fingers continued to fidget, but she didn't drop her gaze. "It's been three weeks. No sign of movement. No sign of future movement. It's impossible for me to make amends or prove my feelings if I can't even speak to you. You don't want me there. It's clear."

My anger increased because her awareness was nonexistent. She had me in the palm of her hand—and she didn't even know it. "If I didn't want you there, I wouldn't have welcomed you into my home. I wouldn't come into your bedroom at night. I'd visit my favorite whore instead. I wouldn't drive all the way here. I wouldn't be sitting here right now at all, looking at you the way I always have, since the moment I first saw you. I kept my promise to you even after you broke your promise to me. You're alive this very moment, when anyone else would be dead. I don't want you there..." I shook my head. "You insult me. You fucking insult me." I rose to my feet and moved to the door, expecting her to get off her ass and follow me.

But she didn't.

I turned back around and gave a deep sigh of annoyance.

"You have to try... Otherwise, I won't come with you."

I bent over backward for this woman. I destroyed my self-respect for this woman. There was no request I wouldn't honor. Anything she asked of me, I would give it to her. It was fucking pathetic.

Almost made me walk out for good.

But I'd lived a life without her...and it was unbearable.

Obsessed. Addicted. Infatuated.

Haunted. Bewitched. Possessed.

This woman was the fucking air to my lungs.

So, I caved—again. "Alright."

I DROVE her back to the palace.

Gilbert greeted us with disappointment, taking her bag with a sigh, as if he'd hoped she would never step foot in this place again. He could barely tolerate her when things were good. I imagined he was worse now than he'd ever been before.

"Gilbert."

He halted and turned back to me. "Yes, Your Highness?"

I just stared him down because he would understand my silence better than my words.

He gave a slight nod then carried her bag to her bedroom upstairs.

I turned back to the office. "I have shit to do."

She looked around the foyer, the gold sconces, the floral wallpaper and the portraits on the wall—like she'd never seen it before. "Can we have dinner together?" She looked at the floor, expecting a no before she heard it leave my lips.

I stared at her fair cheek, the blush that highlighted her prominent cheekbones, that gave her a deeper level of beauty. The answer that came to mind stayed there and never left my lips. "Yes."

THE ANGER WAS impossible to release.

Not when I was this enraged.

But it was a necessary sacrifice to have the one thing more profound than my hate.

My *chérie*.

I stepped into her bedroom and found her at the dining table near the window in her living quarters. Her makeup had been refreshed, and she was in the designer clothes I provided.

Gilbert had her tray set up in front of her, and then he did the same to mine.

I approached, my bare feet moving across the hardwood floor and then the thick rug. My mind was more focused now that the scotch had been siphoned out of my diet. Didn't need it as a form of pain management.

There was nothing to do for the anger, unfortunately.

I sat in the chair across from her, feeling so much rage for what she'd done, but that slowly tapered off the longer I looked at her.

Her beauty dulled the fury.

Gilbert removed the silver lids to our platters then left us to enjoy our dinner.

Melanie stared at me without touching her silverware, her eyes slightly soft, as if she couldn't believe I was actually there with her. Gratitude. Joy. A lot of different emotions moved across the surface of her eyes.

It was real.

Raven was always the wedge between us, but now that she had been permanently removed from the situation, she shouldn't cause any more problems. I wasn't sure what made me hate her more—destroying the camp, or taking Melanie away.

Melanie grabbed her silverware and started to eat.

I dropped the linen napkin in my lap, sliced into the tender meat, and ate in silence. My arms rested on the table as I chewed, looking across the table at the woman in front of me, the living portrait that could entertain me for hours.

"So...how was work?"

I chewed my food slowly, recalling the remains of the camp, a pile of burned ash. Smoke had lingered in the sky for weeks, making it hard for the men to breathe as they worked to rebuild from scratch. The entire organization had been compromised for months because everything went to shit. "It was fine."

Her eyes darkened slightly, like she knew that work would always be a touchy subject. "How long will you be here?"

"No idea." I cut into my food again and took another bite. Even if I knew when I was leaving, I wouldn't tell her. She might reduce my anger with her appearance, and she might soften my heart with the words she said to me, but there was nothing she could do to earn back the trust she'd pissed away.

She stopped asking questions and ate in silence.

Silence. My preferred form of communication.

I stared at her as I ate my meat, her appearance matching the one I'd stored in my memory while she was gone. The whores I'd bedded didn't compare to her. They did whatever I paid them to do—and I still couldn't get off the way I had before. Once I pictured Melanie instead of them, the sex became good, but it still fell short.

"I got a job at a café." She pushed her potatoes around with her fork.

I stared as I chewed.

"I wasn't very good at it." She released a chuckle that came out like a rushed breath. "The manager was a nice guy and didn't fire me, even though I was slow and most of my drinks were wrong."

"He wasn't a nice guy. Just wanted to fuck you." I'd tried to think of her as little as possible after she left. When the dark thoughts broke through the barrier of my scotch, when I'd wondered where she slept at night, if another guy got to fuck her while I lay there in the dark alone, then I would drink more.

She kept her eyes on her plate and continued to push her potatoes around.

I didn't ask because her answer didn't matter. It wouldn't change anything. If I didn't get the answer I wanted, it would just make me angry, and I was already angry enough.

She took a few bites of her food, her eyes downcast.

I kept eating, still wanting to reach for a scotch that wasn't there.

With her eyes still down, she spoke. "I wasn't with anyone..." Even though that was a huge relief, I continued to eat with the same stony expression.

"Were you with—"

"Yes." I didn't tell her it was unsatisfying. I didn't tell her I pretended she was the woman underneath me. I wanted to hurt her—and I hoped it did.

She went back to pushing her food around, like she didn't have an appetite.

Good.

***

WHEN DINNER WAS FINISHED, I rose from the chair and turned to depart. There was tea and desserts, but I didn't enjoy either of those things.

"Wait."

I stilled by her bed but didn't turn around. Her black bag was still there, sitting on top of the duvet cover.

She came up behind me, her hand touching my arm. Her fingertips weren't as soft as they used to be, like her working at the café had callused her rose-petal skin. When I didn't turn away, she came closer, resting her forehead against my bare back.

I stood there and felt her hands grip my triceps, her forehead against my back.

She straightened then turned me slightly, getting me to turn around the rest of the way and face her.

With my arms by my sides, I stared down at her, unsure what she wanted from me. I wasn't in the mood to take her to bed.

Her hands gently slid down my arms as she looked at my chest and stomach, admiring my appearance like another woman hadn't gotten to enjoy it in her absence. She moved farther into me, her hands slid to my biceps, her eyes lifting to mine. Her lips parted as she breathed quietly, her eyes now on my mouth.

She rose on her tiptoes and kissed my jawline, her soft lips like pillows against the hard bones in my chin. She moved to my mouth, kissing the corner, giving me a gentle swipe of her tongue.

My exterior was impenetrable. If she wanted more from me, she'd have to try harder than that.

She brought her face close to mine and stared at my lips, her eyelashes moving down her cheeks, her plumps lips ready for a kiss. Her nails dug into me slightly before she leaned in and pressed her soft mouth against mine, closing her eyes, feeling our lips touch.

My eyes remained open, my lips still.

She rested them together for a long time before she pulled away slightly. But she tried again, tucking her bottom lip between mine, exhaling a quiet breath filled with longing. Her nails dug into me deeper, just the way they did against my back.

My mouth remained lifeless.

She lifted her eyes and looked at me, her lips just a hair away from mine. "Je t'aime..."

Against my will, I inhaled a deep breath.

She moved into me once more, her hand cupping my neck, and she pressed a harder kiss to my mouth.

My eyes closed, and my mouth moved with hers, fire between our lips. My mouth took hers slowly, tasting the rain off her rose petals, inhaling her scent for the first time. My tongue reached for hers, and they met in a beautiful dance we'd shared a thousand times. It felt the same as it always had. Passion. Desire. Heat.

She pulled her lips away and looked at me, her nails slowly releasing my flesh. Her blue eyes showed everything that I'd just felt, that the heat burned her insides too. Her mouth moved farther away as she took a knee in front of me.

Another breath of air was sucked into my lungs automatically. My hands tightened into fists. My dick throbbed in my sweats because he wanted to feel the lips I'd just kissed.

She got to both knees on the rug then hooked her fingers to the insides of my bottoms and slowly dragged them down, letting my cock come free.

My face might be stoic, but my dick gave me away.

Thick. Hard. Long. Drooling at the tip.

She dragged my bottoms to my ankles then gripped the outsides of my thighs as she brought her mouth to my head. Her slightly parted lips pressed a kiss to the tip, a little tongue swiping over the drool.

I sucked in another breath because...fuck.

If I could have any woman in the world on her knees, it would be her.

Always.

Her mouth moved to my base, and she stuck her tongue against the bulging vein that rivaled the ones in my arms and neck, and slowly, she dragged it up, closer to the tip, taking her time.

I stopped breathing.

She made it back to my tip and gave it another swipe of her tongue. With her eyes on mine, she whispered, "Je t'aime..." Her mouth opened wide, her tongue flattened, and she slowly pushed her throat over my dick, taking her time, eyes on me.

I shut my eyes and let out an unstoppable moan. My dick slid across that wet tongue and deeper into her throat, saliva immediately spilling from the corners of her mouth and dripping to the rug below. My hand slipped into her hair, and I started to move with her, eyes on her, her eyes on me.

NINE
THE MOST BEAUTIFUL WOMAN

Melanie

When I went downstairs, his office doors were open.

I stepped inside and saw him sitting behind the large desk, phone pressed to his ear, speaking in French. "Magnus a essayé de lui parler?" He listened to the voice on the other line before he said, "Bien," and hung up.

My French was a little better, so I translated that to, *Magnus talk to her?* It took me a few seconds to figure out the subject of their conversations. *Her* was definitely Raven, and Magnus was clearly staying away from her.

I wasn't sure if I'd ever be able to save her.

When Fender realized I'd joined him, he stared at me from his seat behind his desk, his gaze always hostile.

Things were getting better, but at a snail's pace.

I held up my book then moved to the couch, hoping he would allow me to sit there quietly and read.

His eyes followed me, but he never issued a protest.

I sat down in my old spot near the fire and flipped through the pages until I found my spot.

He walked over a moment later. His large body lowered to the couch across from me, his stomach chiseled even in a seated position. Winter, spring, or summer, he was dressed exactly the same, choosing to wear as little clothing as possible.

I looked up, expecting him to say something.

"I'm leaving in a few minutes." He leaned back into the couch with his fingers interlocked behind his head. Knees apart. His chiseled thighs stretching the cotton of his sweats. His enormous size dwarfing the couch that supported him. He was like a Clydesdale.

"Oh..." My hands moved to shut my book.

"Wait." He leaned forward and ripped off a pink rose petal from a flower in the vase on the coffee table then extended his outstretched hand to me.

I hesitated before I gave him the book.

He inserted the rose petal between the pages, the pink color sticking out at the top, then closed it. He left it on the table then leaned back into the couch once again, one arm resting over the top of the couch, the other on his thigh.

"Thanks."

His shoulders were relaxed, but his gaze was sharp like the tip of a drill. He constantly dug into my surface, burrowing deep down below.

"Where are you going?"

His expression didn't change.

"Sorry...just trying to make conversation."

Dark. Observant. Powerful. He looked at me exactly the way he used to. We could sit together in silence for hours and not speak a word, and he seemed perfectly content with that. As long as his eyes were on my face, that was all he needed.

My eyes dropped down from his face to his body, over the two slabs of concrete forming his chest, the bricks of his abs, the flesh that had remained untouched despite his violent affairs. Even if I'd never seen him before, he would be exactly what I described as a perfect man. If we'd met in some other way, the second I looked at him, I would never look away. He stared at me like I was the work of art—but he was.

If he had somewhere to be, he was clearly in no rush. Unblinking. Potent. Deep. That stare was endless.

I left the couch and came around the coffee table toward him.

His eyes followed.

I stopped in front of him and reached for the zipper at the back of my dress. Slowly, I pulled it down, letting the delicate fabric release its hug from my body, and felt it slide down around my heels on the floor.

His eyes dropped to my free tits. He never seemed to think they were anything less than perfect.

My thumbs hooked into my panties and pushed them over my ass and down my thighs until I was in nothing but pumps.

He inhaled a slow breath, his eyes darkening even more.

I lowered myself to my knees in front of him and gripped his bottoms with both hands.

With his eyes on me, he lifted his hips and allowed me to pull down the sweatpants, reveal his cock that was ready to go. It lay against his stomach, the thick veins matching the ones in his neck.

I leaned forward and pressed a kiss to his balls, which were groomed at all times like he could get head at the drop of a hat.

After a few seconds, he released the breath he held.

My tongue dragged up his length to his tip then I positioned him upward, giving his head wet kisses, just the way I kissed his mouth. Slow. Wet. Deep.

He watched me, his eyes heavy and lidded with pleasure.

I released his heavy dick and watched it plop back against his stomach like a heavy rod before I crawled up in his lap and got on top of him, my thighs over his, my hands planting against his chest for balance.

He'd only taken me with my face down lately, but he didn't try to stop me. His arms remained restrained in his refusal to touch me. He wanted me, but he only wanted to take, not give.

I grabbed his base and slowly slid down, getting his thickness past my entrance in a gentle glide. When I had a good hold, I slowly sank farther and farther, getting every inch of that thickness inside of me.

He closed his eyes, inhaled a deep breath accompanied by a moan, and then his hands were on me. They gripped my ass, his large fingertips kneading my cheeks. When he looked at me again, he was there with me.

In this moment.

Together.

My hand cupped his face, and I started to ride him slowly, rolling my hips just the way he liked, pressing my face close to his. "Tu m'as manqué." *I missed you.* "Tu es le seul homme pour moi." *You're the only man for me.* "Je t'aime..."

THINGS GOT BETTER.

Change was slow with Fender, but it did happen. It was like the blossoming of a rose. It started with a green bud that blended with the vine, but slowly, it finally started to open. Then it opened wider and wider until it was in full bloom.

He ate his meals with me. Carried on a little conversation. Let me get on my knees and blow him when I wanted to please him. Let me get on top of him whenever I wanted to ride him. But he never initiated anything on his own. He never spoke to me in French. He never told me he loved me.

He never called me *Chérie*.

I had to continue to be patient.

At the end of the day, he entered my bedroom. There was no knock or any kind of announcement. He just let himself inside.

I was on the couch working on my French. I closed my notebook and looked at him, seeing him in a suit.

I was taken aback, because I'd never seen him dressed that way.

Handsome. Elegant. Powerful. He could pull off any look, even one as refined as that. The jacket made his shoulders broader, the slacks fit his muscular thighs perfectly, and he stood with a posture that evoked his fortune and status.

"Are you leaving?"

He adjusted the sleeves of his collared shirt underneath the jacket, shifting his watch in the process. "Get dressed."

"I'm...I'm coming with you?"

"I said get dressed." He stepped away like the conversation was over.

I went after him. "If I'd known, I would have prepared myself better." It was clearly a fancy event, and while I had gowns in the closet, my hair and makeup weren't fresh. He must have debated whether to invite me or not, and at the last minute, he did.

He turned back to me, his eyes scanning my face. "You'll still be the most beautiful woman in that room—whether you're prepared or not."

FENDER DROVE US INTO PARIS.

He was a large man in a small car, but he must have preferred speed and luxury over comfort.

I was in a gold gown and decorated with diamonds and jewelry, my hair down and in soft curls, my makeup sultry in the way he liked. "Where are we going?"

When he arrived in Paris, the traffic slowed him down, so there was a lot of stopping and going, but he gradually approached a historic building that was attracting a lot of cars. Men in suits and women in gowns stepped out of their vehicles and ascended the steps to the grand entrance. Despite the traffic and the confusion, he oozed calmness. "Art show."

"Oh, that sounds fun. New artists present their work?"

He always took his time answering me, giving a long pause to determine if he should respond at all. "Yes and no. These private events showcase historic collections, paintings that are hundreds or thousands of years old. Sometimes museums sell their inventory to raise money for something else. Sometimes sellers have had a painting for so long that they want something different. And yes, there are some relatively new artists, but they're the finest artists in Europe." He pulled up to the front, and the valet immediately stepped forward to collect the keys.

We exited the car, and Fender buttoned the front of his suit as he came to my side, like he was a gentleman with a respectable business. When he came close, he regarded my appearance as if he needed a moment to take me in before he placed his arm around my waist. He looked into my face, came close like he might kiss me, but he pulled away instead.

He always teetered on the edge, reacting to his instincts but never giving in. He looked at me the way he used to, but there was also a glaze of resentment and anger that had slowly faded over the past month. It was still there. Just distant. Faded.

WITH A GLASS of champagne in hand, Fender mingled with people he knew. He introduced me as Melanie, but the rest of the time, he spoke in quick French. He seemed to be charming, and he made people laugh pretty often.

I wished I could understand what he said.

His arm was always around my waist, always holding me close, and we moved to each painting to admire it in silence. They were placed on the walls, an art light flooding the art with illumination to make it stand out.

It was obvious which paintings were old, really old, and super-duper old.

With his hand on my back, Fender would admire each one in great detail, standing there for twenty minutes sometimes. Without looking at the man standing to the side, he spoke. "Je vais le prendre." *I'll take it.*

The man nodded then took it off the wall so it could be wrapped and ready for transport.

Fender guided me to the next painting.

"There are no prices anywhere..."

"Doesn't matter." He examined the next one with the same interest, his eyes focused the way they often focused on me.

I turned to study his visage, to see the way he appreciated everything on display as if he were an artist himself. "I didn't realize how much you loved art." It was a beautiful and unexpected quality he possessed, another sign of softness that contradicted his hardness.

"You've seen my home."

"I thought maybe Gilbert picked everything out."

"No." He finished his glass of champagne and held it out in midair, like he would drop it and let it shatter on the floor if a staff member didn't get there with a tray in time.

But they swooped in and took the empty glass before providing another—like royalty.

Fender moved me to the next painting.

I was more interested in him at this point. The art was beautiful, but after a while, it was hard to remain focused when the pieces started to blur together. "Why do you love it so much?"

He took a drink then licked his lips. "Because it's history. Because it's one of a kind. Because it's evocative like fire. Because it's priceless." He turned to look at me, his dark eyes absorbing my face the same way he'd just absorbed the painting. "Because it's beautiful."

WE WALKED into a different alcove that showed one of the biggest paintings I'd ever seen. It would take up an entire wall in a museum. Those paintings usually depicted large battles that required a lot of detail, but this was just a portrait of a woman. She stood in a white dress with the sleeve falling down one shoulder, her brown hair thick and beautiful, her eyes downcast.

A man stood beside the painting, but he wasn't in a tuxedo, so he must be the artist.

The title was on display in front of us, along with the artist's name.

The Most Beautiful Woman -Alexander Pedrotti-

Fender didn't look at this painting with the same luster as the previous ones. It was immense in size and quite impressive, but Fender's eyes narrowed in annoyance, like he wasn't impressed in the least. The energy around him was different, hostile. His hand left my waist, and he stepped forward. "Je vais acheter votre toile." *I will buy your painting.*

The artist stepped forward. "Elle vous plaît, monsieur?" *You like it, sir?*

Fender didn't respond. "Je veux que vous me peigniez un portrait." *Paint for me.*

"Désolé monsieur, mais je ne fais pas ça." *Sorry, sir. I don't do that.*

"Vous le ferez. Donnez-moi votre prix." *You will. Name your price.* Fender stared him down, daring him to defy him.

He gave a sigh in defeat. "Qui est le sujet?" *Who?*

"La plus belle femme du monde." *The most beautiful woman in the world.*

HE WAS in a foul mood for the rest of the night.

Our pleasant conversation was over.

The drive was spent in silence.

I'd assumed we had dinner plans afterward because we didn't eat, but he blew them off.

I didn't understand why a single painting could make him so angry.

We returned to the palace and entered the foyer.

Gilbert immediately came to greet us. "How was your evening, sir?"

"Deliver dinner to my bedroom in an hour." He took my hand in his and pulled me to the stairs.

Gilbert was flabbergasted. "I...I didn't realize you were expecting dinner this evening. I'll get right on that."

Fender took me up the stairs, to the top level, and into his bedroom. There was an urgency to his movements, like the way he sped through the streets even though he had nowhere to go. He gripped my hand tightly as if I might slip away and fall down the stairs. He'd been angry before, many times, but he'd never been quite like this.

His clothes dropped, and he tugged everything off like he couldn't get rid of it quickly enough.

Unsure what to do, I just stood there and watched him.

He got down to his bare skin, his dick hard despite his anger, then flashed me his aggressive stare.

I froze.

He stared at me as his chest rose and fell with his deep breaths, giving me a searing look that was aflame with molten fire. He sprang into action and cupped my cheeks, giving me a passionate kiss full of those deep breaths, full of unbridled need.

My mouth immediately responded, and my hands were on him, feeling him devour me, holding on to him for balance as he backed me up to the bed, his big fingers yanking down my zipper and getting the dress free.

He pushed it down my body, yanked off my underwear, and then carried me to the bed. My back hit the sheets as his arms hooked behind my knees, and he quickly positioned his thighs so he could push inside me.

His tip went in first then he sank the rest of the way. A possessive moan escaped his lips as his eyes burned into my face. He paused as he dug his hand into my hair and kissed me, kissed me like that for the first time since I'd left. When he pulled his lips away, he started to rock hard and deep. "Tu es la plus belle femme du monde." *You're the most beautiful woman in the world.* Between his hard thrusts, he spoke to me. "Toi." *You.* He kept going. "Et tu es à moi." *And you're mine.*

THE NEXT DAY, he was still in a bad mood.

A night of sleep hadn't dulled the offense from the night before. He'd taken that painting personally, even though he didn't know the artist or the woman in the portrait, even though it didn't matter who was more beautiful.

But it mattered to him.

I sat in the office with my book open on my lap, the dried-out petal on my knee so I could insert it once I was finished.

He didn't acknowledge me as he worked, talking on the phone to people in French, typing on his laptop, eating his lunch in silence. Based on the way he'd made love to me all night long, he wasn't angry at me.

He was just angry.

I watched him from my position on the couch, noting the black fire in his eyes as he stared at his computer screen, the hardness in his jawline, the deep level of masculinity that I'd never seen displayed in another man. He thought I was the most beautiful woman in the world—but he was the most beautiful man.

Gilbert stepped inside. "Sir, the crew has delivered your paintings. They're approaching in the roundabout."

Fender was immediately on his feet and across the study.

"I'm very excited to see the pieces you've picked out." Gilbert followed him out of the office and into the foyer. "Once we've decided where to hang them, I'll get them up right away."

I inserted the petal into the book and stepped into the foyer. Maybe I knew Fender better than Gilbert did, because I could tell Fender was not himself right now. When I looked toward the rest of the house, I saw Fender return, carrying a gas can.

Gilbert was right behind him. "Sir, what are you doing with that?"

They walked out the front doors, and I followed them.

The small paintings were already lowered out of the truck, wrapped in brown paper, and the men were just taking the enormous painting out of the truck. It took twelve men to do it.

Gilbert halted. "Uh, sir. Where on earth is that going to fit?"

Fender ignored him. "Leave it here."

The men looked confused because Fender had just asked them to drop the painting on the cobblestone driveway.

Fender held the can and flashed his eyes with irritation. "Now."

They gently set it on the ground, and then the truck drove away.

Fender started to pour gasoline all over the painting.

Gilbert literally gripped his chest as if he might have a heart attack. "What are you doing?"

Fender left the empty container on the portrait then lit a match.

"Sir!"

He tossed it on top—and it burst into flames.

Gilbert ran down the steps. "Have you lost your mind? This painting cost you a fortune. It's going to stain the cobblestone." A chicken with his head cut off, he ran to the painting and started to give orders to the men to put it out. "Get the hose!"

"No." Fender slowly walked away from the flames, like the blazing heat didn't bother him in the least. He did what he wanted, and now that he was done, the urgency was gone. He moved up the steps, eyes locked on me. "Let it burn."

TEN
WINNER

FENDER

I stepped into her bedroom and found her seated in the living room.

In the evenings, she worked on her French. Her textbook was open along with her notebook, and she taught herself when Gilbert wasn't around. She improved with every passing week, able to carry on short conversations in French.

She turned to look at me over the back of the couch when she heard me, her straight hair shifting like panels of a curtain. In her nightgown, she had her ankles tucked under her ass with her notebook on her lap. The fire burned low in the fireplace, just simmering coals at this point.

I walked around the couch and took the seat beside her, eyes hypnotized by the way she looked in the gentle fire-light. Her cheeks were brightened by the glow, her eyes glimmering like diamonds. In silence, I stared at her, still offended that another woman had ever been declared as the most beautiful. In the present or the past, it didn't matter. Melanie triumphed over any other contender.

She broke eye contact and closed her notebook. Her little thumb clicked her pen so the ink wouldn't run everywhere. Everything was set on the coffee table before she turned her gaze back to me.

"Alexander is coming to paint your portrait tomorrow."

Her eyes shifted back and forth subtly. "Do you think he'll still do it if he knows you destroyed his painting?"

"It's none of his business what I did with it. Transaction is complete." I turned my chin forward and looked at the dying fire. "Ugliest painting I've ever seen." I watched the red color underneath the destroyed logs, glowing bright with incredible heat.

Her hand moved to my thigh.

All it took was a touch, her slender fingers on me, to give me that rush of blood to the head. My anger was usually easy to maintain because I was always mad, and I never forgave. But it was impossible to hold on to now. She pulled me under, took me back to a peaceful existence that was quiet like the falling snow. My heart was incapable of resisting her. My eyes incapable of not feasting on her beauty. Nothing in the world softened me the way she did.

Fucking nothing.

I turned back to her, seeing her blue eyes burn a little brighter when my gaze came back to her.

"Make love to me..." Her pretty eyes pleaded. Her fingers kneaded. Her lips parted for an anxious kiss. Her words wrapped around me like an invisible string, binding her to me forever.

My stare lasted several seconds, immersed in the moment, the invisible heat between us, the connection between our souls. We were star-crossed lovers—she was my Juliet. If she died, I'd die.

I lifted her petite body as I rose to my feet and carried her to the bed. She was set at the edge, and I kept one arm around her waist as I lifted her and pulled off her panties. My hand bunched up her dress above her belly button, and I kissed her soft skin, tasting the swell at the bottom of her breasts.

She instantly started to breathe hard, her fingers digging into my short hair.

My hands opened her thighs wide with her ass at the edge of the bed before I lowered myself to my knees. My hands supported her slender legs as I pressed my face into her sweet pussy and kissed her.

Over and over.

Deeper.

Harder.

Making her writhe and grip the sheets.

I pushed her into panting, pushed her into screams and tears.

More delectable than chocolate. Smoother than a Barsetti wine in the cellar. Sweeter than rose hips. My mouth was addicted to her soft flesh, the sex that belonged to me and no other man.

Mine.

I got to my feet and pushed down my bottoms so my slobbering dick could be free. I positioned her again, seeing a tear-stained face and running makeup, and leaned over, sliding inside in one smooth motion.

She instantly gasped at my entrance and hooked her arm around my neck, folded underneath me, her other hand planted against my chest on top of my heart. She could feel it beat for her. Feel it race. Feel it ache. Her eyes glistened with old tears and some new as she whispered to me, "Je t'aime..."

My dick twitched inside her as I thrust, our bodies close together, giving her my length all the way to the base every time even though I could tell it hurt. "Encore."

Her voice grew louder. "Je t'aime."

There was no fantasy that made me burn hotter than this. Whether she meant it or not, it made me thrust harder, made me moan because I wanted to come every single time I heard it. "Encore."

"Je t'aime." She cupped my face and brought my forehead to hers.

My hips were working faster, slamming myself into her at a pace I couldn't control, and I commanded her not to stop. "N'arrête pas."

"Je t'aime pour toujours." *I'll love you forever.*

My hips bucked, and I came inside her with a loud moan. Exquisite pleasure. A good ache between my legs. A load bigger than I'd ever given her. It all happened with an intensity that rivaled the heat of the sun. She was my one and only. I could never be with another woman as long as I lived. I could never go back to the whores like I did before. If she ever wanted to leave, I wouldn't be able to let her go —not again. She'd give me strong sons. Beautiful daughters. I'd hold her against her will, do whatever was necessary to keep her in my bed every single night. It was beyond reason, insanity, but it hit me so hard in that moment. The obsession deepened. The addiction mocked my love of scotch.

I slowed down, my dick still rock hard even though I slid through my come and hers. My hand gripped the back of her head harshly, and I kept going, picking up speed as if the delay never happened. "Encore."

MELANIE SAT on the stool in front of the window, her hair in place, her makeup done by an artist from Dior. Her white dress was tight around her waist but flowed else-where. One strap was positioned off her shoulder.

People gathered around her in the garden room with the perfect backdrop and worked until she was perfect.

Alexander prepared his canvas and supplies, putting every-thing into position for the ideal lighting to capture the moment. "Yes...yes...very beautiful." The canvas was much smaller than his previous one, but I didn't intend to cover an entire wall with this picture.

It was just for me.

And it would be much better than that piece of trash portrait I'd burned.

Melanie looked nervous, unable to stop fidgeting.

"Don't move," Alexander ordered as he prepared his paints. "Stay just like that..."

The hairdresser and makeup artist were escorted out of the house by Gilbert.

I took a seat in the armchair and didn't plan to move.

Alexander continued to mix and prepare his paints, and when he realized I had no intention of leaving, he turned to me. "I work best in solitude."

I gave him a cold look.

"It's part of my process—"

"I'm not leaving. Get to work."

Alexander stared at me for another moment, unsure what to do, but he eventually faced forward again and gave a loud sigh in defeat.

Melanie was in a beautiful white gown with flowers in her hair, looking more stunning than the French aristocrats who used to lounge on sofas with their tits hanging out. But she continued to fidget, as if this level of attention were uncomfortable.

Alexander pressed the wet brush against the canvas and began her cheek line, capturing the exact color of her complexion with such perfection that his title as a master was well deserved. But he hesitated, adding color, stopping, and then adding again, only to stop once more. "Madame, please stop moving."

"Sorry..." She looked down at her hands to still them, but by moving her head, she changed the picture.

"Merde..." Alexander turned to me. "How am I supposed to work like this?"

"Calm the fuck down." I rose to my feet and stared him down, making him immediately take a step backward. I maneuvered around the easel and approached Melanie where she sat on the stool.

Flustered, she wouldn't make eye contact with me.

"Relax." My hand moved to her neck, and I cradled her face, my thumb tracing the left side of her bottom lip.

"I'm just afraid the painting will come out bad."

"If it does, it's his fault—not yours."

Her eyes were still elsewhere. "I just don't want to disappoint you."

My hand turned her face to mine, so she was forced to look at me, forced to let her worried eyes take comfort in the confidence of mine. I dipped my head and pressed a kiss to her lips, careful not to smear her lipstick. "You could never disappoint me."

She closed her eyes, like my words were a breath of fresh air.

My hand moved back to her neck, and I pressed a kiss to her hairline. "Now, relax." I moved back to my armchair behind Alexander and got comfortable for the show.

She straightened her back, adopted her poise, and held her position without moving.

Wordlessly, Alexander got to work.

And I just watched.

LIGHT FADED FROM THE WINDOWS. The spring gave us longer days, so the fire didn't start until deeper into the night. Spring was nearly summer now, and the heat was removing the necessity of the fire entirely.

My eyes watched the final rays of light disappear as the sun officially set and dunked the bedroom into evening. Then I looked at the woman beside me, still in her white gown that was wrinkled and soiled with sweat. With eyes lidded and heavy, she looked worn-out after the way I'd had her for the last hour.

The painting continued to dry in a safe room so it wouldn't be knocked or touched, and once that process was complete, I would finally have it for my own. I didn't take pictures on my phone because a camera couldn't capture a feeling the way a painting could. Paint was superior to pixels.

I lay on my side with her on her back beside me, my hand resting on her flat stomach, spanning the entirety of it from her hips to her breasts. Words hadn't been spoken. Only looks had been exchanged.

Her hand moved to my face, her fingertips feeling the scruff of my jawline, rubbing against the hair to feel its coarseness. Everything about me was rough—except her. She was the boutonniere to my tux. She was the flowers to my vase. She was the clouds to my sky. The sunshine to my winter.

Her hand cupped my cheek, and she leaned in to give me a soft kiss. Spontaneous and affectionate, it gave me a warmth even though the sex was finished. It was a kiss for no reason—and those were my favorite from her. She told me she loved me without actually saying it. Actions spoke louder than words, and those were the actions that affected the beat of my heart.

A knock sounded on the door. "Sir? Sorry to disturb you, but Magnus is here. Shall I let him know you'll be down in a moment?"

I kept my eyes on the treasure beside me, the possession worth more than everything I had earned in the last decade. Like a fire-breathing dragon guarding its hoard of treasure, I watched over her, never wanting to leave her, not for a moment. "Yes."

I got out of bed and pulled on my sweats.

She sat up too, her dress a mess around her, her panties on the floor. She watched me go.

I made it down the flights of steps and through the foyer. His back was to me, a glass of scotch in hand. He looked out the window to the pool in the rear as he took a drink. "You've nearly recouped our losses."

He kept his gaze out the window. "The women are working longer."

"You've negotiated more product?" I came to his side and looked out the window alongside him. Gilbert wordlessly placed a glass of scotch in my hand and silently dismissed himself. Magnus had successfully put everything back in order ahead of schedule, so my rage had dulled significantly. I was also less angry in general—because she'd come back to me.

He was quiet for a long time, as if preparing for a long-winded answer, but this response came out short. "Yes."

"What's the fee?"

"No fee."

I slowly turned my head his way.

He kept his eyes forward.

"How did you manage that?" Now that Raven was no longer a distraction, his true potential shone through. He jumped higher than he ever had.

He shrugged. "Persuasion."

I faced forward and drank from my glass again. "I'm impressed."

He swirled his glass then looked down into the dark liquid. "With the new production schedule, we'll make fifty percent more than we were before on a regular basis. I'm trying to figure out a way to secure more, but it's complicated."

I took another drink then wiped my mouth with my forearm. "How are the men treating you?"

Another pause. "Fine."

I knew the men unanimously hated him, as they should, but they would never cross me and slit his throat in his sleep. But their anger would fade, just as mine had. "Negotiating that increase in product will increase their salaries, so they must have granted you some forgiveness."

Magnus continued to stare into his glass.

"You've definitely earned some from me." I ignored the window and stared at him. There was no amount of anger that could overcome the connection between us, the bloodline, the unspeakable bond. He was my little brother, and like a parent, I couldn't stay angry with him forever.

He turned to meet my gaze, to look me in the eye, his brown eyes and facial features similar to mine. It wasn't just a pause, but an eternal silence. His look said it all, that my forgiveness meant the world to him, that we were still family...even after what he'd done.

I let it linger a little longer before I moved on. "How's the cunt holding up?"

His expression immediately tightened at the mention of her, anger floating to the surface of his eyes like flames. His breathing changed. His posture. Everything. "I wouldn't know."

I believed him, not just because I had a source on the inside to confirm it, but I could see the truth written on his face. He looked like he might kill her with his bare hands. "I don't understand your fascination with her. Melanie is beautiful, petite, quiet...and she's the ugly one."

There was no reaction.

I took a drink and looked out the window again, not expecting him to justify his strange fascination. He could have any woman he wanted, but he chose to risk his integrity and honor for a woman so unremarkable. It was just a dig on my part.

The sound of heels was audible behind us.

I hadn't asked her to come down, but I didn't mind her joining us. It was another shot at Magnus, to show him what real beauty looked like. She was the kind of woman worth life and death, worth your integrity and honor, and it was an opportunity to show him what I had and he didn't.

That I had picked the winner.

He'd picked the loser.

I turned to regard her.

She was in a deep blue dress, cinched around her waist with a slender black belt. Her makeup had been reapplied, and her hair fixed from the tangled mess it'd been just moments ago. Stunning and perfect, she glided to me, like a butterfly about to land on my arm.

Magnus turned to look as well.

She stopped a few feet away, as if asking for permission to be there.

I lifted my fingers and silently beckoned her to me.

My arm outstretched as I waited for her to step into me, to come to my side so I could secure my arm around her waist, so I could squeeze her tight. When I felt her dress against my palm, another rush came through me, like I was in the presence of royalty. She was the countess of this palace without a ring. She was the countess of my heart. I brought our lips close together but didn't kiss her. "Glass of wine?"

"Please."

I squeezed her tight then kissed her before I departed. Gilbert was nowhere in sight, probably with the chef preparing dinner, so I went down to the cellar to get her a bottle of the wine she loved.

I gave Magnus the opportunity to become acquainted with her—since she would be my wife. I also did it for more selfish reasons, to flaunt what I had and he didn't. The bottle was uncorked, the wine was poured, and then I returned with the glass.

The second I rejoined them, I could feel the tension, feel the negative energy. Magnus clenched his hand tightly like he was annoyed before sliding it into his pocket to disguise his anger. "I had to go down to the cellar to get your favorite."

Her eyes softened as she looked at me. "You didn't have to do that."

"You know I'd do anything for you." My hand encircled her waist before I gave her another soft kiss. "Now, let the men talk business. I'll join you for dinner soon."

She gave a nod before she left my hold and walked away, her heels growing fainter and fainter as she disappeared.

"Now that is a woman worth fighting for." I turned back to my brother and took a drink, seeing the anger still on his face.

He hated Raven so much it was even hard to be around her sister.

Guess I had nothing to worry about.

He took a drink before he spoke. "I've never seen you this way with a woman." He didn't ask how I felt. He didn't ask for details of the relationship. He just made his assessment based on a single interaction.

"Because this is the first time it's happened."

ELEVEN

THE LIES WE KEEP

Melanie

It was the first time I'd ever interacted with his brother directly.

Last time I saw him, he was screaming at Raven, telling her to run or he'd kill her.

Throughout the entire conversation, he looked like he wanted to kill me.

I'd taken a big risk, a risk that could ruin what I had with Fender. But when Gilbert had said he was here, I had to take the chance. I quickly scribbled that note and bunched it up in my hand. My heart still raced a million miles a minute because, any moment, I could be caught. I put my faith in the belief that Magnus still felt something for my sister—and would do as I asked.

He didn't rat me out on the spot, so that was a good sign.

But he might change his mind tomorrow.

Or the next day.

The next morning when I woke up, I expected Fender to come at me hard with the news of my betrayal.

It didn't happen.

I went into his office where he worked behind the desk—and everything was exactly the same.

Magnus didn't tell him.

When we had lunch, he stared at me with an intensity that had increased significantly. The portrait had magnified his obsession. The idea of another woman being more beautiful than me was deeply offensive, and now he was on this tirade to prove that they were all wrong. It made him want me more, made him treat me the way he used to, made him forget about what I'd done.

I wondered if I could ask him to release Raven.

Or would I jeopardize these months of work?

I spent the evening in my bedroom before dinner, wondering if Fender would get that phone call from Magnus at any moment. I sat on the couch and tried to study, but the paranoia continued to suffocate me.

If Magnus were going to tell him, he would have done it already.

I had to keep telling myself that.

Gilbert knocked before he stepped inside, carrying a large tray that contained dinner for two. "His Highness will join you in a moment." He set the table, two large plates with silver lids, along with tea and desserts.

"Thank you."

Gilbert silently dismissed himself. He wasn't outright rude to me, but he was never kind either.

Minutes later, Fender silently emerged, letting himself inside my bedroom without announcement. He approached the table then stared at me in my seat on the couch. Shirtless and muscular, he looked like a professional fighter rather than someone who sat at his desk all day and yelled at people.

I set my book and notebook on the end table then got up to join him.

His eyes watched me draw closer, his arm extending slightly so he could get it around my waist when I embraced him. His arm scooped around me and brought me in for a soft kiss, pulling me to him and almost lifting me off the ground. The look that came with it was searing, full of devotion, completely devoid of the previous anger he'd carried for months.

I'd never been loved by anyone the way he loved me.

When he released his hold, he pulled out the chair for me before he moved to the chair across from me.

I watched him go, a tremor in my throat, because I'd finally gotten back what we lost. I treasured it, and the second I asked him to release Raven, it would all be gone. No one saw the good in me the way he did. No one loved me the way he did. No one took care of me the way he did. I didn't want to lose that.

But I had to.

We sat down and ate in silence.

Fender's portions were always much bigger than mine, having enough food for three servings instead of just one. For him to maintain that size, he had to eat the calories to support it, and I wondered what his breakfast was like. I never saw him in the morning, so I had no glimpse into that aspect of his life.

With his eyes on me, he ate. He shoveled pieces of meat into his mouth then washed it down with water. He rarely drank scotch anymore, unless it was socially. "What is it?"

I was about to slice into my meat when I paused at the question. I stared at him for a few seconds, not under-standing the question, and then continued to cut into my dinner and place a bite in my mouth.

He continued to eat, but his eyes remained fixed on me, waiting for the answer.

"Is he your younger brother or older brother?"

He slowly chewed as he listened to the question, taking his time to decide if he wanted to respond or not. "Younger."

"You look a lot alike." When they were in the same room, their similarities were profound. Magnus was leaner, having an athletic build of a runner or swimmer, but he still appeared strong. Fender, on the other hand, looked like a mountain.

"You and your sister look nothing alike."

"We have the same eyes."

"Never noticed." He continued to eat, his mood souring slightly at the mention of Raven.

"You guys seem good again."

He drank from his glass of water and kept his arms on the table, but he didn't eat. It wasn't a question, but he absorbed my statement like it was, searching for a response. "He's made up for his mistake...for the most part." His eyes flicked away, slightly glazing over. "His betrayal hurt. But I know he wasn't himself." His dark eyes came back to me. "A woman can do that to you..."

I felt the waves of his stare wash over me like the high tide had rushed in. The beat against my face as if I were the rocks. They kept coming—over and over. "It's good to forgive and forget—especially for family."

His stare deepened, penetrating my face like needles to the skin. "And love." His hands went back to his utensils, and he watched himself slice the meat and stab the vegetables before putting it in his mouth, his eyes returning to me.

My heart raced because that was the first time he'd said anything of the sort since I'd left. "How did you two get into this line of business?"

He ate his food with no intention of answering.

"I just want to know you better. If I intend to stay here for a long time—"

"For the rest of your life." His voice deepened, as if giving me a command that only had one response—to obey.

He possessed me with just his words, reached across the table and grabbed me without ever touching me. Even when we weren't in the same room together, his hold was unbreakable. I lived on my own in Paris for months, and even then, he still had me. I had options to date other men, to sleep with other men, to move back home, but I never did any of those things. "Then you'll have to tell me."

"I don't have to do anything, Melanie."

It was a deliberate sting, a reminder that he was still upset about my betrayal, that he hadn't quite overcome it. "I just want to know you. That's all. Why does Gilbert call you His Highness? Is that a title you picked out?"

He stopped eating, resting his arms on the table. "No."

"Then where does it come from?"

He gripped the fork between his fingers. "I'm a count."

My eyebrows rose. "A...count?"

"Yes."

The palace. The paintings. The teacups. The butler. His social connections. In an instant, it all made sense. He was handsome, intelligent, well-mannered, like he'd been born into elegance. "If you're a count, why do you have the camp?" If he was already rich, already powerful, then what did he need it for?

His look turned cold.

"I just want to know you…" I egged him forward in the only way I could.

His elbows rested on the table, and his hands came together in front of his lips. He stared me down, for seconds that felt like minutes. "Our wealth and reputation were stolen from us. I had to earn it back to reclaim my title."

"Who's us?"

"My family." He continued to remain tense, the veins popping in his arms, like he was forcing himself to answer, forcing himself to share a piece of his life with me.

"Who took it away from you?"

Silence stretched. Stretched so far that the string broke. "You know me in the ways that matter. My past has nothing to do with us—"

"If it has nothing to do with us, then why won't you tell me—"

"Because I don't want to." He raised his voice slightly, bringing me and the entire house into silence. "I don't want to think about it. I don't want to talk about it. Conversation over."

ONCE WE WERE on the bed, his foul mood evaporated.

He was on top of me, taking me slowly, taking me over and over, his kisses on my neck and jawline, his mouth against my ear so I could listen to him breathe. When we were connected this way, he was the softest—his mind, body, and soul wrapped around mine. Without saying the words, he made me feel loved, made me feel secure in his commitment, safe in his devotion, made me feel things no other man ever had.

When we were finished, he lay beside me, his fingers slightly grazing over my skin. He would press a kiss to my shoulder for no reason. He would stare at me like he hadn't stared at me all day. Whatever he had of me, it just wasn't enough. Never enough.

I propped myself up on my elbow and turned to him, my palm planted against his stomach. I stared at the hardness of his physique, the strength of his abs, his two pecs that looked like concrete slabs.

His fingers slid through my hair, gently brushing it out of my face. His fingers moved underneath my chin and gently lifted my eyes, wanting my stare to meet his. His fingers released me and slipped back into my hair once he had me in the right position. I was the painting—and he savored me like art.

I saw a man who would do anything for me. Anything at all. "I want you to do something for me..." My heart raced because the moment had arrived. I didn't plan it, but it suddenly felt like the best time to make my case, to plead with his heart that was literally in my hands.

His eyes shifted back and forth as he waited for the request.

"I want you to free her...for me."

His expression didn't change for the first few seconds. But when the change began, it was profound. Eyes darkened in rage. The softness of his calm features immediately tightened into a wall of hardness. Now we were back in time, and he stared me down with the same hatred he had on the steps of his home. "I enjoyed your lies. But I never believed them." His hand dropped from my hair, and he left the bed.

The attempt immediately backfired in my face. "I didn't lie to you—"

"You don't love me." He turned back to me, his arms by his sides, his hands clenched in fists. "She's the only reason you came back to me. I'm not a fucking idiot. And as I said before, I will never let her go." His voice was controlled and deep, and somehow that was more sinister than if he screamed. "And I will never let you go either. I love your lies and your performances. I let you go once, but now, I owe you nothing." He grabbed his bottoms and pulled them on.

I was out of the bed and on my feet, naked and covered in a gleam of sweat. "I didn't lie about that, Fender."

He turned away, the conversation over. "The only reason you're alive is because my love is stronger than my hate. Count your goddamn blessings."

Both of my hands grabbed on to his arm. "I do love you...I do." The emotion came out of nowhere, burning the corners of my eyes, making me realize this was no longer pretend. It had never been pretend. "Why can't I have both? Why can't I love you but also want her to be free?"

He yanked his arm away and turned back to me.

"If you really love me, you will do it."

"No. I warned you that I wouldn't change my mind about this. Not now. Not ever. Not for you. I agreed once, and she humiliated me. And then you—" His jaw tightened, and his eyes filled with darkness. "You crossed me just as much as she did. And I still kept my fucking promise to you." He slammed his palm into his chest with a strike so hard it made a loud thud, but he didn't flinch at the hit. "The only reason she's alive is because of what you asked of me. How dare you ask for more?"

Tears streamed down my cheeks. "I don't understand you..."

His eyes narrowed.

"This isn't you." Tears continued to fall, to streak across my quivering lips.

He pivoted closer toward me, looking down into my face with the same hardness.

"The man I know, the man I've fallen in love with, is kind, chivalrous, good... Why do these terrible things if it's not who you are?"

He breathed hard as he stared me down.

"Why?" My voice broke with emotion. "Why do you keep my sister prisoner and punish her for running, when she's doing exactly what you would do if you were in her situation? Why do you keep these girls against their will for forced labor when you've never forced me to do anything? Why do you not give the woman you love the one thing she wants more than anything? Why...?" The tears kept falling. "You have no idea what it's like to love a man with everything that you have...and he stands for everything that you're against. You have no idea what it's like to love a man who's literally keeping your sister a prisoner in a labor camp. And the only way I can justify it is...by believing that it's not who you are. I truly believe that, that you're better than this." Everything broke through the dam and came rushing out, giving me a needed catharsis that I'd bottled inside for so long.

His enormous chest continued to rise and fall with labored breaths. An invisible button had been hit, because for the first time, he didn't have a distinct reaction. He continued to think about every single word I spoke.

"Tell me..." I was on the precipice of truth, so close to understanding this man.

He inhaled one final deep breath then went still. "You're wrong to believe I'm anything more than what you see. I feel *nothing* for anyone besides Magnus—and you. I do these terrible things because I'm a terrible man. My love for you is independent of my crimes and tragedies, and it's not enough to release my hate. Your sister will never be free. She had her chance—and she blew it."

FENDER DIDN'T SPEAK to me for a couple days.

He didn't order me out of his sight. When I came to the office, he didn't tell me to leave. He just didn't talk to me or look at me. He took his dinner alone in his room and never came to mine.

I let him boil until the water was completely evaporated. No point in trying to be with him when he wanted nothing to do with me. But when another day passed, the isolation became overwhelming. It wasn't just that I had no company, but I missed the company I enjoyed the most.

I made a gentle knock against his bedroom door before I opened it.

He wasn't on the bed.

I let myself inside and heard the sound of the fire in his living room. I moved farther into his quarters and found him sitting on his couch, elbow on the armrest, fingertips against his lips. A bottle of scotch was on the table in front of him, along with a glass with a few drops of liquid at the bottom.

I stood at the opposite end of the couch and stared at the side of his face, the dark beard that he hadn't bothered to shave. He usually shaved every morning and got a shadow by the evening. But now, he'd stopped altogether. His dark eyes were focused on something on the wall.

I followed his gaze to the painting.

The portrait of me.

Glowing in the firelight.

There had been another painting there before, but he'd replaced it with mine, so he could stare at it whenever he felt like it, could admire my face even when I was just down the stairs from him.

He turned his chin slightly and regarded me. Longing had replaced anger. Love had replaced hate. Desire had replaced solitude.

A flood of emotion swept through me as I moved to the couch and took the seat beside him. My hand went to his thigh.

His arm moved around my shoulders.

I shifted closer to him and got into his lap.

He brought his face close to mine and closed his eyes.

We sat together in silence, our bodies at ease now that they were reunited, our hearts returning to their peaceful pace.

It reinforced my belief.

That the man and the boss were two different people.

He would release my sister.

And eventually...everyone else.

TWELVE

MON AMOUR

FENDER

We sat across from each other inside the restaurant. It was a round table near the window, covered in a white tablecloth with a small vase of roses in the center. The lights were dim, but the chandelier still cast a glow on her perfect face.

In blush pink, she wore a beautiful sweetheart neckline dress, her décolletage sparkling with diamonds. Her collarbone had a distinct outline, as did her petite shoulders, so slender that the segment of muscle was visible. Her fair skin was kissable. Her full lips were kissable, too. Men couldn't resist a glance. When they stared too long, I stared back.

It was as if nothing had happened.

We went back to our lovemaking.

Our quiet evenings were spent wrapped around each other in silence.

Whether she really loved me or not, it didn't change the way I felt about her. Whether she meant a word of anything she said to me, it didn't change anything either. Nothing would ever change it.

I loved her—beyond reason.

She took a bite of her dinner then slowly chewed as she looked at me.

I had to leave in the morning, so I appreciated her beauty even more.

She returned her utensils to her plate and gave me a long stare. "Why do you love me?"

Her question soaked into my mind for a long time, but a response was never formed. "Because I do."

"If there's no reason, how do you know it's real?"

My eyes narrowed on her face, offended by the question. "Because if there's no reason, it's real. If it were conditional, based on a reason, then when that reason no longer existed, neither would everything else. The fact that there is no reason makes it unconditional. That's much stronger than having a reason...and that's why it's real." My heart had been dead for a long time. Incapable of feeling anything at all except greed and vengeance, it beat for a purpose, but never a reason. Now, it was alive and strong, pounding hard every single day for the woman across from me.

She held my gaze for a long time, her eyes far away, as if thinking about my words on an elemental level. Whenever she was deep in thought, her eyebrows shifted slightly and held the position. That was what she did now.

"I leave tomorrow."

Her concentrated look was instantly shattered by my announcement.

"Not sure how many days I'll be gone." The camp was running smoothly, so it shouldn't require my attention very long. Magnus had restored that camp and improved it beyond its former glory. It basically got a remodel we didn't know we needed.

She immediately looked disappointed, just as she did every time I left, like she truly missed me, wanted me home with her because, without me, she was lost. Her need was the sexiest thing in the world to me. She needed to be taken care of—and I got to be the one to do it. I got to be the one to cover her in diamonds and kisses. I got to be the one to keep her full with the most delectable food possible. I got to dress her in the finest designer clothing, the finest lingerie.

Me.

She looked down at her plate for a moment, absent-mindedly moving her fork around. "Take me with you." She lifted her eyes and looked at me through her thick eyelashes.

Those nights together in her cabin had never left my memory. Sometimes when I stared at her painting, flashbacks came to me—the first time she gave herself to me, the first time I earned her. That was the beginning of the end for me. My obsession grew into something deeper. "Why?"

"I want to see my sister." She gave her answer immediately without having to think twice about it.

Her response disappointed me.

"And I hate it every time you're gone..."

My eyes locked on to hers and saw only sincerity. She told me her primary reason with blunt honesty. She told me her second reason with conviction.

"It's not the same without you—"

"You're perfectly safe there—"

"I'm safe *with* you. The palace, the men, the luxuries...are nothing without you."

My visage was made of stone. I didn't release the breath I held. Stoic as ever, I kept my expression and my heart disconnected. But inside, I felt that blinding heat through my chest, felt that rush of blood to the head. Her love and affection were my fantasy—and every time it happened, it was a greater high than the last. "I'll bring you—but that doesn't mean I'll allow you to see her."

SHE ACCOMPANIED me in the passenger seat on the drive, and she sat behind me in the saddle as we rode down the dirt path. The snow had melted everywhere except the top of the peaks, and now wild flowers were visible on the sides of the well-beaten path. Green bushes and plants replaced the white powder that once covered the ground.

We arrived at the camp, and I climbed off my horse before I guided Melanie down and safely got her to the ground.

The guards immediately stared at her.

She was in tight jeans, boots, and an olive-green shirt. Despite our location, she still wore her diamonds. She kept her eyes down and didn't look at any of them.

With one stare from me, they all turned away, like scattering flies.

Magnus waited for me at the entrance of my cabin. His hood was back, revealing his hard features that matched mine. He had the same dark stare, the same intensity, something we inherited from our dead father.

I approached him and stared him down, the guards standing there to watch. His betrayal still gave me so much rage, so much pain. We hadn't spoken for a long time, because the one person I trusted implicitly had turned on me. But he took his punishment like a man, and he busted his ass to right his wrong. The shame in his eyes was the reason my hatred had faded, because he sincerely regretted what he'd done to me. I could see it on his face. "Brother."

He exhaled a long, slow breath, closing his eyes briefly, like my affection meant the world to him. "Brother."

I extended my hand to his.

He hesitated before he took it, staring for several seconds before he gripped the inside of my forearm and stepped in, his hand moving to my back.

I did the same.

I embraced my little brother.

The brother I loved like a son.

When we pulled away, I nodded to the cabin.

We stepped inside, Melanie following behind me.

The door closed, and Magnus moved to one of the couches. Melanie moved to the other, taking a seat with her knees together, her back straight, her hair back elegantly to show the diamonds in her ears. She took the road with me on horseback, but she looked as pristine as ever, French aristocracy.

I poured two glasses of scotch and grabbed a bottle of water for Melanie. I took a seat beside her, put the drinks on the table, and then moved my hand to the beautiful woman beside me, the woman who was so beautiful, she didn't look like she'd ever been here in the first place.

I gripped her thigh until she looked at me. "Men need to talk. Wait for me."

She gave a silent nod before she dismissed herself into the bedroom and shut the door.

Magnus waited until she was gone before he grabbed his drink. "I'm surprised you brought her here."

"She wants to see her sister."

He couldn't hide his surprise. "And you'll allow it?"

I stared into my brother's face but didn't see it. It was all just a blur to me right now because I was picturing Melanie across the table at dinner, picturing the most beautiful woman I'd ever seen, the woman who made me bend over backward more times than any man ever should. She made me weak—and not always in a good way. "Haven't decided."

We talked about operations of the camp for a while, and Magnus informed me he was in the process of increasing production by negotiating with the Colombians. There were hiccups along the way, but I wasn't going to let any obstacle get in the way of my riches.

Magnus shared his negativity, as always. "Don't let arrogance turn to complacency."

"It's not arrogance—greed." I took another drink then set my glass on the table. "And you know how greedy I am."

There was never enough money. I wanted more money, more power, even if I'd already reached the top of the hierarchy.

Magnus took a long drink. "Trying to figure out how to make it work. But if it's too risky, we'll have to accept what we have."

I gave a slight nod, even though I still didn't like that response. "When you leave in a few days, take care of it."

My hand grabbed my glass once more to nurse my cold lips. Conversation had concluded, and there was a beautiful woman waiting for me. I waited for him to leave, but he lingered on the couch, the glass in his hand. My eyes shifted back and forth as I looked into his, seeing a hesitation that I couldn't recognize. "What is it?"

He broke contact and stared at the bottom of his glass. There were only a few sips left. He spun the glass around to get the liquid to swirl in a vortex before he returned the glass to the coffee table. Whatever he had to say was significant because he took an eternity to say it and fidgeted along the way. "I've taken Raven as my own."

My eyes immediately narrowed when I heard that godawful name.

"I want to take her with me."

Slowly, my features tightened and changed, because I couldn't believe the words coming out of his mouth. Eyebrows furrowed in anger. Nostrils flared even though I hadn't taken a breath. When my words came out, they were loud, maniacal. There was no chance that Melanie didn't hear me scream. "What the fuck is it with this cunt?"

"I'm not asking for her freedom. I'm asking for her to be bound to me—the way Melanie is bound to you."

Once he mentioned the woman who'd claimed my heart, my anger simmered down.

"When I leave, she comes with me. When I return, she's back to work with the other prisoners. I want her to be mine. That's all."

I stared at my brother for a long time, unable to believe that his dick had such bad taste. This woman had haunted us both in different ways. She was like a fucking witch in the woods. "I don't understand your fascination. What about Stasia? She's far more beautiful. What about all the women in Paris? You can have any woman you want, and *this* is who you choose?" Melanie was the only woman who'd earned my fidelity because she deserved it. Her beauty was unparalleled, a work of art. A taste of her had made every other woman undesirable. But Raven...looked like a fucking car wreck.

"Yes."

I shook my head slightly.

"But it's not monogamous. It's not affectionate. She betrayed me, so I want her at my beck and call whenever I wish. She's mine to use. She will make up for what she did to me. That's all."

My anger slipped further away when I began to understand. This was a form of revenge because working at the camp just wasn't enough. His affection died with her betrayal, and now he just wanted to fuck her like a whore. "She's your plaything?"

He nodded.

I bowed my head slightly as I considered the request, eyes on the glass on the table.

Magnus was silent.

As always, I wanted to grant any request my brother made. I was like a parent who couldn't resist giving their child the toy they really wanted in the store. But I could only grant it with a set of hard restrictions. "If she escapes...I'll cut off the rest of you and watch you bleed out."

His expression didn't change as he stared at me, as if he'd expected those kinds of terms. "I understand."

"It doesn't matter if you let her go, or she betrays you. If she's out, it's your head." If it happened, I would have no choice but to kill him. Surely he would see that she wasn't worth that risk.

But he nodded. "I know."

I clenched my jaw slightly and shook my head. "I'll never understand it, but I'm not going to try anymore. If this is what you're into...so be it. I grant your request." I grabbed my glass, finished the scotch, and then slammed it down again before I rose to my feet.

Magnus stayed put, in disbelief.

"Melanie." I raised my voice slightly, with a hint of affection.

The door opened, and she came back into the room, her eyes on me like there was no one else in the cabin. Her petite frame had an hourglass shape, a flat stomach with large breasts. She had long, slender legs. I usually detested American women. But there was something different about her.

When she was close, my arm circled her waist as I brought her close. "We'll have dinner then go to bed. I have a lot of things to do tomorrow."

"Can I see her?" The words flew out of her mouth like she'd been holding them back since we got here. "Please." Her arms circled my neck, and she brought her face close to mine, leveraging my love to get what she wanted. "I just want to see my sister...please." She leaned in and gave me a gentle kiss on the lips.

It was hard to deny her anything when she mirrored my affection, when she made me feel like I was the only man she'd ever touched. My hands squeezed her ass before I stepped away. "Take her to the cunt's cabin. Give them five minutes. Nothing more."

She grabbed me by the arm, her nails digging into my flesh like it was life or death. "Thank you, *mon amour*..."

I stilled at the nickname she'd never used before and turned back to her. My eyes took in her features, seeing sincerity that was so true, it couldn't be forced or faked. We saw what we wanted to see, so perhaps it was all wishful thinking on my part, but when she told me she loved me, it rang clear and true like the bell of a chateau. It seemed real. It felt real. It was real.

She came closer to me, cupped my face, and gave me another kiss.

I forgot my brother was standing there. Like always, it felt like it was just the two of us.

THIRTEEN
UNDER LOCK AND KEY

MELANIE

Magnus led the way, guiding me to Raven's cabin that was a short distance away. He didn't seem interested in conversation, keeping a few strides ahead so I wouldn't have the opportunity to talk to him.

I rarely had alone time with Fender's brother, so I took advantage of it. "I heard you and Fender talking. What did you say about Raven?"

He kept going, his silence his answer.

"Please tell me—"

"Haven't I done enough for you?"

I stayed behind and turned quiet again.

We approached the cabin, and he unlocked the door. "Five minutes. That's it."

I looked into his hood, no longer able to see his face. "Thank you...for giving her the note."

His annoyance was palpable in the air around us.

I stepped inside and found Raven sitting up in a little bed, reading. There was a desk with a laptop, a TV, men's shoes on the floor.

She dropped her book with shaky hands and looked at me in shock. Slowly, her hands went to her face, her eyes glistening with tears, and her chest suddenly gave a jerk with emotion.

I lived in a palace with a butler and a private chef, and she was still here, still wearing the ugly work clothes, still forced into labor for someone else's gain. It hurt more than I'd expected it to. "Oh my god..."

"Sister." She scooted to the edge of the bed.

I rushed into her embrace, nearly knocking her over, and held on like the storm surrounded us once more, like it would blow us apart if we let go. Tears sprang into my eyes as I kept her close, as I treasured the person I loved most in this world.

The hug lasted a long time before she pulled away first. "How...how are you here?"

"I asked Fender to bring me."

"It must be hard...to be here again."

I saw Mom when I looked at her. I saw a strong person who only thought about others instead of herself. "I wanted to see you so bad... I guess I didn't care." The camp didn't look the same, not without the snow.

Her hands grabbed mine. "I just can't believe you're here..."

I squeezed her fingers. "Me too."

She inhaled a deep breath, her eyes watering with more tears, staring at our joined hands.

"Magnus continues to help you." It was such a relief, to know that he looked after her when I was powerless to do anything for her. "I gave him that note and thought he'd rat me out, but he didn't."

She shook her head. "I'm living in his cabin right now."

That explained the men's shoes. "Why?"

"Only way he can protect me."

I couldn't believe that Magnus and Fender were brothers because they were so different. Magnus exposed his softness and allowed himself to be vulnerable. Fender was stubborn, holding on to his power like he'd collapse if he let it go. I didn't understand it.

"I don't know why he wants to protect me at all, because it's not the same." Her eyes started to water more, for a whole other reason. "He won't forgive me for what I've done to him. And I miss him...so much."

"He will, Raven." Fender forgave me. Magnus would forgive her too.

Her bottom lip trembled.

I could see myself in her that very moment. I could see the conflict, the pain of loving someone you shouldn't love. I thought I was the only one. "I didn't know you felt that way."

She gave a slight shrug. "I didn't either. I guess...I've always known. Just didn't want to admit it to myself."

I dropped my gaze to our joined hands. "He'll come around."

"I don't know..."

"He will—because he obviously feels the same way." I lifted my chin and looked at her once more, wanting her to feel hopeful rather than drowning in despair. Because I really believed both of these men were more than what they seemed. "I will convince Fender to release you. Not right now. Not tomorrow. But eventually...I will."

"You shouldn't have gone back to him, Melanie." She sniffled and pulled her tears back into her sinuses. "You shouldn't have done that for me. I never would have wanted you to do that."

"It's not so bad..." Images flooded my mind. The way he placed his hand on my neck when he kissed me. The way his dark eyes burned into my face with love, not hostility. The way he took care of me like I was a burden he wanted.

"Does he treat you well?"

Gowns. Diamonds. Gourmet meals. Parties. Lovemaking. A man who loved me with all his heart. It was the first time I'd felt at home since Mom died. "Yes...he does."

Raven breathed a sigh of relief.

"I'm going to get you out of here, okay?"

She shook her head. "He'll never let me go, not after what I did. Not that I have any regrets about it."

"I know he will." I believed that man had a soul. I believed it was beautiful like his heart. And I believed that his love for me was real, not just infatuation, not just obsession. But there was something in the way. "He'll do it...for me."

WHEN I RETURNED to Fender's cabin, dinner was laid out on the dining table.

Magnus shut the door the second I was inside and departed.

Fender sat forward with his elbows on the table, his glass full of scotch, the bottle beside him. He lifted his gaze and stared at me in silence.

He probably saw my red eyes, my puffy cheeks, my ruined makeup. I moved to the seat across from him like we were home in his bedroom, having dinner together as our night-time ritual.

I placed the linen napkin over my lap and grabbed the silverware to eat.

He was still, his fingers interlocked as they rested against his mouth. It wasn't an intense stare that shone with his obsession. He was clearly angry.

Like a deer in the headlights, I went absolutely still, too petrified to move.

"I'm waiting."

I swallowed, confused by the statement.

"I'm waiting for your gratitude." He was a different man when we were here. He wasn't the man who could be entertained for hours just by looking at me. He was the boss. He drank his scotch, barked his orders, and his need for power increased tenfold.

"Thank you..."

Satisfied, he dropped his hands and began to eat.

THE SEX WAS ROUGH TOO.

He wanted me on top, one hand deep in my hair, the other on my ass. He spanked me to increase my pace, making my skin redden because he did it so many times. He wetted his fingers in his mouth before they returned to my ass and slipped inside.

I slowed down and held on to his shoulders because I'd never experienced that before.

His eyes deepened in desire. "First time?"

I nodded, feeling his fingers pulse inside me.

That seemed to be the answer he wanted, because he gave a loud moan as the pace of his fingers increased. "I'll do the honors when we get home."

When sex was finished, he showered then moved back into the sitting room down the hallway. He had his laptop, so he worked on the couch, drinking scotch like water.

There was only one bedroom, so I wondered if he would sleep with me.

I lay there alone for a long time, drifting in and out of sleep, until I eventually got up and went to the living room. "Are you coming to bed?"

He was lying down on the couch, in just boxers. The scotch was on the coffee table beside him. His eyes were closed, so he opened them and looked at me. "I was in bed...until you woke me up."

"Sorry, I didn't know you'd fallen asleep." I eyed the bottle, which was now empty. "You don't drink this much at home."

He sighed as he sat up and got to his feet. He moved down the hallway and into the bedroom.

I followed him then got back into bed.

He stepped back into the hallway, closed the door behind him, and locked it.

I was back on my feet instantly. "What are you doing?" I tried the knob, but it wouldn't turn. "Fender? Why is the door locked?"

"I'll unlock it in the morning."

"That wasn't my question. Why is the door locked?"

No answer.

"Fender?"

"I'll see you in the morning." His footsteps sounded down the hallway.

"I don't want to sleep alone in here!" My voice turned hysterical, and I pounded on the door. I'd had to sleep alone in my cabin for a long time, and it brought all that stress back. "Please don't leave me in here...please."

His footsteps grew louder as he returned. "No one will hurt you. I'm right here."

"Please just unlock the door..." I banged my fists against the wood again.

Now his voice grew louder, angry. "If you didn't want this, you shouldn't have asked me to bring you with me. Fault's on you."

"Open the fucking door! I don't want to talk through a piece of wood."

The knob turned, and he unlocked it, opening the door quickly and staring down at me with eyes filled with the underworld. He breathed hard, his jaw clenched tightly, like he was pissed off at me the way he'd been with Magnus. "What?"

My eyes welled up with tears. "Please don't make me sleep in here alone. It brings back so much."

His anger didn't wane, not this time. "You insult me. You think I'd ever let something happen to you?"

"It's not that, okay? I just don't want to be alone...with my thoughts...my memories."

Still nothing.

"You've slept with me before—"

"That was when I trusted you. I don't trust you anymore."

My eyes closed at the comeback. "*Mon amour*—"

"Nothing you say will change my mind. You're the only woman I've slept with my entire life—and you threw it away."

"Why are you like this—"

"None of your fucking business." He slammed the door and locked it. "That's why."

———

FENDER WAS a different man when he was here.

Hostile. Angry. Venomous.

I hardly recognized him.

He was out of the cabin most of the day, so I stayed inside alone. I didn't get much sleep, during the day or at night, because just being at the camp was so traumatizing. He was the one thing that could make me feel better, but he refused to comfort me. He didn't give in to my demands, and every night, he locked me in the bedroom.

Thankfully, we were only there for a couple days.

When it was time to leave, I was so relieved to get the hell out of there.

The fact that Raven had to stay just made me feel worse.

I had a choice—she didn't.

We rode on horseback back to the main road, took his car into Paris, and then pulled up to the palace at dark. The windows of his bedroom were lit because Gilbert had it prepared for Fender's return. The grounds were maintained. The flowers were in bloom. It was such a beautiful place.

I was so happy to be back I nearly cried.

I could never go back to the camp again.

We entered the palace, were greeted with pleasantries from Gilbert, and then headed upstairs.

Fender went into his bedroom, still in a foul mood.

I didn't follow him and went to my bedroom. It was prepared for my arrival as well, with fresh flowers everywhere, the bed already turned down for bedtime. There was a hint of floral fragrance in the air, and sometimes I wondered if the housekeepers sprayed a scent in the room when they cleaned to make it smell like that.

I took off the dirty clothes, showered, and then got into bed.

I was so happy to be home. Could finally get some sleep.

I was on my side, the lights off and my eyes closed, drifting off instantly.

Then the bedroom door opened.

My eyelids rose at the sound, seeing Fender approaching the bed in his sweats, like this was every other night.

I sat up in defense, wanting him to leave for the first time ever.

He stilled at my reaction, his eyes narrowing in surprise at my response.

"No." That was all I said. There was no better way to describe my feelings. Even if he wanted to sleep with me now, I wouldn't allow it. It was the first time I really wanted to push him away, to get him as far away from me as possible.

He continued to stand there, reading the unspoken words in my stare.

"Leave."

His eyes narrowed. "I—"

"I said leave."

He remained still, absorbing the command slowly. He probably had never been spoken to that way in his life, and it took him a while to understand reality. But he stepped away from the bed and walked out without saying a word.

I STAYED in my bedroom the next day.

I woke up refreshed after a good night of sleep, had breakfast and lunch in my living room, and spent my time reading. As the sun moved, I sat in different places to feel the warmth coming through the windows. Sometimes I was on the couch, and sometimes I was on the rug in the center of the room, just to feel those rays.

In the evening, I was on the couch, still reading, when the door opened.

I knew it was him—and anger immediately flooded my body.

His footsteps came across the hardwood then turned muffled on the rug. They stopped altogether when he was in my living room.

I kept my eyes on my book. "I still don't want to talk to you. Leave."

He inhaled a deep breath, full of irritation.

I turned the page and kept reading.

"What—"

"I said leave." This time, I looked up and met his eyes.

He was livid. His face was tinted red, and all the muscles of his body were flexed. But he kept his mouth shut and clenched and left.

THIS WENT on for a couple days.

He would come into my bedroom every night and stare at me.

I'd ask him to leave.

He would obey.

It didn't matter how angry he was, he respected my wishes and excused himself. That didn't stop him from trying, from hoping that night would be different, but when it wasn't, he listened.

I didn't understand how he could be two men. When we were home, he was Fender. When we were at the camp, he was the boss. Different personalities. Different hostilities. Different everything.

When he came into my living room that night, I was finally ready.

The space had been necessary, but once it went on for too long, I started to miss him. I closed the book and set it on the end table beside me before I looked up at him.

The anger slowly left his face when he realized he wouldn't be asked to leave. He moved to the couch across from me, his forearms on his knees, and he leaned forward as he stared at me. "I told you I don't sleep with people—"

"Why?"

He clenched his jaw at the interruption. "The only reason I'm allowing you to talk to me this way is because—"

"What?" I purposely interrupted him just to press his buttons.

He shook his head and clenched his jaw, keeping his rage restrained. He dropped his eyes and stared at his hands, rubbing them together slightly as he let the seconds trickle by, as he let his anger fade before he spoke. "Because you're the only person who's allowed to speak to me this way." He lifted his chin and looked at me again, still angry, but substantially less.

"Answer my question."

His eyes narrowed. "You're still upset about that? Because I didn't let you sleep with me—"

"What kind of man are you?"

His face flushed with anger at being interrupted again, but he didn't interrupt me. He didn't want to risk being ordered to leave, and watching him cooperate despite the way I treated him showed how much I really meant to him.

"Your woman is having a panic attack because she's back in the very place where she was held prisoner, and you do nothing? I needed you, and you weren't there for me. Because of what? You just don't like sleeping with people? I'm not *people*, Fender."

"I never offer to take you with me for that very reason." He didn't raise his voice. He stayed calm, because he wanted to resolve this, to get me back into his bed so he could kiss me and make love to me. "You wanted to come."

"You locked the fucking door—like I'm an animal."

He rubbed his hands together again and didn't refute that.

"I barely slept the entire time we were there."

"You. Wanted. To. Come."

I shook my head in anger. "What do you think I'm going to do to you? Stick your hand in a cup of warm water and make you pee yourself?" I turned sarcastic when I was really angry, and I knew I got that from Raven.

His eyes darkened at my words, but he didn't say anything.

My voice trailed off, the hurt rushing in. "You really think I'd ever hurt you?" I could have snuck into the kitchen, grabbed a knife, and hid it behind my back. I could have gone into his office, and when he came to me, I could have stabbed him right in the throat. There were countless ways

I could have retaliated, but the thought never crossed my mind. I wasn't a murderer by nature. But I also had no desire to cause him pain. Even if his death would result in Raven's freedom, I still wouldn't do it.

He dropped his gaze and rubbed his palms together. "I'm the reason you were in the camp in the first place. I'm the reason your sister is there now. I'm the reason she'll be there for the rest of her miserable life." He lifted his chin and looked at me again. "Yes. I think you'd hurt me—and I wouldn't blame you."

I held his gaze as the pain engulfed my heart. My eyes even watered a bit, hurt by the mere idea of ever causing him any kind of harm. "I would never...ever...hurt you." My voice broke, so I stopped talking and shifted my gaze away.

He stared at my face for a long time. "The only way your sister gets out of there is if I'm dead. Surely you've come to this conclusion."

I shook my head. "That's not the way she gets out of there. There's another option." I turned back to look at him.

His gaze was as hard as ever. "No, there's not."

"I know you'll let her go."

He shook his head. "Never."

"You'll change your mind."

His voice was quiet, as if he regretted having to say the words. "I won't."

I stared at him for a long time, seeing a distant softness in his eyes, a glimpse of who he really was. "I don't know what made you this way, but I'm so sorry that you had to go through it."

He immediately shifted his gaze to the window, his demeanor turning rigid like the door of an impenetrable vault.

"I wish I had been there for you..."

His eyes didn't shift. He didn't breathe. He was stone.

That was his reaction to trauma—to turn everything off and feel nothing.

He wasn't a monster. He was just...heartbroken.

I left the couch and walked over to him, his expression not changing even when I was right in front of him. My hand went to his shoulder, and I gently directed him backward as I straddled his hips and got into his lap.

He allowed me to guide him, but he still didn't look at me.

My hand cupped his face and forced his eyes on me.

He allowed that too. He gave up all his power to me, let me cross lines that others would be killed for. He let me speak my mind without punishment. He let me order him to leave—in his own home.

His eyes moved with mine, dead inside.

I brought my forehead to his. "I can see you—who you really are. You're the man I've fallen in love with."

He pulled away so he could look me in the eye, life coming back to him.

"Je t'aime..."

His eyes reacted instinctively, contracting at my words. A kaleidoscope of emotions filled his gaze, showing the depth of his love, the goodness in his heart. Because a man couldn't love this fiercely if his heart were full of evil. He couldn't treat me so well if he weren't willing to sacrifice his life for mine. He couldn't forgive his brother if he possessed too much hate. He was a good person—even if he resisted. "Chérie, je t'aime..."

FOURTEEN
NEVER LET GO

FENDER

She lay with me in bed, cuddled into my side with my arm hooked around the small of her back. Her face was on my chest, her hair was everywhere, and she breathed slowly because she'd fallen asleep almost instantly.

I wondered if she drifted off as quickly when she was alone.

The fireplace was cold because it was too warm for flames. The chandelier above was dimmed to the lowest level, so little light highlighted her face. Her hand was on my chest, over my heart, and I grabbed it and held it there.

A quiet knock sounded on the door. "Sir?"

I didn't speak because I didn't want to wake her up.

Gilbert poked his head inside.

I raised my hand slightly to tell him I'd be down in a moment.

Magnus was supposed to stop by tonight. Just didn't expect him so late in the evening.

I hugged her to my chest then gently rolled her to her back before I left the bed.

She stayed asleep.

I went downstairs and found Magnus waiting in the living room. In silence, I sat across from him and stared at him, knowing Raven was in Paris since he was in Paris. She was staying at his estate, exposed to luxuries she shouldn't ever get to experience.

I'd thought his betrayal was in the past, but now that she accompanied him, it was in the present—and it was hard not to think about. My love for my brother outweighed my hate, but I did still hate him because of this. "How'd it go?"

His answer was blunt. "I don't like him."

"You don't like anyone, Magnus." Except ugly cunts.

Magnus ignored the insult and told me all the reasons why dealing with Napoleon was a bad idea.

All he ever had were reasons not to do something. I was used to it.

"We have enough money, Fender. Risking the empire we have isn't worth—"

"That empire can grow into a regime—if we work for it." I wanted this enterprise to exist outside of France, expand into the other European countries, even into Russia if I could make that happen. It didn't stop here. When we were big enough, we would take on the Skull King in Italy.

His eyes filled with irritation. "We have enough money."

"No amount of money is enough. Not unless it's all the money."

"I have more than I can spend in a lifetime—"

"Well, I don't."

He fell silent.

"Napoleon is a good partner. He can increase our distribution."

"I told you I don't trust him."

"We don't trust anybody."

He took a deep breath then pushed it out of his flared nostrils. "Why would someone like him work for someone like us—"

"Me. Everyone works for me—including you."

His annoyance was impossible to hide, but he didn't voice it. "I don't think he's right for us. We will find someone else."

"And you won't like that someone else either."

Magnus took a long pause, simmering underneath the surface. "I know it's difficult for you to see, but I'm doing everything I can to protect your back when you're looking the other way. I want to preserve everything you've built. I want to preserve what we've accomplished—because I know how important it is to you."

I believed every word, but I was in a foul mood since she was in the city.

"Why did you ask me to screen him if you don't value what I say?"

"For a couple reasons." I grabbed my glass and took a drink. "And you know what those reasons are, Magnus."

Guilt flooded his gaze.

"Fender?" Melanie's voice came to me from the foyer.

"*Chérie*, in here." I kept my gaze on my brother but instantly responded to her call.

She stepped into the room, wearing one of my t-shirts that fit her like a dress. She obviously didn't expect me to be with company because she wouldn't have dressed that way if she'd known.

I thought she looked exquisite.

She hesitated when she spotted Magnus but came to me anyway. "I woke up, and you weren't there."

"I'll be up in a minute."

She looked at my brother again. "Is she here—"

"Yes," I said with anger in my veins. "She's in Paris."

"Can I see—"

"Go to bed." I didn't mean to snap, but I couldn't control it. I would never allow that cunt to enter my home—not again anyway. I tried to smooth out my voice to make up for my hostility, because if I pissed Melanie off, she wouldn't talk to me for days. Really didn't want to experience that again.

She walked away.

When her footsteps were gone, I looked at my brother again. "All she ever talks about is her obnoxious sister. Maybe I should kill her, so I don't have to hear about her anymore—from either one of you." I grabbed the glass in front of me and downed the rest of it.

He watched me for a while, studying my face. "Why do you hate her so much?"

It was a stupid question, and I gave him a look that made it clear what I thought of it.

"It's more than that, Fender." His eyes shifted back and forth as he looked into my face. "We both know we would do the exact same thing if we were in her position. Her actions aren't personal. So why?"

I grabbed the bottle and refilled my glass. "Because she is the one thing that stands between Melanie and me." She would always be the wedge. She would always be the hesitation. Her hatred for me would never die, and she would force Melanie to choose between us. I already knew what that choice would be.

"Then let her go. Problem solved."

I gave a shake of my head. "What happened last time I let her go?"

He stared, his arms on his thighs.

"Melanie left me." I threw my head back and took another drink like it was a shot rather than a full glass. "And she would leave me again."

He dropped his gaze.

"Raven's hatred for me will never fade. She'll ridicule Melanie for wanting to be with me. She'll turn her against me. She'll take away the single greatest thing that had ever happened to me. So, no, I can't fucking let her go."

***

I SAT at my desk with my lunch tray beside me. I took a few bites as I worked, pulling numbers from the file Magnus had sent to me in an encrypted format. When I looked up from the screen, I saw her standing there.

In a beautiful dress with a bracelet on her wrist, she stood in front of me.

I waited for her to speak her mind.

"Can I see her?"

I knew this would come up again.

"Please."

I shook my head.

She inhaled a deep breath, her eyes full of emotion. "Why not?"

"Too risky."

"In what way?"

"The second you're united, she'll try to run with you."

"If she's allowed to come to Paris with Magnus, I doubt she would risk that just to get caught again."

"I think she'll feel differently if she sees you."

"Well, I won't run. I promise." Sincerity burned in her eyes with undeniable brilliance. She seemed to mean every word she said to me, like this wasn't some kind of stunt to get what she wanted.

"She might make you."

"I...I...I don't think she would. And again, what does it matter? Because we won't get far."

"It does matter."

"Why?"

Because I'd made an oath that I would have to keep. "When Magnus asked to have her accompany him during his trips to Paris, I granted it with a condition. If she runs— I'll kill him. It's in my best interest to give her no incentive to do that."

Her eyes dropped as she fidgeted with her fingers.

"I'm sorry."

She lifted her eyes and looked at me again. "She wouldn't have to run...if you let her go."

Under no circumstances could I do that—because I would lose Melanie too. I turned back to my laptop and went back to work. Her final words hung in the air, echoing unanswered.

She stood there for a while, her gaze burning into my face with fierce hope. But she eventually gave up and walked away.

———

I HAD her at the edge of the bed, thrusting inside her until I hit my release, giving a loud moan in satisfaction. My desire for her figure never expired. She brought me so much satisfaction, but also constant need. Some was never enough. All of her was more, but still fell short. My dick remained hard time and time again, when for other women, it went soft after the first round.

I stayed inside her as I slipped my fingers to her back entrance.

"Whoa..." She immediately arched her back and grabbed on to my arms. "What are you doing?" Passion left her eyes as she considered my intentions.

"Getting you ready." Two fingers were inside her, pulsing, forcing her to stretch.

With her knees pushed up against her sides, she lay there and breathed, her skin slightly sweaty even though she was only lying there while I did all the work—not that I minded. Trepidation was bright in her eyes, a look I hadn't seen since our first night together in the cabin.

"*Chérie?*" I held myself over her with one arm, my hard dick inside her, my wet fingers inside her, forcing her tightness to expand.

She breathed hard at my ministrations then gave a shake of her head.

Instead of pulling my fingers away, I brought our faces close together.

"I'm just not...into that."

"But you've never tried it."

"Well...you barely fit inside me as it is."

I fit inside every woman I'd taken before. Melanie was no different. "I've never really made love to you if I haven't made love to all of you. It will hurt, but it'll get easier. I'll be gentle and slow."

Hesitation was still in her eyes.

"Then, one day, you'll like it."

Her blue eyes shifted back and forth as she looked into mine.

She had all the power in this situation, so if she said no, I'd remove my fingers and try again at a later time. But I hoped she would trust me enough to at least try.

"Is this a French thing?" she whispered.

"It's common."

"Okay..."

Shivers ran through my muscles before I started to thrust inside her once again, getting her to relax once more, to get back into the moment. Two fingers turned to three. Breaths turned to moans. Heat rose to the ceiling.

Soaked to the base, I pulled out my dick and removed my fingers.

Gently, I pressed, getting my crown inside.

She gave a slight cry as she grimaced.

I stopped, gave her a moment, and kept going.

She clawed her nails deep into my flesh, nearly puncturing the skin and drawing blood. She breathed harder as she took more, panting in pain as I slid inside, her skin tinting red. Tears formed in her eyes when I was halfway.

I paused as I looked down at her, more aroused than I'd ever been. She was stronger than she gave herself credit for. Tears shone in the corners of her eyes and slid down her cheeks as her lips panted with deep breaths. "*Chérie*, tell me to stop, and we stop." I didn't want to pull my dick out, not when it already felt right, not when I knew what we would have if she allowed it to happen. But I would—in a heartbeat.

"It's okay..."

I moved farther inside, getting my dick sheathed to the base.

She breathed louder and harder, holding on to me, more tears coming.

Then I started to move, slow and easy, making love to her asshole as I watched her cry. "*Chérie, tu es si belle*..."

FIFTEEN

MAGNUS

MELANIE

He seemed to understand how much it hurt because the next two days were filled with massages, kisses, and sexual fantasies just for me. He ate whipped cream and strawberries off my body before he made love to my pussy with his mouth. Sometimes he would have me sit on his face, and he would go for hours, making me feel good, doing things just for me since I'd done something just for him.

It made it worth it.

The sun had just set, and I was in the Olympic-size pool in the backyard. Gilbert had brought me drinks and snacks on a tray, so I snacked while I splashed around. The sun faded, but it was still warm. The lights from his gardens came on at the moment the sun set, and I could see the acres of his property that looked like a public park. My arms rested on the edge of the pool, and I stared at the view, unable to believe I lived in such an estate. The only experience I had with places like this was in the movies, and even then, they paled next to the real thing.

Footsteps sounded on the deck behind me, and the fact that I could hear them at all told me it wasn't Gilbert. He moved like a ghost, providing pristine service without being seen or heard. He faded into the background the second his job was complete, like a shadow.

I turned around to see Fender there, stripped down to his nakedness. From my angle below, he looked like a living statue stepping into the pool to join me. He was so cut and so strong that every movement he made caused a ripple effect to the rest of his body.

He moved into the heated water, his pecs and shoulders above the waterline. He headed straight for me, his eyes dark like espresso beans on the counter at the café. Every time I'd looked at that jar, I would think of him, remember the way he looked at me.

My chin was just above the waterline, and when he came to me, he lifted me so my legs wrapped around his waist. His hands held on to my ass even though I didn't need the support, and now that we were at eye level, we stared.

Quiet as a mouse, Gilbert brought another tray of drinks and snacks for Fender then excused himself back to the house.

Fender didn't look away from me, as if he didn't notice or care.

Gilbert and I had never really talked again. He wasn't rude to me, but what little friendship we'd had was forever severed. It was strange to think that the butler was more stubborn than his master.

I'd never had a relationship with a man that required no conversation. Fender and I spoke with our touches and our looks. When two people were as close as we were, it was unnecessary to fill the silence with words. We just existed in the same moment—and that was enough.

He guided me against the wall of the pool then slipped his fingers underneath my bottoms and found my clit. With his eyes on me, he rubbed me in a circular motion, his pressure growing harder and harder.

My arms wrapped around his neck, and I breathed in his face, climaxing against his fingers within a few minutes.

As if nothing had happened, he grabbed his glass and took a drink, like his only interest was getting me off and receiving nothing in return. He kept me against the wall, looking at me as he enjoyed his drink, sometimes a drop catching in the corner of his mouth. He stared at me like an artist who couldn't decide what to chisel off his sculpture next because it was already perfect.

"As much as I'm enjoying all this...you've made it up to me."

He finished his drink then put it down. "Watching you come is foreplay for me."

"That's several days of foreplay, then."

"Worth the wait."

My arms circled his neck again, and I held him close, never feeling safer than I did in moments like this, when his powerful hands were on me, when his bulletproof chest was against mine. "Well, I don't think I can wait any longer."

He gave a slight smile, a rare glimpse into his boyish charm. "When we go to bed." The smile disappeared an instant later, leaving no trace behind. His eyes were dark and intense all over again.

The silence lasted a long time, and we just floated in the pool together, drinking and snacking, the night deepening.

He spoke. "I'm attending an event tomorrow night."

"What kind of event?"

"Cocktail party."

"Do you want me to come?"

The annoyed stare answered my question.

"Just wasn't sure..."

"Don't be unsure again." He released me and drifted away slightly, turning around to take a look at the house as if to check on something before he returned to me, standing on his feet so his chest was above the water. He could say something so harsh, but it somehow felt romantic to me.

"Who will be there?"

"Socialites. Same characters you see me with. Magnus, as well."

The mention of his brother immediately made a lightbulb brighten in my mind. My interactions with him were rare, and I'd only been alone with him for minutes at a time. But with a house full of people, it might be possible to slip away and speak to him without Fender knowing. I hid my reaction and enthusiasm. "I guess I'll have to find something to wear."

"Gilbert has taken care of it."

"Of course, he has."

Fender studied my face. "Has he been good to you?"

The two of us would never be civil again. Gilbert had taken the rejection worse than Fender did. Or maybe he was just upset that I was back in the house and he had to watch us together. But I actually liked him because he was so loyal to Fender. No other butler would care so much, would be so trustworthy. "Yes. He's great."

He seemed to believe me because he admired the grounds behind me, his hand moving to the back of his neck to give himself a quick scratch. He was so strong, with such hard features to his face that made him undeniably handsome. He could walk into any bar and get any woman he wanted, even if they spoke different languages. With every passing month, every week, every day, I found him more irresistible.

It was hard to believe that I was his one and only, that I was enough for him.

Masculine, with a libido that took several sessions to quench. Rich, with more money than he could spend in several lifetimes. Ripped, hitting the weights the way some people attended church. Handsome, with hard features, a shadowed jawline, sexy lips, dark eyes.

How was I enough for someone like him?

What had I done to deserve to be loved so unconditionally?

Weak and stupid, I couldn't survive on my own. I'd had two roommates back in America because I was just a bartender who couldn't stand on my own two feet. I had no ambitions in life.

His eyes homed in on my face. "Don't do that."

My eyes flicked to his face.

"You look like that every time you hate yourself."

For a man so...manly, he had unparalleled intuition. He could read between the lines when other men couldn't. He could see what others could not. Or maybe he just knew me the way I knew him. "Is that something you would notice with your French girls a lot?" I didn't say whore because it seemed demeaning, even though that was exactly what they were. If I got paid to have sex with Fender, I'd probably do it too.

His eyes focused on me for a while before he answered. "Yes."

I could barely tolerate it, and no amount of money would make me tolerate it better. I wasn't one of his French girls. Nor would I ever be.

"Don't compare yourself to them. I don't."

I studied his face.

"Because every time I was with them, I wished it were you."

THE ESTATE WAS FILLED with people.

Women in gowns. Men in tuxedos. Flutes of champagne were delivered to guests, as well as tiny appetizers guests could enjoy in a single bite. The house was decorated with extravagant flowers, and a string quartet played instrumental music that made the moment identical to a scene in a movie. I'd lived a life of luxury for months now, and I never got used to the wealth Fender possessed. I never got used to the things money could buy.

My look was achieved by professionals. All I had to do was sit there as the team transformed me into an image I'd never be able to replicate without weeks of practice. My hair was done beautifully, my makeup pristine, and my gown was probably as expensive as one of his cars.

But the hours and money were all worth it when Fender looked at me.

His gaze seared into mine as we walked up the stairs. Possession burned bright, like he wanted to push me up against the wall and take me right then and there. Pride was there too, like he was the only man who could ever have a woman like me. A million emotions and thoughts happened in just a few seconds. I saw love, devotion, and commitment in there, too.

It went against everything I believed in—but I felt like the lucky one.

With his hand on my lower back, he spoke to his acquaintances in French, and I chimed in whenever I understood enough to say something intelligent.

Whenever I did that, he gave me a look of pride and brought me closer, pressing a kiss to my cheek.

It made me melt every time.

Made me feel good about myself.

Caught up in Fender, I forgot about the reason I'd looked forward to this evening.

Until I saw him.

Magnus walked up and greeted his brother with a stare.

I didn't know what to do, so I looked away.

They exchanged words in French, and one word stood out the most. Napoleon. Quick words were exchanged back and forth, too fast for me to pick up on, but I could tell that Fender was irked.

I'd hoped Magnus would bring my sister, but it was clear he was stag. "You didn't bring her?"

"Why would I?" He switched to English, and his tone was clipped and angry, like the mention of her infuriated him the way it infuriated Fender.

Fender drank from his glass, changing the subject. "Stasia is looking for you."

His face remained stony at the mention of this person.

I should keep my mouth shut, but I was instantly hit with a need to defend my sister, who loved this man. "Who's Stasia?"

Magnus dismissed himself without giving an answer. He walked off and headed down the hallway.

This was my chance.

Someone else walked up to us and engaged Fender in conversation, so while he was distracted, I excused myself. "Excuse me, just need to use the restroom." I kissed him on the cheek, received a quick look of approval as he continued his conversation.

I went down the long hallway, a hallway I guessed was correct, and searched for Magnus. He must be in the bathroom, so that was where I was headed. Then I heard his voice from a room—with a woman.

"C'est le cas. C'est juste que je ne suis plus intéressé, Stasia." His voice was even more annoyed than it'd been before. I could roughly translate it. *I don't. No interest, Stasia.*

Her entitled voice responded. "Les hommes ne se désintéressent pas des femmes comme moi. Alors si tu la gardes dans ton froc, ça veut dire que tu te réserves pour quelqu'un d'autre. Intéressant. C'est qui ?" *Men don't lose interest in beautiful women like me. Who are you fucking?*

Magnus didn't answer before he stormed out and kept going down the hallway, not seeing me because he headed in the opposite direction.

Stasia remained inside, probably recovering from his rejection.

I went after him. "Magnus?"

He stopped in front of the bathroom and slowly turned to look at me, his eyebrows raised. He immediately glanced behind me to make sure Fender was nowhere in sight. "What the fuck are you doing?"

"Thank you...for being loyal to my sister." I had a whole other agenda, but I had to show my gratitude for the one man who looked after her, who was loyal to her despite the dangerous position it placed him in. "I really... It means the world to me...that she has you." I got choked up when I didn't expect it, but this man deserved every ache of my heart. "You love her."

Just like his brother, he had a face carved out of stone. No reaction of any kind. "What do you want from me?"

"Just to talk."

His eyes filled with irritation, and he glanced over my shoulder several times to make sure Fender hadn't come looking for me. "You better make it quick, because I won't be able to help you if he catches us."

I ran with it and didn't waste a second. "I know you don't agree with the camp. I know you don't agree with the way it's run. You wouldn't risk your life for my sister repeatedly if you did."

His gaze remained hard.

"Do you believe...that Fender can change?"

Subtle differences moved into his face, a softness he couldn't fight.

"Because I think he can. I just...don't understand why he is the way he is. If I knew...it would help."

His eyes shifted behind me before he responded. "Yes."

I inhaled a breath of relief, like Magnus had literally lifted a burned-down cabin off me. "Then can you talk to him—"

"I've tried."

"Again—"

"I've tried more times than I can count."

Disappointment hit me like a punch to the gut. It took me a second to recover. "Then why do you think he can change?"

He inhaled a slow breath, like the answer was so complicated that a response was daunting. "Because he's a good man. He's just obsessed with a goal to the exclusion of everything else. It doesn't matter who he hurts in the process...since he was hurt."

"What hurt him?"

Magnus shook his head. "Can't tell you."

"Why—"

"Because I'm literally the only person in the world who knows—so he'll know your source."

I inhaled a deep breath in disappointment. "I won't tell him."

He shook his head. "I won't betray my brother. If he wanted you to know, he would tell you."

"But if you tell me, I might be able to get him to stop."

Magnus stared me down for a while, like the thought was tempting. But his answer cut through my dreams. "Then get him to tell you. Not my place." His eyes flicked past my shoulder. "You should go back now. I'm surprised he's left you unattended this long." He turned away.

"He won't sleep with me. Why?" I barked out my question because I knew the conversation was over and I'd never get this opportunity again.

He hesitated before he turned back to me. A deep stare ensued. "Same reason."

"What do you mean, same reason?"

"Everything he says, everything he does, everything he's become—it's all for the same reason." He glanced behind me before he turned to the bathroom door. "Go."

SIXTEEN
DEATH OF INNOCENCE

Fender

Days passed, and we barely shared a few words.

She read in my office while I worked. We had dinner together in my bedroom, sharing looks across the table, but having no conversation. Clothes came off, and we made love in my bed. We'd done it a hundred times, knew the other's body better than our own, and it was somehow just as fascinating to me every time.

My life had always been full of money, power, and sex.

But it was filled with something more now.

I pictured her walking around the palace with her hand over her bulging stomach, chasing down a little boy with my dark hair and eyes. She gave me back the very thing I'd lost—a family.

She was propped on her elbow with her hand on my stomach. "What are you thinking about?"

My eyes shifted to hers, seeing the way she absorbed my stare. She knew when my thoughts were outside the four walls of this bedroom. She knew when my thoughts strayed, when my heart changed its pace, when a glaze settled over my eyes. I held her look and never answered, my hand moving to her flat stomach. That fantasy was for a time in the future, a dream on the horizon. Not today. Not tomorrow. Time would ravage our appearances, but my love for her was a candle with an endless wick. It would burn—always. For her and no one else.

She didn't ask again. "So...who is Stasia?"

The party was days ago. Already forgotten about it. "Socialite."

"I mean, was she his girlfriend or something?"

"No. She's trying to hook him because he's rich and powerful."

"How do you know that?"

"Because she did the same with me."

Her eyes immediately changed, reacting in jealousy.

"Before we met." I'd always tell the truth, and if she didn't want to hear it, she should stop the line of questioning. "She went for me first since I'm the count."

Her eyes dropped, looking at her hand on my stomach.

My hand slid up her neck and to her cheek. "But I've found my countess. And she's far more beautiful than any other woman in that room."

Her eyes lifted again, a slight smile entering her gaze. The tightness of her features faded when she heard my praise. The previous jealousy faded until it disappeared entirely. "Je t'aime..."

My thumb brushed her bottom lip, and I stared at her mouth, the source of those poetic words. The waves of her love washed over me, brought me deep under the sea until I couldn't breathe. But I'd rather suffocate with her than take a full breath without her. "Je t'aime."

———

"*MON AMOUR*..." Her quiet voice came from the couch in the sitting area. Her book was on the coffee table in front of her. The daylight streamed through the open windows and blanketed her beautiful face in a wondrous glow.

I stared at her from my seat at the desk, taking in the scene like a work of art. It could easily be painted and hung over someone's mantel. I closed my laptop and moved to the couch across from her. Arms on my thighs. Hands together. Eyes on her face. Work required my attention, but it became secondary to her needs. "Oui, *chérie*?"

Her legs were crossed, and she held herself with poise, her back straight, her hands together on her lap. She had all the qualities of royalty without even trying. Most of the qualities she possessed were innate and didn't need to be taught. "You'll give me anything I ask for?"

The softness in my features immediately turned stony. "Except one."

"Then I want to ask you something—and I want an answer."

My eyes immediately narrowed at the bait and switch.

"You can't tell me you love me without giving me this answer. You can't say you want me forever without giving me this answer. I want this answer, and if you love me, there should be no hesitation to oblige."

I felt like I'd walked into a negotiation unprepared. She set the tone, manipulated me into denying her only one thing, so she could ask for something else and get the answer she wanted. I was annoyed. Irritated. A little pissed off. But I also felt respect. "I never want to hear you say you're stupid ever again." Her sister had destroyed her self-esteem with lies. She'd ripped her apart and held her to a standard she never asked to be held to. The only reason Raven was alive was because of her. The only reason she was spared time and time again was because Melanie fought for her. Raven was just jealous that Melanie was far more beautiful—as she should be.

Her eyes softened in a way they never had before. Her entire face changed, her breathing included. Her stare lasted a long time, looking at me like I'd just given her wings. Her insecurities were erased by my confidence, because I knew my *chérie* better than Raven ever did.

"What is your question, *chérie*?" I'd been the provider and the protector since Magnus and I fled in the streets with gunshots ringing behind us. I became the man of the family because my father was a coward. There had been no one else I wanted to take care of until Melanie, and it was my greatest joy. It wasn't the fancy clothes and expensive makeup that I provided. It was the love that she needed. It was the confidence that she needed. It was being the man that she needed.

She hesitated, her fingers starting to fidget in her lap.

Still and silent, I gave her the floor to speak her mind. No one else could command my attention the way she did. No one could yell and interrupt me and live to tell the tale. But I let her do whatever she goddamn well pleased. Because she was my *chérie*.

Her eyes were reinvigorated with confidence. "I want to know what happened to you."

With my hands together, I gave her the same look I had for the last few minutes.

"I want to love all of you, not just the man I know now. I want to love the man I never met. I want to...know you. I want to know you in a way no one else does." Her eyes pleaded with mine, desperate to get this answer.

My thumb moved over a knuckle on my right hand, the knuckle that always ached in the cold because I'd dislocated it so many times. "It won't change anything, *chérie*." I knew she believed I was capable of change, but she was dead wrong about that.

"Then you should tell me, so I'll understand."

I massaged my knuckle again as I kept my eyes on her. My future wife. The future countess. The future mother of my children. My future widow. With every day and every week, I let her in, let her deeper inside, shared my life with her without barriers. The night she left me never happened. Those months apart had been erased. For the first time, I didn't live in the past. I cherished the present. "My family was murdered."

She inhaled a deep breath, her eyes instantly watering.

"Mother. Sister. Brother. All of them." So much time had passed that their images had faded from my mind. Their pictures were in my safe, and sometimes I would look at them and remember my childhood with my siblings, the cookies my mother would make every Sunday, the house at Christmastime.

"Magnus and I are the last of our line." I spoke without emotion because I was numb to the loss. It was factual at this point. Grief was complicated, and sometimes it would arrive at my shores like a hurricane, and other times, it was silent for years. Right now, it was silent. Probably because of her.

"I...I'm so sorry."

I gave a curt nod.

"Your father?"

"He was the one who killed them."

A quiet gasp left her lips as her hand cupped her mouth. The watery film over the surface of her eyes increased, reflecting the sunshine coming through the windows behind me. "Why...?" Her voice broke, and she gave a loud sniff. "Why would someone do that?"

"Because he'd rather kill us all than suffer the public shame of his financial ruin." I hadn't talked about this in years. My voice was sterile. Emotionless. It was just a story to me now, not something I'd lived through. "He gambled our wealth on bets he could never pay. Then he gambled more to recoup those losses. Just went deeper into the hole." It was the reason I never gambled. I went to the horse races for sport, not for money.

She was silent in her disbelief.

I let her soak it in before I continued. "I came home later than I was supposed to. He must have assumed I was already in bed or thought he could just shoot me when I walked in the door later. He'd drugged everyone during dinner, and in their sleep, he shot each one in the head."

She inhaled another strained breath, on the verge of sobs.

"By the time I got there, it was too late. Mom was dead. My sister was gone. He was executing my other brother when I discovered Magnus was still alive. He was the last on the list because his bedroom was the farthest down the hall. I was young and weak at the time, so I struggled to carry him." I could still remember the way he felt in my arms, the way I clenched my teeth together so tightly as I strained my arms. It was the last time I allowed myself to be physically inadequate. I hit the gym every single day, no exceptions. "I dropped him on the stairs. He hit his head and woke up. Thankfully."

She continued to breathe hard, hanging on to every word of the story.

"That got my father's attention, so he came to the top of the stairs. Gun in hand. Hatred in his eyes." I'd never forget the way he looked. It was forever seared into my brain. He was actually angry that I'd halted his plan. Angry that I got my little brother to the door. Angry that we wouldn't die like he wanted. There was no love. There was no remorse. Nothing. When I tracked him down later, I showed him no remorse too. "Magnus and I got out the door and missed the bullets. We ran for our lives down the street in the pouring rain, the sound of gunshots following us until we turned into an alleyway."

With wet eyes, she was completely absorbed in the story. "Then what happened?"

"Magnus and I lived like rats in the street. We couldn't go to the police because they would just put us in an orphanage, which would make it easier for our father to find us. We took food out of the dumpsters so we wouldn't starve. We stole from people so Magnus could get me to the doctor when I got pneumonia. We lived that way for a long time, scrounging for food, trying to survive, growing weak and emaciated."

Tears broke and dripped down her cheeks.

"We eventually got into the drug trade—and the rest is history."

Her makeup ran. Her cheeks puffed. Her eyes turned bloodshot. The story haunted her as if she'd been there, digging through that garbage with me. Perhaps now she would understand. Perhaps now she would accept me as I was. "You...you killed him?"

I nodded. "Eventually." When I had the money, the resources, and the strength, I came for him. "It took a long time. A decade ago. Like a coward, he was hiding in the middle of a forest in Romania. He must have known that we would grow into strong, ruthless men. He must have known what we would do to him."

"What did you do to him?"

I'd spare her the gory details that would give her nightmares. "He died a coward. My family got the revenge they deserved. He tried to kill me as a boy, but I came back and slaughtered him as a man."

Tears continued to run down her cheeks, the pain too much for her to carry.

"I became the biggest kingpin in this country. I earned back the wealth that was taken from us. I earned back the respect that his scandal caused. I left that house as a weak boy, but I became the strongest man who could carry all of my siblings out of that house to safety. I became the man who would have kept my mother safe. Never in my life will I be weak again. Ever." My hands tightened in anger because I'd failed my family. "If I'd been stronger, I could have saved my other brother. If I'd been smarter, I could have suspected his intentions and killed him before he put that gun to my mother's head." My voice rose entirely on its own. "I will protect the brother I have left. I will protect my family name. And I will protect the woman I love." My knuckles turned white as I tightened my fists more than I ever had. I forced them to release before I ripped all the tendons underneath my skin.

She moved into my lap, her arms hooking around my neck as she pressed her face close to mine, rivers of tears down her cheeks, her eyes filled with remorse for crimes she'd never committed. She looked at me before she pressed her forehead to mine. "I'm so sorry..."

My arms wrapped around her and held her against me, smothered by her love and affection, smothered by her smell. She was the single most important thing in the world to me, and as I felt her delicateness with my hands, I knew I would protect this precious thing to the forfeiture of my own life. In a heartbeat. "Now you understand why I won't change. Why I'll never change."

WE DIDN'T SPEAK of it again.

Days passed and she didn't mention it, but I knew it was on her mind because of her silence. Her mind always seemed elsewhere, living in the memories I'd shared with her, dissecting the tale that no one should have to tell.

We sat together on the couch in my bedroom, the game on the TV above the fireplace and next to her painting. It was a nighttime ritual we did now, spent the evening together watching TV before dinner.

She was snuggled into my side, her hand planted on my thigh, her head against my shoulder. She was in her dress with her heels kicked off, and I was in my sweatpants. She pushed off me then regarded me, her eyes filling with that same sadness she'd showed days ago. "Tell me about your family."

I ignored the TV even though it was a game I wanted to watch. My focus was on her—like always. "Mother was a homemaker. Magnus and my sister were twins. My older brother was a great soccer player."

"Magnus had a twin?"

I nodded. "He lost his other half. It still bothers him."

"I can only imagine…"

"You would never guess I had a great childhood, judging by the way it ended. But I did. We had a nice home in Paris. We all went to private school. My mother was the best cook. She could have had the nanny chauffeur us around, but she also chose to do those things herself. She'd make us breakfast, take us to school in the morning, be there for all the performances and games. We'd spend our summer vacation at our other home in Tuscany. Attended events in society because of our status. But our mother never allowed our wealth to turn us into smug kids. She kept us humble."

"She sounds like a great mom…"

My head turned back to the TV. "She was." She thought money was the root of all evil, and she was right, because it was the reason she was murdered in her sleep.

"Is that why…you won't sleep with me?"

I turned back to her. "Yes."

She gave a slight nod, but her eyes suggested she'd already figured that out. "I understand now."

I looked at the TV.

Her eyes remained on my face. "But you know I would never…" She shook her head, her voice getting choked up. "I would never hurt you." She leaned into me and pressed a kiss to my shoulder.

I did know that.

"I won't ask you again, but...I just want you to know that."
She kept her lips there and breathed against me, her hand
planting against my chest as she plastered herself to me,
like she wanted to crawl inside and live there.

My chin turned back to her, and I pressed a kiss to her hairline. I left it there, my hand cupping the back of her head,
cherishing her for the gift she was. The moment our eyes
met, I knew.

EYES LOCKED.

Our bodies in unison.

Her body engulfing mine.

My body weak for hers.

Breathing the same air. Breathing at the same time.

The beat of our hearts.

I wanted her every night. I wanted her always. But it wasn't
her body that satisfied me.

It was something else.

Something I couldn't get when I went into her bedroom
and fucked her like a whore. I got what I needed and left,
but it was never close to what I felt when we were together
like this.

It was therapy.

It fixed my broken heart. It faded my scars. It brought me peace.

We moved together. We came together. We lay together. It was perfect every time, satisfying despite its repetitiveness. It was beautiful like the art that I admired. She captured me so deeply, so completely, that I was lost without her.

We lay together in the darkness, still close together despite the heat on our skin and underneath it. My arms enveloped her, bars of a steel cage, to keep everything out, not to force her in.

Her fingertips brushed against my jawline, feeling the coarse shadow that darkened my face. With eyes on me, she spoke. "I understand you. I feel closer to you. I feel the pain that you carry... I can't explain it."

Neither could I.

"I would never ask you to change. I would never want you to."

My lungs sucked in a breath at her admission, feeling a deeper connection to her than before, because she accepted me.

"But that doesn't mean it can't be different..."

My eyes narrowed on her face.

"I know you know what you're doing is wrong...so just change that aspect—"

"No." My voice rose out of anger because she'd dangled her acceptance then took it away. My arms loosened on her body. My touch withdrew.

Her eyes filled with pain. "You can still operate the camp. Just release the girls—"

"I said no." I got out of bed and pulled on my boxers.

She sat up. "Why?"

"Because it doesn't work in any other way. I've tried." I sat at the edge of the bed, looking out the dark window.

"Then try again—"

"Enough." I rose to my feet. "Go to bed."

She left the sheets and stood on the rug naked, her eyes following me as I moved around the bed toward her. "After everything that happened to your mother and sister...you really think this is okay?"

My eyes shifted back and forth as I stood in front of her. "Never said it was."

"Then stop—"

"I can't."

Her eyes filled with pain as she breathed harder, losing a battle she'd assumed she would win. "You have the money. You have the title. You have the woman. You have—"

"It will never be enough. Not after what he stole from us."

She shook her head, looking at me with sheer disappointment. "Your mother wouldn't want this—"

That look just killed me. "She didn't want to be killed in her sleep either. My mother would have wanted a lot of things but didn't live long enough to want them in the first place. Bad shit happens to good people." My voice rose in my rage. "It doesn't make it right, but that's life. Accept it."

She shook her head as her eyes watered. "Let it go—"

"Never." I stepped closer to her, my eyes drilling into her face with anger.

"This isn't who you are."

"It's exactly who I am." I got in her face, nostrils flaring, arms shaking. "Accept me."

Tears dripped down her cheeks. "I accept you. I love you. But I don't accept this part because it's not who you are. I believe there's more to you, and the reason I believe that is because I love you so much." She cried harder in front of me, pleading, tugging on my heartstrings in the way I hated. "I won't give up on you. I know you'll let the past go...and do the right thing—"

"Get out." I wouldn't listen to this bullshit anymore. I shared my past with her so she could understand, not so she would try to change what was unchangeable. There was no other way—and nothing would stop me.

She continued to cry in front of me.

"Don't make me ask you again."

Her clothes were left behind as she fled, the tears loud through the hallway when she left. Her door slammed shut a moment later. Even though it was impossible, I could still hear her cries.

I could hear them haunting me.

Torturing me.

I LEFT the next morning without saying goodbye.

It was an impromptu visit to the camp, but that was how I liked to work.

No one knew when I would move.

And I didn't want to see Melanie for a few days. I was pissed she'd made that attempt after I'd bared my soul to her, and I was pissed at myself for making my woman cry like that.

I hated her for doing that. For making me hurt her. For making me disappoint her. For making me the villain.

When I was the victim a million times over.

I made the drive with my hand tight on the steering wheel, speeding around the cars that wouldn't get the fuck out of my way. Music didn't distract me from my thoughts, and I was hit with a flood of flashbacks.

All of *Chérie.*

The men were surprised at my arrival, but they had a fresh horse for me to ride across the well-beaten path flattened by wagons and horses. I rode hard and made it to the camp right at dusk.

Torches were lit. The last bit of light left the sky. The camp was quiet. I dropped down from the horse and threw the reins to one of the guards who waited for me. When the men tried to follow me, I gave them a look that clearly said I wanted to be alone.

All I wanted to do was see Magnus—and get to work.

I passed between two cabins then moved past the clearing, seeing the empty picnic tables where the women worked. My eyes flicked to the noose there. The ground below wasn't covered with red snow—but the earth was tinted red. My gaze lingered for seconds, a chasm forming in my chest and filling with sensations I couldn't understand. I looked away and kept going.

Then I heard a scream pierce the night.

"*Magnus!*" A woman screamed with the full capacity of her lungs.

I stilled. My eyes scanned the area. I searched for the source.

"Please!" Tears broke her voice. "Please let me go."

I moved forward, circumvented a cabin in my way, and then spotted the scene.

Alix had Raven by the hair, and he dragged her naked body across the ground, her skin getting caked with dust. Tears stained her cheeks, and the identical eyes she shared with Melanie showed the exact same look of despair I'd seen dozens of times.

My eyes lifted to Alix, who was too busy sneering down at her to notice. He gave her scalp a painful tug to make her cry out again, as if torturing Magnus, who was nowhere around. There was only one reason he wouldn't be around.

I stopped in front of Alix and stared.

He seemed to feel my presence because he looked up.

And paled.

He stopped dragging Raven. He stopped breathing. He met my gaze and swallowed. Alix was a grown-ass man, but he turned into a boy when he was the recipient of my stare. There were no breaths. No movements. It was as if he were scared to move.

If Raven looked at me, I didn't notice.

Rage burned inside me, bubbling like boiling water. "Let her go."

Alix obeyed and let her collapse to the dirt.

The door to the guards' cabin burst open—and Magnus ran out and nearly tripped on the stairs because he was in such a rush to get to Raven.

Eric and Nathan emerged from behind him.

I didn't look at my brother again, my fury reserved for the man I wanted to butcher with a butter knife. My anger was audible without my voice rising a single decibel, so I didn't need to scream to express my disappointment. "This woman doesn't belong to you—and you know that."

Alix was stupid enough to argue, to somehow justify his actions, to somehow pretend he hadn't been caught with his pants down. "She's a prisoner—"

"Don't. Speak."

Alix inhaled a deep breath, growing so timid at my stare that he dropped his gaze.

Good. "She belongs to Magnus." I pulled a blade from my pocket and placed the tip right against Alix's heart, the point digging into the fabric of his shirt. "Touch her again, and I will not hesitate to slam this deep into your heart and make it stop."

Alix didn't even breathe.

Magnus yanked his shirt over his head and dropped it over Raven's body when he reached her.

She pulled the shirt to her thighs before she clung to him, holding on like she was too afraid to let go. Silent tears still dripped down her cheeks. Her body convulsed in a way I'd never seen before, even when she was whipped.

Magnus displayed the kind of affection I gave *Chérie*—cupping her face and brushing away her tears. It was a quick moment, only lasted a few seconds, but it showed a side to my brother I'd never seen. He helped her to her feet.

My eyes shifted back to Alix to continue the showdown. "Magnus was punished for his crimes. He's increased shipments to distributors, lost his own pay to make up for losses, rebuilt this camp, and has atoned for those sins. If you can't let your need for revenge die, then perhaps you need to die." I meant every fucking word—because no one crossed my brother. Fucking no one.

Alix kept a straight face, but it was obvious he was scared, judging by the way he didn't have strength in his gaze anymore. There was no sinister smile, no confidence in his posture. His shoulders sagged, like he wanted to disappear.

I turned to look at my brother head on. Terror. Rage. Trauma. Eric and Nathan must have held him down in the cabin while Alix dragged her away. I turned back to Alix. "This has been going on a while, hasn't it?"

I spoke to Alix, but I was actually speaking to my brother.

Silence.

I shifted my gaze back to Magnus.

His mouth was shut tight.

Alix looked at him, like he knew Magnus would throw him under the bus.

But he didn't.

I looked at Alix again. "He's not a snitch. Looks like it's your lucky day, Alix." My knife was sheathed. "I won't pretend to understand my brother's fascination with this unremarkable cunt, but as long as she is his, she's off-limits. Do you understand?"

Alix nodded. "Yes, sir."

"The only reason I won't kill you is because Magnus stirred unrest in this camp. But you're even now. Cross my brother again, and I won't hesitate to kill you." I turned to see the guards on the porch of the cabin and raised my voice. "All of you." I stepped away and moved to my brother, ignoring Raven altogether, and nodded in the direction of my cabin. Then I took the lead, knowing he would follow.

We made it into my cabin, and after we took our seats and poured our scotch, the guards brought my dinner—a well-done steak with potatoes and asparagus. The guard dismissed himself, and we were surrounded in solitude once more.

Magnus was quiet, as if he needed time to process what had just happened.

I was hungry, so I cut into my steak and shoved pieces into my mouth.

Magnus stared at me, his palms together. "Thank you. I know you probably did it for Melanie, but—"

"No." I shook my head. "I did it for you."

Magnus stilled at my admission, his eyes filling with a look of gratitude. "Then I appreciate it even more."

I was so pissed at Melanie right now that I couldn't see straight. I didn't want to save her sister. I didn't want to spare someone who would never spare me. But I did it for her, too—even if I wouldn't admit it. "How long has this been going on?"

We talked about the events in the camp as I ate my dinner, washing it down with scotch that hit me harder than usual because I had weaned myself off it. My plate was wiped clean, so I sat with my glass in hand.

"You didn't bring Melanie with you."

"No." I took a drink.

He must have detected my tone because he said, "Everything alright?"

I pictured the way she'd sobbed in front of me in my bedroom, pleading for me to be someone I wasn't. "Just need some space."

Magnus let it go, and our conversation turned to Napoleon. When I returned to Paris, we both had an event where he would attend. My brother couldn't contain his objection and reminded me once again that it wasn't a good fit.

I didn't care.

"I'd like to bring Raven, if that's okay."

My eyes narrowed on his face. "Beauty is in the eye of the beholder, but Raven doesn't hold a candle to Stasia, so I have to ask...what's wrong with your dick?" His expression remained hard, doing his best to keep back his offense. "I don't think Melanie is as remarkable as you claim."

I couldn't suppress the grin on my face because I didn't believe that for a second. Melanie was the best cut of meat, but I'd beat him to the punch. He was stuck with the cut no one else wanted.

"Raven would like to see her."

"Yeah, bet she would." I set down my glass and released a long, drawn-out breath. I didn't want to see Raven in any capacity, but after what my brother just had to go through, I wanted to honor any request he made. "Fine."

He couldn't hide the look of surprise on his face. It quickly turned into a look of gratitude.

Silence lingered. I nursed the scotch with my lips, my eyes on the unlit fireplace. When Melanie woke up and realized I'd gone, she would probably be angry with me. After I returned home, she would probably ignore me the way I ignored her. I hated that cold shoulder. I hated that anger in her eyes. But if she didn't want me to leave, she shouldn't have demanded something I'd never offered. I never pretended to be anything less than what I was. My honesty was prevalent in every word, every look, every touch.

"I have another request."

My thoughts were so deep that I'd forgotten he was there. My eyes shifted back to him.

"I'd like to buy Raven's freedom."

The glass was held to my lips, but I didn't take a drink. My hand shook slightly before it lowered back to my knee. The look I gave him must have been sharp because his eyes turned guarded in preparation for my wrath. "No."

"I will pay you whatever you want—"

"There's not enough money in the world, Magnus." I set the glass back on the coffee table.

He should just let it go, but he didn't. "She'll still be a prisoner. But she'll be my prisoner—"

"Not good enough."

"Melanie would appreciate it—"

"And she's asked many times. My answer has never changed." The only reason I didn't scream at him was because of the scene I'd just witnessed. He wanted to remove her from the camp because she was clearly unsafe here. When I vacated the premises, the guards might creep in once more. "It won't change for you either. She had her opportunity to be free, but she chose to spend that freedom burning down my camp, the place I built with my bare hands alongside you. She chose to destroy the thing I care most about. So, no, she will never get the offer again. I granted her mercy once—and she chose to piss it away."

MAGNUS ASKED to leave the camp early.

He wanted to give Raven a change of scenery after what she'd suffered.

I allowed it because I didn't want to look at her anyway.

Magnus and I walked together to the wagons that were tied to the horses. The drugs were packed and covered in the rear, ready to be transported to their next drop-off point. Magnus offered to do the job so I could keep an extra man at the camp.

Raven was somewhere behind us. I chose to believe she didn't exist, so I genuinely forgot she was in my presence.

Magnus cupped my forearm in a salute of goodbye before he turned to the wagon. "Brother."

I repeated the phrase. "Brother."

But then Raven walked up to me.

Right up to my face.

She looked at me, having the same eyes as Melanie.

Magnus turned back and stilled.

Her eyes shifted back and forth as she looked into mine, closer to me than she'd ever been before. There was a hint of fear, but also something else. She studied me like I was an animal thought to be extinct a very long time ago.

Fury swept through me. Deep in my veins. Deep in my blood. Deep in my bones. I'd spared her from a violent crime, and she had the audacity to look at me—like we were fucking equals. She was the one thing standing in my way. She was the one thing that kept Melanie and me apart. I felt hatred. Pure hatred.

"I just wanted to say thank you...for what you did." Her eyes searched mine, as if she expected to see humanity in my gaze.

There was none. "Your appreciation means nothing to me because my intervention had nothing to do with you. My only interest was keeping my brother's dick clean. Speak to me again, and I will cut those blue eyes out of your skull and feed them to my dogs."

Magnus grabbed her by the arm and pulled her away. "Get into the wagon. Now."

I abruptly turned away and marched back into the camp, trying to forget that shit ever happened.

Melanie

He left without saying a word to me.

If he'd stayed home, I would have ignored him anyway, but it still upset me that he'd left without saying goodbye.

I had no idea when he would return.

I couldn't ask Gilbert because he wouldn't know either.

So, I spent my time reading, in the swimming pool, keeping myself busy.

Waiting for him.

A week had come and gone, and he didn't return. Despite how angry I was with him, I missed him. Every time I went to bed, I hoped that he would be there the next morning. I lay in bed in the dark, cold despite the summer heat outside, and struggled to fall asleep because I replayed our final conversation over and over.

I knew he was more than that.

I knew it, and I think he'd gotten angry because he knew it too.

My eyes flashed open when I heard it.

Gunshots.

Lots of gunshots.

I sat up in bed and looked around, even though the sound was coming from the front gate. There was no one in my bedroom. I was alone. My heart raced a million miles an hour. Anxiety like I'd never known hit me so hard. Fear. Pure fear hit me. "Fender..." I got out of bed and tripped to the floor. I got to my feet and turned on the lamp so I could see two inches in front of my face. I dashed to the windows and opened the curtains.

The gate was broken down.

Dead men were on the ground.

Three black SUVs drove up the roundabout to the house.

"Oh my god..."

Did they come because Fender wasn't here?

Or did they come because they assumed he would be here?

Or...was he dead? "Oh god..."

The door flew open, and I screamed.

"It's me." Gilbert rushed to me, holding a handgun. "Come on." He spoke in loud whispers and waved me toward him.

I ran to him and took his hand. "What's happening?"

"Be quiet. We have to make it to the safe room. That's where the staff hides." He hurried me out the door and peeked down the hallway before he pulled me with him.

I was breathing so hard, I thought I would pass out. I let him drag me along in the dark, heading to the stairs.

Three men were running up, all dressed in black.

Gilbert yanked me back. "Shit." He moved quicker, hurrying down the hallway and taking a right.

"Where's the room?"

"Bottom floor."

Oh no...

We ran as quietly as we could.

"Not here." A voice drifted out from where we had just escaped. The sounds of doors being thrown open, furniture being pushed aside were so loud, it was as if they were right behind us. "Bitch, we'll find you."

They were there for me.

Gilbert took me to another set of stairs, one that the staff used, but it was blocked by guys at the bottom. "Fuck." He tugged me again, pulling me into a random room where he left the door open. He quickly ushered me around behind the bed, and we both ducked down.

"Did they kill everyone else?"

"They're already in the safe room." He held his gun at the ready, ready to turn and shoot someone when they came looking.

Despite my terror, my breathing paused to look at the side of his face, to look at him in a way I never had before. "You came for me..."

He pressed his forefinger to his lips to hush me.

The sounds of the house being ripped apart were audible. Plates shattering. Glass breaking. Men yelling to one another.

Sitting there in the dark and listening to it all made the experience so much worse.

I held on to his arm because I was scared, more scared than I'd ever been. "They're here for me, which means they probably won't kill me. Give me your gun and hide under the bed."

He put his forefinger to his lips again, giving me a fiery look that said, "Shut up now."

Footsteps grew louder.

They entered the bedroom.

I was so fucking scared, I was about to pass out.

The closet doors were thrown open. The bathroom was checked.

Maybe they wouldn't look on the other side of the bed.

But they did.

A man stepped around and stilled when he saw us.

Gilbert pulled that trigger, shot him right in the chest, and he went down instantly.

I covered my mouth to stop the scream that wanted to burst out.

The men heard the shot and came running. "She's here!"

Gilbert moved in front of me, covering me with his body as he prepared to face off against the men who came.

I held on to him, tears streaming down my face.

One man came around the corner of the bed, carrying a shotgun. He pointed it right at Gilbert.

Gilbert was still, staring down that barrel without fear. "He'll come for you. All of you."

I was barely coherent because the sobs racked my chest. "I'll come with you. Just—"

He pulled the trigger.

"Ahh!" My hands immediately released him when the blood hit me.

Gilbert went limp and slid to the floor, his eyes still open, his chest still rising and falling.

"No!" My hand immediately went to his chest to stop the bleeding...even though nothing could be done.

The man grabbed me by the hair and dragged me away. "Come on, bitch."

I screamed as I was dragged across the floor. "No!" I tried to fight back, but that just hurt my scalp harder.

Gunshots rang out in the house.

The man stilled and looked out the door before he grabbed me by the arm and yanked me to my feet.

The gunshots grew louder, making my ears ring as they echoed down the hallways.

He pulled me into the hallway then abruptly yanked me back like he saw something. He pushed me back and aimed his shotgun, as if expecting someone to round the corner any moment.

It must have been Fender's men, so I kicked him in the back of the knee so he would falter and drop his aim. "Help!"

A man rounded the corner and moved too quickly for me to see what actually happened. But there was no gunshot. A knife sliced across the man's throat and made him collapse in front of me.

I crawled backward to get away.

Then I saw Fender standing in front of me.

Covered in blood. Expression maniacal. His breathing fast. His posture still. He took me in with a rage I'd never seen before. He was on his knees instantly, his arms grabbing me and checking me, his hand planting itself on my chest to see if I had a gunshot wound. "*Chérie*, are you hurt?"

"I'm fine." I heaved and heaved, breaking down in mental agony. "Gilbert...help him... He's been shot."

When he realized I was fine, he moved to the floor where Gilbert lay on his back, staring at the ceiling, giving labored breaths as he clung to his last few minutes of life. When Fender bent down over him, Gilbert shifted his eyes to Fender's face.

I crawled over, tears pouring down my face. "He saved me. Everyone went to the bunker, but he came to get me."

Fender's face turned stoic, and he planted his hand against his bloody chest. He inhaled a deep breath as he stared at his blood-soaked hand. Blood pooled underneath him, staining the rug with so much blood, it was incredible Gilbert was still alive.

I choked on my sobs. "He...he wouldn't let them take me."

Fender kept his hand on Gilbert's chest and looked into his eyes. He didn't tell him he would be okay. He didn't try to move him so an ambulance could take him away. "Thank you."

Gilbert moved his arm weakly so his hand could reach Fender's. He held it against his chest.

Fender reciprocated and squeezed his hand.

Gilbert breathed deep and hard, his breaths becoming more labored as the blood supply to his lungs grew less and less. "I...I...did it...for you...sir."

My hand cupped my face, the amount of my tears rivaling the amount of blood everywhere.

Fender inhaled a deep breath as he looked down, his eyes growing soft. "Not 'sir.' Fender." He held Gilbert's hand on his chest and stared into the eyes of the man who had served him so faithfully, so loyally. There wasn't deep emotion on his face, just a quiet sympathy, and he watched Gilbert struggle to breathe as their hands remained clasped. "Your family will be taken care of."

His breathing grew deeper and deeper, gasping for air that he couldn't get. His eyes started to glaze over, and his hand immediately went slack in Fender's. His body went rigid, all the muscles tightening, and then his head turned slightly because he went limp.

When he was gone, Fender closed his eyes and bowed his head, sucking in a deep breath that showed the pain he'd been restraining until Gilbert was no longer with us.

My tears stopped for a few seconds before they resumed once again, louder and harder.

Fender released Gilbert's hand and placed his hand over his heart. "I'm sorry."

EVERYTHING THAT HAPPENED after that was a blur.

Fender carried Gilbert outside and placed him on the grass in the backyard, so he could look at the stars with his closed eyes, ascend to heaven easier. More men were dispatched to the palace, cleaning up the dead men in the hallway and disposing of them. The rest of the staff came from the safe room, unharmed, and the news of Gilbert devastated them all.

It devastated me more—because he'd died for me.

Once Fender knew I was unhurt, he ordered his men to work and left me alone in my bedroom. He didn't comfort me. He didn't speak to me. He had a lot more on his mind at the moment.

I was covered in blood, so the first thing I did was take a shower. My nightgown was ruined, so I sealed it inside a bag and threw it in the trash. I didn't bother to dry my hair or do my makeup. I just sat on the bed with my arms crossed over my chest, replaying the events over and over in my mind. Gunshots echoed. Their voices sounded like they were still in the hallway. Gilbert's bravery. His dead face. The bloody rug. It cycled over and over—endlessly. Night deepened, but I was too flustered to lie down and try to go to sleep.

Not without Fender.

My bedroom door opened, and I immediately looked up to see him walk inside.

He was in fresh clothes. The blood had been washed off his hands. But he wasn't in his sweatpants—like he intended to leave. His eyes were soft as they looked into mine, coming to the bed with his heavy footsteps. He lowered himself on the mattress beside me, stared at the floor for a few moments, and then turned his chin to regard me.

I had stopped crying, but looking at him now made me want to cry again.

"I'm leaving."

"Can I come with you?"

He shook his head. "I won't be gone long."

"Are you...getting the people who did this?"

He nodded.

"Please be careful."

His dark eyes had no reaction.

"But yes...make them pay for what they did."

His response was immediate. "I will."

My hand went to his, holding on tight.

He squeezed my fingers in return. "While I'm gone, I want you to move all your things to my bedroom."

His eyes remained steady as they looked into mine, but mine turned confused.

"I never want to be apart from you again, *chérie*."

EIGHTEEN

MACHETE

FENDER

I piled into the SUV with my men, and we left the palace.

I took twenty men—but left forty behind.

With my elbow propped on the windowsill, I held the phone to my ear and called Magnus.

He answered even though it was the middle of the night. "What is it?" His voice was quiet and his footsteps were audible, as if he were trying to vacate the room before Raven woke up.

"Gilbert is dead."

He was silent, waiting for an explanation.

"We have a snitch. The Renaldi Brothers hit the palace in my absence."

He released a loud breath that came out as a snarl.

"By the time I returned, all of my men were dead. Gilbert had been hit with a shotgun. Nothing I could do for him."

"And Melanie?"

"Unharmed."

"Are you okay?"

"Physically, yes." If I hadn't returned when I had, Melanie would have been taken. Used for ransom, but they wouldn't have hesitated to hurt her until I'd negotiated her release. They came into my home, killed my butler, tried to take my woman, and to say I was livid was an understatement.

"We rejected their partnership. This is a bad way to change your mind."

"They never intended to change my mind. If I'd wanted Melanie to be free, I'd have had to offer my own life instead —and I would have. They would have killed me, taken over the empire, and then killed you if you resisted."

He digested that in silence for a while. "You know where they are?"

"Yes."

"What can I do?"

"Kill the snitch. When they realized I was gone from the palace, they called it in. It has to be Jeremy." Based on the timeline of everything that happened, it had to be him. "Must have been paid a fortune. Enough to take care of his family when he's executed."

"You're certain it's him?"

"Yes."

"I'll take care of it."

THEY WERE in their private plane on the tarmac, taxiing to the runway.

We hopped out of our SUVs, and in the third one was the rocket launcher. I carried it out, loaded it, and took a knee on the ground with the weapon in place. My eyes watched the plane move, waited for the perfect moment, gauged the distance and the speed, and then fired.

It hit its mark perfectly—setting fire to the left wing and toppling the plane over.

We got back into the SUVs and drove to where the plane burned on the asphalt.

No one at the private airport came out to intercede. Police weren't dispatched. They stayed inside and knew this wasn't their concern.

I hopped out and nodded to my men.

They climbed up onto the plane, pulled the door open, and then dropped inside.

I stood there and waited, my knife held at the ready.

Victor Renaldi was pulled out of the plane in an unconscious state. He was carried down until he was dropped on the concrete.

I nodded to another one of my men.

He kneeled and injected the needle into his skin, giving him a high dose of epinephrine so he'd be forced to walk up.

His eyes opened and he came to, taking in the scene, immediately panicking. When he tried to get up, a gun was shoved in his face.

His brother Carl was taken out as well, but he was awake.

He was dropped on the ground next to his brother. Then my men backed away, letting me do the honors.

I stared down at them for a long time, my large knife held in my grip, the blade reflecting the flames and the smoke behind them. It was a summer night, but the heat from the flames made it an inferno. Only a few minutes were left before the flames torched the engines and caused an explosion that could kill us all. "Who's first?"

They remained on their asses in front of me, looking up at me with false bravado. Their deaths were inevitable, but they still breathed in fear, still shook with the revelation of their demise.

I raised my voice. "I said, who's first?"

Victor exchanged a final look with his brother before he got shakily to his feet.

I grabbed him with lightning speed, kicking the backs of his knees, and forced him back to the ground. My boot pressed into his back, pinning him to the ground. "Machete."

He inhaled a deep breath when his punishment was revealed.

I was handed the large blade before I nodded to one of my guys.

His boot replaced mine.

I kneeled and looked at Victor, my blade held at the ready. "You tried to take my woman. Now I'm going to take everything from you."

He didn't look at me, his cheek pressed to the tarmac.

I raised my blade and slammed it down hard, severing his neck, blood squirting everywhere. "One."

A gurgle came from his lips, blood flooding out of every orifice he possessed.

Carl closed his eyes.

It always took at least three hits to sever the head from the body, so I did it two more times. "Two. Three." I decapitated him completely then rose to my feet. "Carl, you're up."

NINETEEN

WITH ALL MY HEART

MELANIE

It was nearly morning when he came home.

The sun had just peeked over the horizon. It was a beautiful summer day, the dawn after the dark night. My things were moved into his bedroom, and the staff put everything back in place. The men had ransacked his suite, looking for me everywhere. But now, it looked exactly as it had before.

I couldn't sleep, not until I knew he was home, not until I knew this was really over.

When he finally walked through the door, he was covered in blood again. He didn't say a word to me as he pulled his shirt over his head and undressed, putting his clothes in a big plastic bag, as if there were a procedure for this sort of thing. He took a quick shower before he emerged in a pair of black boxers.

I sat on the edge of the bed, my racing heart slowing down as he came closer, bringing me peace.

He joined me on the bed. "It's done."

I nodded. "So...it's over?"

"Yes. They won't return."

"Why...why did they do this?"

His arms rested on his knees, and he stared at the floor as he considered the question. "They wanted to do business with me. I said no. So, they decided to eliminate me and take it over themselves." He turned back to look at me, his dark eyes giving me a look that said more than his words ever could.

Our fight never happened.

It was irrelevant now.

His hand moved into my hair, cupping my cheek, his thumb brushing my bottom lip slightly. The stare was endless, going on and on, and his expression slowly began to change. A slight shine moved to the surface of his eyes, a subtle redness, a tightness to his face. "If something happened to you...I wouldn't have gone on." He brought his face to mine and rested his forehead against mine. "Je t'aime, *chérie*. Je t'aime de tout mon cœur et de toute mon âme." *I love you, sweetheart. I love you with my heart, my soul, my everything*. He inhaled a deep breath and closed his eyes, gaining control of his emotions. "Je ne te quitterai plus jamais. Je te protègerai. Toujours." *I will never leave you again. I will protect you. Always.*

IT WAS the first time we went to bed together but didn't make love.

We got under the sheets in the dark, my body on top of his, his thick arm wrapped around me, keeping me close. His lips rested against my hairline, and his deep and slow breaths became less frequent once he drifted off.

It only took a few minutes.

Like there was no hesitation anymore.

I was awake longer, the memories still so fresh, but knowing he was there helped me drift off too.

When my eyes opened the next day, it wasn't morning.

It was two in the afternoon.

Fender wasn't there.

I showered and got ready for what was left of the day before I went in search of him.

The staff had restored the palace to its former glory, cleaning the blood and dirt that had stained the walls, rugs, and floors, and replacing the broken items that had been damaged beyond repair. There was a heavy solemnness to the house, rain clouds in every room, a sadness that hummed in every ear. Maids would break into tears unexpectedly, the rawness of the night before hitting them again and again.

A night of rest hadn't dulled the pain for me either.

I was about to ask where Fender was when the front door opened and he walked inside. Dressed in all black with his customary boots, he shut the door behind himself then stilled when he spotted me.

I inhaled a breath of relief at the sight of him, feeling comforted by that look that no one else could give me.

He walked over to me, a solemn expression in his eyes. "I took Gilbert to the funeral home so they could prepare him for burial."

My eyes filled with pain all over again.

"And I went to his parents to tell them what happened."

"Oh my god..." My hand immediately went to his arm, knowing how painful that must have been.

His expression was hard and stony as if nothing had happened, because his true nature was so much deeper beneath the surface. Sometimes he looked like he didn't care, but that wasn't true. He just didn't know how to express it.

"That must have been hard."

"It was." His eyes dropped for a moment, a quick replay happening in his mind. "I gave them enough money to be

very wealthy for the rest of their lives, for several genera-
tions of their family."

I knew they wanted their son—not the money.

"I've found a replacement. He starts today."

My eyes watered—because Gilbert couldn't be replaced.

He inhaled a deep breath at my reaction, the look paining
him. "I know, *chérie*..."

I cupped my mouth to stifle the tears.

His strong arms wrapped around me, and he held me in the
foyer, his body supporting mine, his love cushioning the
blow to my broken heart. His fingers gently ran over my
hair and down my back, treating me with such gentleness
that contradicted his entire nature.

"I...I miss him so much."

He pressed a kiss to my forehead. "I do too."

A WEEK PASSED, but that week felt like an eternity.

Gabriel was the new butler. He was a young man who had
recently left his previous employer because they'd relo-
cated to the Netherlands. He learned fast, was quick on his
feet, and didn't talk much.

But he was no Gilbert, even though Fender refused to learn
his name and insisted upon calling him Gilbert. Gabriel

seemed flustered at first, but given his salary, he adapted to his new identity quickly, soon answering only to Gilbert.

There wasn't that extra effort, that drive to make Fender's life absolutely perfect at all times. It was just a job to him, doing it the best he could before he was excused to live his own life.

My old bedroom had been turned into a guest room that no one ever used, and when I stepped into Fender's closet, I saw his clothes on the rack across from mine. The sheets always smelled like him. There weren't vases of flowers because he didn't care for them in his private room. They were replaced with glasses of scotch that he left behind on tables and nightstands.

He was quiet. Quieter than usual.

But I was too.

After we attended the funeral, we didn't speak for two days.

Fender worked in his office while I read a book on the couch during the day, we had our meals together, and every night, he slept beside me like dropping his guard was the easiest thing in the world.

It was what I'd always wanted—just under the wrong circumstances.

We sat together in his living room, the TV above the fire-place showing the game. In his sweatpants, he sat with one ankle crossed on the opposite knee, his elbow on the armrest, nursing the glass of scotch on the table beside him.

I read my book.

He kept drinking and drinking, and then he took it to another level when he opened a brand-new bottle and refilled his empty glass.

I'd never seen him drink like this—unless he was at the camp. I shut my book and looked at him.

After he took a sip, he turned his face to regard me, like he felt my stare because he could see it.

"You're drinking too much." It was a mystery to me that he wasn't stumbling around everywhere, losing his footing and knocking over furniture in a stupor. Whenever we kissed, I could taste the scotch—even in the morning.

He kept up his deep stare.

"I know it's hard right now. I'm depressed too. But...it's not good for you."

I knew how much things had changed when he didn't tell me off for telling him what to do. He poured the contents of the glass back into the bottle, tightened the lid, and then ignored it.

I couldn't believe it. "Thank you."

His eyes turned back to the TV.

I stared at the side of his face, the chiseled jawline that made a pronounced shadow down his neck, saw a man who was so hard but so gentle too. Our last conversation about my sister had disappeared from our minds, but it lived on in my heart. Because I knew he would do the right thing —eventually.

There was no doubt.

I left my book on the table then scooted closer to him, my arm hooking through his, my cheek moving to his shoulder.

His hand went to my thigh, and he turned to look at me, his thumb brushing over my skin.

"Are you okay?"

The stare lasted a long time before he gave a nod. "He knew the protocol. He knew to stay in the safe room with the rest of the staff. He chose to go after you, something I never would have asked him to do. You're my responsibility —and I would have gotten you back on my own. I can't carry the guilt of his decision." His eyes flicked away for a moment. "But the loss does hurt. He didn't deserve that. I got the revenge he was owed, but it'll never be enough."

WITH HIS ARMS behind my knees and his heavy body on top of mine, he rocked into me, his gaze on mine, his dark eyes filled with a deeper level of commitment than before. His lips would kiss me between moans. His eyes would saturate me with a look of love. His hips would drive him farther inside when he needed more. He made me his every night, made me feel like there had never been anyone else but him.

It made me forget the life I'd had before this.

It had always been this way.

He already loved me with everything that he had, but now he loved me much deeper than before. He loved me every night like it was our last night on this earth. He loved me like he could lose me any moment.

We lay together once it was over, and despite the heat of our bodies, he held me close. His arm was draped over my stomach as he lay beside me, his face close to my cheek on the same pillow. His large body was a wall beside me, blocking the window from my view.

My arm rested on his as I turned to look at him, to see this handsome man protecting me with his massive body. Every night, I was wrapped in his protection, wrapped in his scent, his possessiveness.

He opened his eyes and met my look.

I stared, my fingers drifting over the endless muscles of his arms. "Je t'aime."

He stared for a few seconds before he pressed a kiss to my shoulder. "Je t'aime, *chérie.*"

I loved my new home in this very spot—right next to him. "I don't know what I would have done if I'd lost you."

A new look entered his eyes, a gaze I hadn't seen before. Windows opened to his soul, and the softness underneath was truly visible for the first time. "You never have to worry about that."

"Why?"

"Because if I die, there's no one to protect you. So, I can never die."

A WEEK LATER, Fender held a party at the house.

He stood in front of the mirror and adjusted the sleeves of his tuxedo, his eyes down on what he was doing, his jaw cleanly shaved, his shoulders broad in the jacket. Tall. Muscular. He looked good in anything, but he looked particularly good in that.

I took a seat in the armchair in my gown and waited for him to finish.

When he was done, he turned to me and stopped.

I looked up and met his gaze.

His eyes combed my appearance, taking in the sight of me with my hair and makeup done, wearing the gold gown that matched the sconces of his palace. I was the trophy—so he wanted me to be gold like a trophy. He walked over to me then extended his hand.

I took it and let him pull me to my feet.

His hands went to my hips, and he squeezed me as he looked into my face, his eyes drilling holes into my appearance. Sometimes he stared at me so hard that he looked furious. But now he backed me up to the wall, undid his trousers, and lifted my dress.

My back planted against the wall, and I felt my thong leave my body. "There are already people downstairs—"

He hiked up my leg and shoved himself inside me.

The back of my head tapped against the wall, and I released a moan at his abrupt entrance. My hands clung to his shoulders, and I lifted my leg farther to rest it higher on his arm, feeling him pound into me right away.

Hard. Fast. Territorial. He was like a dog marking his territory. His eyes burned into mine as he fucked me hard, fucked me in a way he hadn't in weeks.

My arms wrapped around his neck, and I moaned as he took me up against the wall, plowing into me, forcing me into a climax even though I hadn't been ready for it just a minute ago. I did my best to steady my tears so they wouldn't ruin my makeup.

He finished with a moan, giving me a load like he hadn't just done so that morning. Then he pulled out and got redressed as if nothing had happened, his dick still hard and forced into his trousers.

I lowered my leg and breathed hard against the wall, needing more than a second to recover.

"*Chérie*." He moved to the door and beckoned for me to join him.

"I just need to clean up."

"No."

I stilled at his answer. "I look like I just—"

"Exactly."

WHEN I SAW her across the room, I almost couldn't believe it.

Dressed in a beautiful gown with her hair done, her makeup heavy, and having a strong posture that defied her labored imprisonment, she practically glided across the floor, her arm in Magnus's.

I turned to Fender. "My sister is here."

His mood immediately soured at the mention of her.

I squeezed his arm in gratitude. "Thank you."

He continued to ignore me, drinking the champagne that he said tasted like cat piss.

Magnus approached his brother, ignoring me the way Fender ignored Raven. They greeted each other in silence, with notable hostility, as if something had happened between them when Fender was at the camp.

Raven stood there, her eyes down, trying to disappear.

All I could do was stare because I couldn't believe she was there, right in front of me, looking more beautiful than she ever had. "Raven, you look so beautiful." Everything was perfect, from her earrings to her eye shadow. A whole different woman.

Raven looked at me—and all she gave was a nod.

Why wasn't she talking to me?

Magnus had his arm around her waist, wearing a tuxedo like his brother. "I'm going to put the girls in the parlor so we can speak in private—"

"No." Fender squeezed my waist to secure my position against him, like leaving him was not an option, not in any scenario. His resistance probably came from his hatred for my sister, but it was deeper than that, from a fear that would fill his heart always.

I leaned into him. "*Mon amour*, please..." My face came close to his, so I could share a whisper no one else could hear. "I'll just be in the other room."

Fender took a drink to cover his fuming anger. "You're lucky I permit her in our home at all."

Something had happened at the camp to make him hate her even more. He never told me about it, so he either forgot in light of Gilbert, or he just didn't want to spend his time discussing her. Either one was possible. "For me..." He loved me more than life itself, and he would give me anything I asked for—in time.

He looked at me head on, his look icy cold. But he gave a nod in agreement.

Because he was weak for only one person—me.

I kissed him on the cheek before I whispered to him, "Thank you, *mon amour*."

Magnus guided us across the foyer and into the parlor, a room neither Fender nor I ever used. His palace was big and luxurious, but most of it was vacant. There were never visitors, so the rooms were filled with the same energy you would find in a museum after hours.

Raven and I moved to a couch, and Magnus stayed near the door.

I couldn't believe she was here, next to me, looking like an old-fashioned movie star. Every moment I had with her was a gift, a gift so pure it usually brought me to tears. The connection between us, even at our worst, was unbreakable.

She gave a slight smile before she opened her arms and pulled me in.

I held her and squeezed her tight, my face in her shoulder, holding on to this feeling as long as I possibly could, soaking up every single moment. The hug lasted a long time because it was the only way to truly share the way we felt about each other. Words were insufficient.

When we pulled apart, she looked at me. "You look so gorgeous, Melanie... Wow."

I shook my head. "That dress was made for you. Magnus can't stop looking at you—along with everyone else."

She gave a slight smile. "I guess black is my color."

A long stare ensued, full of questions neither one of us wanted to ask.

I went first. "How are you?"

She didn't answer the question directly. "I like being in Paris with Magnus." She told me she was allowed to go shopping and get coffee on her own, that the two of them had a relationship built on a bedrock of trust. She wouldn't run and put him in jeopardy—and he knew that. "What about you?"

I wanted to tell my sister the truth because I told her everything, but the shame was too big to conquer. If I told her the way I really felt about Fender, her reaction would be explosive. She would probably hate me the way she hated him. "No complaints." I took the path of a coward and shared very few details of my life, of the deep and profound connection I had to the man who slept beside me every single night. We were unmarried, but he felt like my husband, a husband I'd had for years. He was everything I could want in a man—except one thing. How could I possibly justify that when my sister was his prisoner? It made me feel like shit just thinking about it. "He'll let you go. It's taking me some time, but he will."

She released a sarcastic laugh. "Yeah, that will never happen."

"It will." Confidence burned in my voice, because I knew him better than she did. I knew his heart—because he'd given it to me.

A long silence passed before she gave me that look—a look that said she had an idea. "You know...if you were to kill him...it might fix all our problems."

Shock hit me like an electrode was attached to my finger. My back straightened with the jolt, and my eyes widened at the suggestion because it was so innately repulsive.

"In his sleep or something."

An image flashed across my mind, a faceless man putting a gun to his wife's head and pulling the trigger, wiping out an entire family—except two survivors. The thought nearly brought me to tears. "I...I can't do that."

"If you do, the camp will belong to Magnus. He'll let everyone go—"

"I said I can't." Ashamed, I dropped my gaze to my lap. My loyalty was divided between the two people I loved most. It shouldn't be divided at all—but it was.

Raven looked disappointed, but after a few seconds, she hid that expression. "Why?"

"Because...I can't do that to him." The truth was locked in a safe inside my heart.

Raven took a deep breath, and as she slowly released it, revulsion spread across her face. "Melanie, this is the man who raped you—"

"He didn't." My voice strengthened, because it was such a terrible accusation that didn't fit Fender in the least. He could never do something like that. Not to me. Not to anyone. He always treated me like a queen, even when he didn't know me. I raised my chin and looked directly at her, offended even though it wasn't her fault for jumping to that conclusion. I hid every thought and feeling from her because the truth was worse than the assumption. "I never said that."

"But he took you from the cabin, put you in another... He dragged his fingers against your cheek and said you tried to get away from him."

I shook my head. "He put me in a different cabin so he could be alone with me, but he never forced me. He would just have dinner with me and said he would wait until I was ready. And then...I was ready."

The look Raven gave me...was indescribable.

I couldn't handle that stare. I just couldn't. I looked away.

Raven was quiet, and the energy around her was so hostile that it seemed as if she might get up and storm out. She took a moment to calm herself before she spoke again, speaking to me like I was a child. "Melanie...I understand we've been in dire circumstances and it's easy to grow attached to anything that's comforting, but this is the man who enslaves and kills innocent women, women that we've known. How can you possibly feel that way about him?"

That was the million-dollar question. We didn't have enough time for me to explain the depth of my feelings, how they started, how they became so strong. There was nothing I could do to make her understand. But then an idea came to mind, something she could definitely comprehend. "The same reason you feel that way about Magnus."

The anger that appeared on Raven's face happened instantly, her breathing deeper, her cheeks flushing slightly. She was livid. "They are not the same, Melanie. Magnus is nothing like that monster."

"How are they different?" Defensive when I shouldn't be, I met her head on. "Both men don't hang the women themselves, but they both work there. How is it different? Magnus is just as guilty, and yet you look at him the way Fender looks at me."

Raven took a few breaths before she responded. "Magnus doesn't agree with the way the camp is run and has expressed that many times to Fender, but Fender ignores it. Magnus is the one who risked his neck to save us both. What has Fender done other than buy you pretty things?

I'm sorry, but to compare the two men is fucking insulting. How can you feel any affection for the man who's the boss of that camp? How?"

My eyes started to water in shame. Our time together was rare, and we were spending it at the gallows, the noose around my neck, her hand on the rope. "I just... I can't explain it."

Anger flew from her lips like bullets from a gun. "Well, you better try."

"He's just...more than that. He takes care of me, he's good to me, he's...a man. He's not like the other boys out there, and I like that. I know it's wrong, but I can't change the way I feel. I can't kill him. I can't do it, okay? I'm sorry." I knew that was a terrible explanation and totally missed the mark. Hot tears left my eyes and dripped down my cheeks.

Raven held her silence, but it was obvious that she struggled to process all of that without losing her temper. "If you don't kill him, I'll never get out of that camp. The women will never get out of that camp. Magnus will never be able to be free."

I kept my head down because the weight was so heavy. I witnessed Fender's relationship with Magnus from the front row, saw the untouchable connection between them, so I just said something to get her off my back, knowing neither man would ever hurt the other. "Why can't Magnus do it—"

"Because Fender will kill him. And Magnus won't kill his brother, so..."

I wanted this conversation to end because I was a mess. "You can kill Magnus and run—"

"Don't say that again." Raven lost her temper, her eyes like daggers. "You know Magnus is not like him. I don't even need to say it. Lie to yourself all you want, but it won't change reality. Magnus is the hero...and Fender is the villain."

I couldn't look at her. "I'm willing to sneak around and carry your secrets. I'm willing to do anything and everything to help you and those girls that are stuck there, but I can't kill him. I'm sorry..." I started to cry—full on.

Her anger was immediately sheathed, and her hand went to my shoulder then into my hair, tucking it behind my ear like Mom used to do. "Melanie, it's okay... Don't ruin your makeup."

I took a few deep breaths to make myself calm, to stave off the tears. "I know I can get him to set you free. I know I can..." Any other plan was pointless to me because this one would work. It would just take time. That was all.

"But that doesn't fix the problem, Melanie. Even if I'm free, the camp is still continuing."

I shook my head and went quiet for a long time, thinking about what she'd said.

Raven stared, waiting for me to address her last words.

"We went back and burned that place to the fucking ground, and it didn't change anything. I know you want to put an end to it, but you need to understand this is bigger than the two of us. I told you we shouldn't go back, that we had no chance, but you forced us to do it anyway. We lost our freedom because of it. I'm never going to be able to walk away from Fender at this point, so I need to make the best of it. Yes, I feel something for him, but how can I sleep beside the same man every single night and see his goodness and not feel something?" I paused to take a few breaths, my eyes filled with emotional intensity. "You need to understand there's nothing we can do. There's nothing Magnus can do. There's only one person who can make any difference—and I know he will. He will let you go. He will end that camp. He will walk away from it all."

Raven stared at me, her eyes skeptical. "And you really believe that?"

I slowly released the breath from my lungs and looked her straight in the eye. "With all my heart."

TWENTY
MAKE A WOMAN CRY

Fender

My eyes continued to shift back to the parlor, waiting for Melanie to return to me.

Every moment we were apart, my dread increased.

Unless she was right beside me where I could block her body with mine, the anxiety would deteriorate all the tissues of my heart. I never panicked. I never had anxiety. But she was the one thing that inflicted both of those sensations on me.

Napoleon approached Magnus and conducted a brief conversation.

My brother's face said it all—he didn't like the man at all.

No surprise there.

Stasia came next.

I lost interest and looked at the door again, not even bothering to pretend to listen to the guest speaking to me.

Raven stepped out of the room and approached Magnus from the rear, but she must have gotten angry at the sight of them together because she marched off and headed straight to the door.

Good.

But Melanie didn't come.

Oblivious to Raven's anger, Magnus continued to speak to Stasia.

Why didn't Melanie come back to me?

I drew breath with more anxiety. I squeezed my flute until it started to crack. Wordlessly, I excused myself from the conversation I wasn't participating in and moved past Magnus to the parlor.

She sat there alone, her eyes on her hands in her lap, her posture drooped.

Puffy cheeks. Red eyes. Smeared makeup.

Nothing hurt me more than seeing her like this.

It made me hate Raven more than I already did.

I moved to the seat beside her.

She turned to look at me, flinching slightly because she was so deep in thought that she didn't know I was in the room until that moment. When she'd assumed it was a stranger, her features had tightened to hide her discomfort. But when she looked at me, her eyes watered again—because she knew she didn't have to hide from me.

My hand moved into the back of her hair, and I brought her close to me, kissing her tears away, kissing her soft lips, kissing her jawline and neck, erasing her pain with my love. "Ne pleure pas, *chérie.*" *Don't cry, sweetheart.* My hand cupped her cheek as I pulled away and looked at her.

Her eyes were dry now, but the effects of her sadness were still on her features.

I pulled a tissue out of my pocket and placed it in her hand.

The smile she gave was so genuine. I was always there for her—and she knew it. She clenched the tissue in her closed fingertips before she brought it to her face to clean up her tear-stained cheeks.

"Talk to me, *chérie.*" My entire world collapsed when hers did too. When she was unhappy, I was unhappy. This was a woman who deserved the world, and every time I failed to give that to her, my self-hatred grew.

She sniffled before she wiped her nose. "Raven..." She shook her head and said nothing more.

"You continue to wonder why I hate her. There's your answer."

Her arm hooked through mine, and she came closer to me. "She's a good person. Better than me."

"Untrue." I looked at the most beautiful woman in the world, a woman who cared about people she shouldn't, saw the good in the evil. That made her a saint in my opinion.

She sniffled again. "She doesn't understand how I can feel anything for you."

"It's not her business to understand it."

"I try to explain it to her, but it doesn't come out right."

Coming between us. Again.

"And the way she looks at me...it just makes me feel so terrible."

"Hypocritical."

"She said Magnus is different."

He was different—but not that different. "He can leave the business any time he chooses. He voices his disagreements, but he doesn't put his money where his mouth is. So, no, fucking hypocritical."

"She said you're a monster..."

"I am a monster." That was one thing we could agree on.

She stared at me for a long time, her eyes still a little wet because the tears hadn't dried. "I told her that you're more than what you seem. I told her that you'll let her go. I told her that you would release all those girls." Her hand moved to mine, and she squeezed it. "And I believe that so deeply..."

We hadn't revisited this topic since our last fight, and I didn't want to have this conversation again, let alone right now. My instinct was to pull away and leave her there by herself, to grow angry at her choice of words, but my need for her was greater than my anger. It would always be greater than my anger. Never again would I let my temper separate us. Never again would I let anything divide us. "Let's get back to the party." I rose to my feet, pulling on her hand to get her to join me.

She stayed seated, looking up at me. "I believe it with all my heart."

AT THE END of the night, everyone left. The staff was left to clean up while we went upstairs to bed. She'd composed herself and chatted with my guests like nothing was wrong. It seemed to be forgotten—until we went to bed.

She let the gown slide off her body, but with a melancholy gaze. Her shoes were kicked off, and then she went to the bed, sitting on the edge and looking out the window.

I stared at her back as I got my clothes off, annoyed that Raven was still in her head.

The only person who should be in her head was me.

Stripped down to my boxers, I sat beside her. "Forget about it."

She slowly turned her head to look at me, and the surprised look on her face suggested her mind was somewhere else. "Raven left abruptly, and I'm not sure why. I hope she's okay. Hope it wasn't because of me."

It was probably because of Stasia, but I didn't tell her that. "Don't worry about her."

"Hard not to. She's my sister."

The annoyance sank in my skin like a sharp knife puncturing my flesh. That woman would always be the bane of my existence. She would always be in the room with us. Her words would always haunt Melanie with their endless echoes. "Magnus will give her what she needs. Just as I give you what you need."

That seemed to provide her comfort because she gave a slight nod. "Yeah...you're probably right."

MAGNUS and I met with Napoleon to begin the distribution process.

Then Magnus voiced all his concerns—for the millionth time.

I ignored him.

He came to the palace, joining me outside by the pool. Gilbert brought us scotch and a cheese board. Everything was on the table, and our chairs were turned to the pool, the sun setting but light still in the sky.

Melanie was swimming in the pool, far away and unable to hear us. She was in a revealing bikini with her hair and makeup done, looking like an angel without wings. It was hard for me to take my eyes off her—like always.

Magnus stared at the pool for a long time, his glass in one hand. "How's the new butler?"

I shrugged.

"The palace looks the same."

"Most of the blood was on the third floor." I turned to him. "You took care of Jeremy?"

He nodded. "Last week."

I would have done the dirty work myself, but hunting him down wasn't a good utilization of my time, not when it would take me away from Melanie.

"I'm sorry about Gilbert."

I looked at my brother again.

"He worked for you for a long time."

It'd been a couple weeks since he passed away, but it was still hard to think about. He had been the closest thing to family that I had besides Magnus. He was loyal—always. I knew the reason he died was because of his feelings for me. If they hadn't been a factor, he would have made the pragmatic decision to save his own ass. His feelings never bothered me, but now I wondered if I should have let him go once he had issues with Melanie. It obviously had had an effect on his work. And he'd still be alive.

Magnus continued to watch me. "I can tell it's affected you. I'm here...if you need to talk."

All I did was shake my head. I didn't talk about things like that to anyone—except Melanie. "You know what I want to talk about?" My gaze left the pool and stared at him head on. "Raven. That's what I want to talk about."

Magnus immediately tightened in unease, hearing the rage in my voice.

"She came into my fucking house and brought my woman to tears."

He looked away.

"Asshole, I'm talking to you."

He gave a loud sigh in frustration then turned back to me.

"If she does that shit again, she can't leave the camp. Understand me?"

All he did was stare.

"Fucking bullshit." I grabbed my glass and took a drink, turning my gaze back to the pool once more, my anger slowly fading away when I saw Melanie look at the grounds with her drink in hand, oblivious to the tension between us.

Magnus turned quiet, letting the hostility fade away in the silence. But then he picked at the same scab. "We agreed from the very beginning that we would only have small distributors, that we would keep them oppressed so they couldn't rise up and defy us. But recruiting someone like Napoleon, you're risking all of that. And who the fuck names themself Napoleon? He's not even European."

I kept my eyes on Melanie, practically tuning him out. "We're expanding. That's how it works."

"There're a lot of other ways to do that..."

I turned to him and couldn't bite back my retort. "Who's in charge? Me or you? Better yet, how many times do I have to ask you this question?"

Magnus held my gaze with his own anger then looked away.

Melanie got out of the pool and wrapped herself in the towel waiting for her at the edge. Her hair was pulled back into a bun with gold hoops in her lobes, looking like royalty even when she was swimming.

I watched her round the pool and approach, my heart slowing down more and more at the sight of her. Even from a distance, she gave me peace. She gave slow rivers. Tall mountains. Gentle breezes. Leaves that turned gold in the fall and green in the spring. "Most beautiful woman in the world, isn't she?"

Instead of holding his tongue, Magnus chose to piss me off. "I disagree."

I would have looked at him if my gaze weren't already entranced. I would have grown furious if my heart weren't embedded in calm. I would have given a damn if I weren't too busy giving a damn about the gorgeous woman who approached me.

Chérie.

She came to me, wrapped in her towel, and immediately helped herself to my lap before she picked up a slice of cheese off the cheeseboard.

My arms immediately enveloped her and brought her in for a kiss, my hands anxious to touch her despite the wetness and the chlorinated smell. My lips moved to her shoulder and pressed a kiss there as well, worshiping her body with my affection.

Melanie lifted her gaze and looked at Magnus as she ate. "Is Raven okay? You two left suddenly."

Magnus didn't look directly at her. "She's fine."

She drank from her wineglass, her eyes still drilling into his cheek because she was desperate for her answer. "You're lying. You and Fender make the same face when you do that."

Magnus turned and looked at her, his eyes darkening in annoyance. "I'm not lying. She's fine."

She wouldn't let it go—like always. "Maybe now she's fine, but she wasn't."

I didn't want to spend any more time talking about that infuriating woman. "She wasn't feeling well. Supposedly."

Melanie set down the glass and ignored the gourmet food in front of her. Every glass of wine she drank was from a vintage bottle, and my staff always took care of every single need she had. She swam in a big pool in a palace, and sat in the lap of a man who adored her. Why did she care if Raven was okay after she'd made her feel like shit? "Please tell me."

Magnus exchanged a look with me before he answered. "One of my old lovers said something to her."

"What?" Melanie asked.

He shrugged. "That she doesn't understand why I left her for someone much less attractive, basically. Which is completely untrue. She just said it to start shit."

Melanie erupted like a volcano, dormant one moment, then explosive the next. "I'm gonna knock that bitch out! Who the fuck is this skank?" She had more fire than she'd ever had before, grew angrier than I'd ever seen her.

I couldn't help but chuckle because it was amusing coming from her. Never heard her say anything like that, even when she was jealous of the women I'd been with. "Come on. She's right. Stasia is sexy, and your sister is a swine."

She could pretend she didn't see it, but I didn't buy it. Melanie was the pretty sister. Period.

Melanie turned to me and gave me a look I'd never seen before. Never once in our time together had she been angrier than she was right now, with fire in her eyes and my body as the kindling. She was still for a second before she pushed off me and got to her feet.

I was cold the second she was gone.

Then she shook. Shook hard. Shook like she didn't know how to channel so much rage.

She made her move. Her palm slapped across my face so hard that an audible smack echoed across the grounds. It was packed with more strength than I would have thought her little body could ever produce. The blow had so much momentum that it made my head turn slightly. The sting was profound the second her palm collided with my face. "Don't talk about my sister like that, asshole."

When I turned back to look at her, my eyes were filled with surprise.

There was no remorse on her part.

Melanie marched back to the estate, her legs moving quickly because she wanted to get away from me as fast as possible.

I watched her go and didn't follow. My hand rubbed my cheek as I glanced at my brother, who looked completely shocked. But I brushed it off and dropped my hand because I didn't regret what I'd said. "Kinda liked it."

WHEN I WENT TO BED, she wasn't there.

I undressed down to my boxers then checked the bathroom and the closet.

She was gone.

I went down the hallway into her old bedroom and found her there. She was in bed with the sheets pulled to her shoulder, facing the window with her back to me. Her breathing told me she was wide awake but trying to pretend she was asleep.

I knew her better than she gave me credit for.

I approached the bed and stood over her, watching her inhales increase because she knew I was there, standing over her, staring her down. My hand went to her arm and gently pulled her toward me.

Her fire obviously hadn't died down because she twisted out of the hold instantly. "Don't touch me."

I continued to stand there, waiting for her to turn and look at me.

She didn't.

I didn't apologize.

I went around the bed to the other side, so she would be forced to look at me.

Her eyes narrowed in anger. "Leave."

I grabbed the top of the sheets and pulled them down.

When I didn't obey like usual, she sat up. "I said, leave."

I got into bed beside her and pulled the sheets to my waist. "No."

In complete bewilderment, she just stared at me, unsure what to do next now that her power had been taken from her. Then she kicked the sheets off and got out of bed. "Fine. Then I'll go." Her feet hit the rug, and she marched off.

I followed her.

She looked back at me in the stairway, her eyes vicious. "Stop it."

I kept going.

She went into my bedroom and shut the door in my face. She locked it too.

That was cute.

I stepped back a couple feet then slammed my body against the door, breaking it clean off the hinges. I stepped inside and ignored the debris underneath my feet.

She looked at the door then my face, her eyes wide in disbelief.

I walked toward her. "Where you go, I go. So pick a fucking bed."

Her blue eyes were livid. Her chest rose and fell with her deep breaths. The anger was too much for her to process, and she had no idea what to do with it. My behavior had never instilled this level of rage, and her loyalty to her sister was the only explanation for it. "I want you to leave."

"No." I stepped closer to her, ignoring her fury and approaching without caution.

Smoke was practically coming out of her ears.

I stood in front of her. Stood over her.

She reverted to her previous behavior and slapped me again.

I turned with the hit, aroused when I should be furious. She'd never been disobedient. She never displayed the qualities I despised. But when she did, I liked it.

"Don't talk about my sister like that again." Her eyes shifted back and forth as she looked into mine, her anger still rampant as if that last slap still wasn't enough to cool her rage.

I didn't understand why it mattered what I said. I spoke the truth. Melanie was beautiful, and Raven was garbage. She knew it, even if I never said it again. But I gave her what she wanted. "Alright."

Her anger dimmed. "Apologize."

"No. I meant what I said."

Now it flared up again.

"You're the most beautiful woman in the world. By default, every other woman is the ugliest."

"You said Stasia is sexy and my sister is a pig." She threw her arms down.

"In comparison. Stasia is a pig in comparison to you too."

The anger dropped a bit, and she crossed her arms over her chest.

Even in her anger, she was beautiful. Breathtaking. I moved in, watching her step back, and positioned her ass against the bed.

Her hands went to the bed behind her, and she looked up at me with guarded eyes.

I grabbed her hips and lifted her onto the bed.

She smacked my hand away.

My eyes narrowed, and I grabbed her hips and tugged her down, getting her to lie down so I could get her thong off.

She kicked me.

"You want me to stop? Tell me." I pushed my boxers down and let my hard cock come free.

She continued that vicious stare, but she didn't say a word. She wanted me—she just wished she didn't.

I positioned her hips at the edge of the bed before my hips moved between her thighs.

She slapped me again.

My hands reached for hers and pinned them above her head. "Tell me."

There was only that furious stare.

One hand kept her wrists together, and I directed myself inside her, sheathed in her typical wetness. "Fuck, *chérie*..." I kept her wrists in place because I liked it, and I fucked her at the edge of the bed, moving into her hard and fast, desperate for her the second she'd slapped me across the face.

She didn't rock with me, but she moaned against her will.

My eyes burned into hers as I pounded into her slickness, feeling her tighten around me only to purposely distance herself, like she wanted to resist me as much as she could. She didn't want to give me that satisfaction. But I already took all the satisfaction I needed. This wasn't a game to me because I wasn't a man who played games. "Je t'aime, *chérie*."

She immediately softened at my words. Her hips started to move. Her moans became louder. And she pulled her hands free from my hold and hooked her arms around my shoulders to bring me closer. "Je t'aime, *mon amour*..."

MY HAND REACHED for her beside me.

Nothing.

My eyes opened and saw the sunlight poking through the closed curtains. Bits of dust were in the air. The room was considerably warmer in the morning than it was at bedtime —even with our lovemaking.

My hand clenched the sheets, disappointed that she'd left me to wake up without her. She made sleep easy. Knowing she was beside me, that nothing could touch her unless it pierced my flesh all the way through first and hit her afterward, gave me a deeper level of peace.

I would never let anything happen to her.

Not again.

I got out of bed and pulled on my sweats.

The door leaned forward, only attached to the wall by a single hinge. Pieces of wood were kicked to the side so the entryway was clear. She wasn't in the bathroom, so I went down the stairs and through the foyer.

"Morning, sir." Gilbert greeted me, in his full tuxedo with his hands behind his back. "Is there—"

"Melanie." I stared him down.

He was getting better at recovering from my harshness, so he gave a quick nod. "She's having breakfast on the terrace. Would you like to join her?"

"Yes."

He nodded and walked away.

"Gilbert?"

He turned back to me. "Yes, sir?"

"Fix my door." I walked past him. "It's broken." I headed out through the French doors in the rear and found Melanie sitting under an open umbrella, an assortment of breakfast items on the table. Chocolate croissants. Pot of coffee. Vase of pink roses. Savory crepes. Bowl of fruit. More food than she could possibly eat. But that wasn't the point.

When I came close, she drew her gaze away from the pool and the acres beyond and turned to me.

I pulled out my chair and sat across from her.

Her chin was on her closed fingers, and she watched me with guarded eyes, like her anger wasn't gone despite all the fucking we'd done, all the whispers we'd shared, all the tears she'd shed. Her eyes dropped back to her coffee, and she brought it to her lips for a drink. She was in a sundress with her bathing suit underneath, sunscreen on her face instead of makeup. The bridge of her nose had a distinct whiteness to it, like that was where she'd slathered on the most lotion.

She was beautiful—like always.

I was content just to sit there and stare.

Our nights and mornings were the best parts of my day. Our nights were filled with a kind of passion I'd never had with another woman. Our mornings were only about need, taking what we wanted before we began our day. Quick. To the point. A good start. I appreciated them both in different ways. So, when I woke up without her, it turned my entire day upside down.

Gilbert appeared and served me the same crepes. Chicken with asparagus with a creamy sauce on top. A white mug was placed there so I could fill it with coffee. Everything else on the table was communal, so I could grab anything I wanted.

She drank her coffee again. Took a few bites. Looked out to the gardens of perfectly manicured rosebushes and trees. She looked like she belonged here, like she was born here, like this was her fate.

Her mood was cold, like she didn't want to spend her morning with me but wasn't angry enough to ask me to leave.

Or maybe she just knew it was pointless to try.

I ate everything on my plate then had a few pieces of fruit. Sips of coffee happened in between. My fingers rubbed the scruff along my jaw as I repeatedly took in her appearance. My morning should be spent in the gym, but all I wanted to do was see her right away. "I thought we were past this."

She turned her chin to look at me, her blue eyes turning a bit sharp. "You called my sister a swine. No, we aren't past this."

"We seemed to be fine last night..." I gave her a slight smile. All she'd had to do was tell me to stop, and it would have been over. But she didn't. Not once. She got on top of me and bounced on my dick while I gripped her tits.

Her eyes sharpened even further to points of daggers. "It's not funny."

"Didn't laugh. I gloated."

She rolled her eyes and looked away. "I don't understand how you can say you love me and then talk about someone I love that way. How would you feel if I said Magnus was hideous?"

"I've always been the better-looking one. No surprise there."

"What if I said I hated him—"

"I hate him most of the time too."

She shook her head, releasing a sigh of irritation.

I'd done worse things, so I didn't understand why she was so hung up on this. They were just words. Insults. Nothing more. "*Chérie*."

She slowly turned back to me.

"Tell me."

She brought her mug closer then looked down into the fair liquid, coffee loaded with cream and sugar. "I know it bothers her..."

My arms rested on the armrests, and my hands came together over my lap, just listening.

"She'd like a boy, but the boy would like me. We'd go out as adults, and if there were two guys, they would fight over me instead of one pairing up with her. She was seeing this guy for a while, and when she introduced him to me, it got weird...and he'd hit on me when she wasn't around."

No surprise there.

"I think that's another reason she ran away from me...so she could stop being compared to me. It made me really angry, but I can't really blame her anymore. I've caused her nothing but grief since our mom died."

"I disagree. The only reason she's alive is because of you."

"That's all I've ever done for her." She grabbed her spoon and stirred her coffee, still looking down into the liquid. "Magnus isn't like that. I can tell when men are attracted to me, and he's not."

Maybe he'd told me the truth. Maybe Raven wasn't his second choice after all.

"That's why I love him for my sister...along with other reasons." She tapped her spoon against the edge to get rid of the drops before she set it back on the linen. "She deserves to have a man who looks at her the way you look at me. Every woman deserves that. And maybe I'm more classically pretty, but she is more than I ever will be."

"Such as?"

She shrugged. "Smart. Independent. Ambitious. Brave. Compassionate. Full of integrity. Kind..." She drew a deep breath then slowly released it. "All I have is my looks... nothing more."

My heart started to increase in pace—because that actually pained me. "She compares herself to you. But you compare yourself to her too. Makes you both miserable."

She lifted her chin and looked at me.

"I wish you saw yourself the way I see you. Because I disagree with everything you just said."

She dropped her gaze and dismissed me.

"I know you killed my executioner."

Her eyes lifted to mine instantly, all the features of her face tightening at the accusation.

"Yes, I know everything, *chérie.*" I knew everything she'd done in that camp when she'd helped burn it down. "Don't sit there and tell me you aren't brave. A woman doesn't go into a blizzard with her sister, expecting to die, if she isn't brave. A woman doesn't love a man like me if she isn't brave. You're the bravest person I've ever met."

She was still, emotion moving into her eyes.

"You're the compassionate one. She is not." I shook my head. "Magnus is as guilty as I am, but you understand her feelings—because you've gone through the same thing. You love me even when you shouldn't, and she gives you no compassion for that. I don't expect her to ever understand me, even if Magnus tells her what happened to the two of us when we were just boys, but I expect her to understand her sister."

She remained still, the emotion continuing to rise.

"Gilbert treated you like shit, but you were kind to him anyway. He was the one who forced you on that diet—and you still didn't throw him under the bus. And yes, I know about that too. *Chérie*, I know everything."

Her breathing increased.

"And you forgot one—loyal. Anyone else would cherish their good fortune and live a life of luxury, but you've remained loyal to her, through and through. She breathes because of you. She's gained immunity because of you. She treats you like the villain when you're the fucking hero, *chérie*."

MELANIE

We went out to dinner.

The entire menu was in French, but I was able to decipher better than I used to. I was even able to order for myself without getting a weird look from the waiter. A ten-thousand-euro bottle of wine was on the table for us to share. Candles cast a glow throughout the restaurant, which was full of couples speaking to each other quietly, hands held together on the table.

Fender was dressed in all black with a suit jacket on top, his jawline shaved, his eyes dark. An expensive watch was on his wrist, solid black. He spent the evening sipping the wine, looking at me, eating, and looking at me some more.

There was never a time when we stepped into a room and his gaze strayed.

I imagined he never did, even when he was alone.

His commitment to me was obvious in everything he did, but that didn't stop women from casting glances his way.

I didn't even care. Couldn't blame them. I didn't realize men like him existed until I met him. Tall. Dark. Handsome. Brooding. Powerful. Rich. Passionate. Loving. Dedicated. How could a man that desirable be so committed to a single woman?

Our dinner was mostly spent in silence. He didn't seem to mind that.

We finished our meal, he paid the tab, and then we got into his car and left.

But we didn't head home. We moved deeper into Paris.

His hand held mine on the center console, and he drove through the busy streets of Paris, everyone enjoying the summer evening.

"Where are we going?"

His eyes remained on the road.

When I didn't get a response, I looked at our joined hands, his big hand wholly encompassing mine.

He turned down a few streets before he stopped and waited for a car to move from its position at the curb. It seemed to be one of his men holding the spot for him because he immediately drove off the second Fender approached.

We parked, walked up many steps, and then stopped at the sight.

The Louvre.

The stone plaza was empty of tourists. The windows of the palace behind it were lit like there were guests inside. And the space around the glass prism was full of lit white candles everywhere.

Everywhere.

There was a narrow path down the middle for the two of us.

With my hand in his, he guided me forward, approaching the pyramid made of glass.

My eyes surveyed the sea of candles around us. They flickered as we passed. Flickered again when a summer breeze moved through. The fountain was the only audible backdrop. All the entrances to the area were blocked off by ropes.

I looked at him, waiting for an explanation for the most beautiful sight I'd ever witnessed.

He ignored me and took me to the base of the pyramid, a wider area that was open in the field of candles.

I looked at it close-up, felt the wind ruffle my hair, felt the heat lick my skin. My heart raced now, pounded in my chest because something was about to happen. "It's beautiful. But...what's it for?"

He pulled his fingers away from mine and slid both of his hands into his pockets. He looked up at the structure before us, his gaze casual, like arranging this was no big deal. He could do anything—because he owned everything and everyone.

"I've always wanted to come here... It just never worked out."

He turned to look at me, hands still in his pockets.

I went still, paralyzed by that stare.

He pivoted to face me head on. Drew close. Stared into my eyes like he hadn't gazed at me over dinner.

Something was about to happen. I could feel it in the air around us. I could breathe it in, and every time it reached my lungs, it burned.

He pulled his left hand from his pocket, and within his fingers was the biggest diamond ring I'd ever seen.

I sucked in a breath. My heart did a weird somersault. My stomach dropped to my feet.

He stared at it in his fingertips for a moment, turning it slightly so the diamond reflected the array of candles around us. "This belonged to Countess Baudelaire—my great-grandmother." He continued to admire it, the enormous rock made small by his big hand. "I tracked it down. Paid a fortune. But it's a family heirloom—and it should stay in the family."

Oh my god.

He lifted his gaze to me. With a hard stare and a depth to his eyes, he grabbed my left hand and slid the ring on to my finger. "Now you'll be Countess Baudelaire—my countess."

The ring was snug on my finger, and the second it was in place, it held a weight I could barely carry.

He pulled his hands away and waited for my reaction.

I looked down at my hand, seeing a diamond that belonged in a museum, seeing a history so rich and deep. My thumb brushed over the diamond, a rock that could easily cut me if I weren't careful. I lifted my gaze and looked at him again, realizing he'd never asked me to marry him.

He just told me that I would.

There was a short moment of euphoria, because everything about this proposal was perfect. The scene. The ring. The man. It was a Cinderella story, but instead of a prince, I got a count. I got a palace.

But it wasn't enough.

I slipped the ring back off my finger.

There was a subtle change to his expression, but that slight difference conveyed so much.

"How can you expect me to say yes?" With the ring in my fingertips, I stared at him.

He was quiet, moving his hands back to the pockets of his slacks. His eyes were trained and steady, focused on me, like the barrel of a gun pointed at a target.

"I—I can't." I held the ring back out to him.

He didn't take it.

I continued to hold the ring in front of me.

He didn't move.

"I'll say yes—if you free the girls."

His answer was immediate. "No."

He'd put his heart on the table, and I leveraged that against him as best as I could.

"You have no say in how I run my business. Nor will you ever." His voice remained low, but it was so hard and callous.

I looked at the ring again, seeing a future I still wanted, inexplicably. "Then release my sister." My fingers moved the ring back over my knuckle, the weight back in place.

His eyes glanced at the ring on my finger before he looked at me again.

"You said I'm loyal. So, you can't expect me to marry you while my sister is in that godforsaken place. Let her go— and I'll marry you."

His stare was endless. Hostile. Annoyed. Furious. A breath escaped his lungs and made his nostrils flare. But slowly, he let all of that go. He came back to me. He drifted back to the moment we shared. "Alright."

ROSE PETALS WERE on the bed. White candles glowed on every surface, filling the room just the way they did at the Louvre. The door had been fixed, and a line of red petals led to the bed.

I moved forward, constantly aware of the weight of commitment on my left hand.

Clothes dropped behind me.

My heart raced. It was the same room, same kind of evening, but tonight was different.

My life was forever different.

A powerful arm slid over my stomach and pulled me into his bare chest, his head dipping to kiss my exposed neck. He sucked the skin as he bunched the dress in his grasp, treating the designer dress like a dirty rag. His hand moved up and cupped my ass, his breaths moving straight to my ear.

I closed my eyes and felt my insides melt.

He whispered into my ear, "You will give me strong sons. You will give me beautiful daughters. You will be my one and only until death takes me. My countess." His hand pulled down the zipper until the dress came apart and slid to my feet. His kisses turned more heated, his hand dipped into the front of my panties and rubbed my clit as he devoured me, his lips growing harder, more aggressive.

I held on to his arm for balance and writhed at his touch, my hips rocking to press into his fingertips because it felt so damn good.

He brought me to the edge before he removed his fingers.

I exhaled in frustration, but I knew he only stopped because he could give it to me better than that.

We made it to the bed, his body crowding me on the mattress, and after my thighs were separated by his narrow hips, he slid inside me, eyes on me, possessing me with more than just his touch, but his mind, body, and soul.

With his eyes on me, he made love to me.

Over and over.

Telling me he loved me. I was his one and only. Till death do us part.

MY EYES OPENED to a view of the windows.

Sunlight didn't break through the gaps in the curtains like every other morning.

Because it was noon.

I was immediately aware of my left hand because of the brand-new weight I'd carry for the rest of my life. My hand lifted to my face, and I looked at the oval-shaped diamond, the rock that was so big you wouldn't be able to miss it if it fell on the ground. It shone in the light, a million little prisms with every slight movement I made.

The man who gave it to me was still asleep.

He was on his back, sprawled out and taking up most of the bed, his hand stretched out to me like it'd been on my stomach at some point during the night. Gentle breaths filled and depleted his lungs. The sheets were bunched at his waist, as if he'd gotten warm sometime during the night. He was a behemoth of a man, giving more protection than an automatic weapon.

I stared for a while, taking in the sight of the man I would marry.

My fiancé.

Guilt pulled at my stomach—but not for the reason it should.

I slowly crept out of bed and got to the edge. My feet planted on the rug, and I ran my fingers through my messy hair. My makeup had never been washed off, so now my eyes were puffy from the eye shadow and mascara. My fingers rubbed the corners, getting piles of goop on my fingertips.

The candles were dark because Fender must have blown them out at some point. Rose petals were in my hair, and one fell out and drifted to the floor. I got to my feet then slowly tiptoed around the bed toward the closet.

"Get back here." His deep voice was raspy, his vocal cords still asleep.

I turned back to him.

He looked at me with tired eyes before he patted the sheets beside him. His hair was messy, there was a streak of lipstick at his jawline, and his sleepy look was sexy. It was one of the rare times he looked harmless.

I slowly crept back, stopping to grab one of his shirts from a drawer on the way. I got back into bed beside him.

He immediately pulled me close, his arm hooking around the small of my back, his lips brushing my hairline. "I'm tired of waking up and you're gone." He closed his eyes once more and held me there, his fingers lightly caressing me, holding me as he slowly woke up.

We lay there for a while before a quiet knock sounded on the door. The noise of the tray settling against the hardwood floor was audible, along with the sound of Gilbert's retreating steps.

It must be breakfast.

I moved from his hold again and retrieved the tray, placing it on the dining table in the sitting room. I used the drapery pullers next and opened the windows, letting the daylight invade every corner of the bedroom.

Fender sat up in bed, his arms moving to his knees, and he rubbed his eye with his palm.

I set the table then took a seat, pouring a hot cup of coffee.

He joined me a moment later, in his black boxers, scruff on his jaw, a slight look of annoyance in his gaze. He sat across from me but didn't reach for the coffee or anything else. His look pierced me from across the table.

I added cream and sugar, eyes down.

He continued to stare, drilling harder, demanding an explanation for my behavior.

When my fingers gripped the handle of the mug, I noticed my ring there, brilliant and beautiful. I released the mug and tightened my fingers into a fist, seeing the diamond reflect different spectrums of light.

I lifted my gaze and looked at him.

He could convey so much with just his expression—and right now, he was borderline furious.

"I...I have to tell you something."

Instantly, all the tightness of his features relaxed. He'd probably expected me to give the ring back because I'd changed my mind.

I didn't just agree to marry him to save my sister. I did it because I couldn't picture myself with anyone else but him. That made me feel guilty for my dishonesty. Made me feel disloyal. Made me feel like I didn't deserve him. "When I came back to you...I did it to save her." I dropped my gaze because I couldn't look at him, not when I was admitting that the foundation of this relationship was a lie.

The silence lasted a long time.

When he said nothing, I looked at him again.

His expression hadn't changed. "I know, *chérie*."

I inhaled a breath in relief. Whenever he called me that, I knew we would be okay.

"I know that was why you told me you loved me too."

Guilt flooded my heart then circulated into all my veins.

"But I didn't care. Still don't."

My fingers played with my ring, spun it back and forth. The diamond was too big to spin all the way around my finger, so I had to turn it back and forth between the two fingers on either side.

"Do you love me now?"

The question caught me off guard because it hurt so much. It hurt that he had to ask that, because what we had was real. Even if it was wrong, it was true. I shouldn't love a man like him, but I did anyway, and that told me it was undeniable. Tears burned my eyes, provoking emotions that hadn't been there just a second ago. "With all my heart."

His hard gaze continued for a while. Then his eyes lightened. His energy changed.

And he smiled.

INSTEAD OF WORKING in his office, he chose to spend time with me.

Our mornings were spent in bed, making love like we hadn't done that all night long. Then he would take me to Paris. We would get lunch, do some sight-seeing, go shopping, stuff that regular couples did.

With his hand in mine, he led the way.

Giving me a life I'd never thought I could have.

He bought me anything I wanted, whether it was a scarf or diamond earrings. Whenever a man came too close to me, he literally gave them the death stare until they scurried off. If a woman hit on him, he acted like she didn't exist.

I was the only thing that mattered to him.

His head never turned.

And I knew it wasn't for show.

We returned to the palace, and Fender carried my shopping bags into the foyer before he set them down for Gilbert to retrieve.

Gilbert emerged when he arrived. The old Gilbert would be ready the second the guards notified him that Fender was at the gate, but it was wrong to compare them, despite the now-same name. "Dinner is almost ready. Will you be dining in your room this evening?"

"Yes." Fender barely looked at him before he took the stairs.

I followed behind him, and we entered our bedroom.

He removed his watch and pulled his shirt over his head, standing shirtless near the bed.

"You don't like Gilbert."

He turned to me, undoing his jeans. "I don't like anybody."

"I know it's hard, but you can't compare him to..."

Fender didn't talk about the first Gilbert, didn't talk about anything really, but it was obvious it still haunted him. He'd lost someone he cared about, and it made him shut down in many ways. He ignored what I said and pulled off his shoes then stripped down to his boxers.

I let it be.

After he'd said he would release Raven, we hadn't talked about it. I assumed he would make good on his word next time he went to the camp—which was probably any day now. I kicked off my shoes and got undressed, choosing to wear one of his t-shirts instead of my fancy clothes. We'd become fully domesticated now, like a couple that sat around in their pajamas when they were home.

He walked up to me, his gaze dark, like he had something to say.

I waited. I knew him better than anyone else, so I recognized all his subtle cues. I understood what he said without saying a word. I didn't have to see his anger because I could absorb it through my skin. I didn't even need to hear him say he loved me—because I could feel that too.

"I leave tonight."

Like I received devastating news, I inhaled a deep breath. "Why do you always tell me at the last minute—"

"Because you hate it every time I leave." His big hands cupped my face. "I hate it too."

The last time he left, everything fell apart.

"I'd stay...but I can't. I have work to do." His eyes were full of apology. "I'll bring you with me if that makes you more comfortable."

I wanted to say yes. I wanted to be with him always. I wanted his massive size beside me every single night.

He watched my eyes, studying my reaction.

But that place was the source of my nightmares. The source of my pain. The very reason we shouldn't be together. My sister would be removed from the camp, so it was best never to think of it again, to pretend it didn't exist. I couldn't pretend if I was there.

His hands slowly dropped from my face. "I understand."

I hated to disappoint him, but I just couldn't do it. "You'll release my sister when you're there?"

He nodded.

"And when she's in Paris...can I see her?"

His look suddenly turned angry. Out of nowhere. Like an asteroid that appeared in the sky with no warning whatsoever. He stepped back, nostrils flaring, eyes closing, hands clenching. "No."

In shock, all I could do was stare.

A knock sounded on the door, announcing Gilbert's arrival.

As if the conversation was over, Fender turned away. "Enter."

Gilbert let himself inside and carried the tray of food to the table.

My eyes never left Fender. "What do you mean, no?"

He turned back to me, surprise in his eyes, like he expected this conversation just to go away.

"You expect me to marry you but never see my sister? Who's with your brother?"

His voice boomed like someone had cranked up the volume on a stereo. "I'm letting her go. Why isn't that enough for you?" He turned on me, skin tinted red with rage, his eyes hostile.

Gilbert stilled at the table then quickly arranged the platters, trying to get out of there as quickly as possible.

My eyes narrowed on Fender's face, all the love in my heart gone. "How do you expect me to be happy when I can't see the only family I have left—"

"Why am I not enough for you?" He rounded on me, his powerful arms clenched at his sides, staring me down like I was the enemy, not the woman he loved. "I've given you everything. I've given you every single part of me. Why the fuck is that not enough?"

I stepped back, my eyes shifting back and forth between his, realizing there was something I was missing.

Gilbert hurried out the door and silently shut it behind him.

"What aren't you telling me?" My voice escaped as a whisper, because when he was irrational, it somehow made me turn calm.

He looked away, his hands moving to his hips.

"Fender."

He looked out the window for a long time, his thoughts somewhere else.

"Tell me."

He turned back to me, his look less angry and more restrained.

"Your hatred for her can't outweigh your love for me. I need her in my life—period. She escaped, burned down your camp, turned your world upside down. But let's not forget that you took her against her will, and the only reason you despise her is because she's given you nothing but hell. I'm proud of her. I'm so fucking proud of her for not giving up. So, you're just going to have to let that go—"

"That's not why." His voice turned quiet and calm, which was somehow more intimidating.

"Then why?"

His eyes shifted back and forth as he looked into mine, as if debating whether he should tell me. His arms crossed over his chest, the muscles becoming more pronounced. "I'm scared of her."

My reaction was uncontrollable. Eyebrows spiked. A breath escaped my slightly parted lips. Unbridled surprise entered my features. Fender wasn't scared of anyone—let alone a woman. "You think she'll try to kill you?"

"No. If she wants to keep Magnus in her life, that's not an option for her."

"Then...I don't understand."

He stared at the ground for a moment before he looked at me. "This is exactly what will happen. She'll talk in your ear. Poison your mind. Remind you of all the reasons you shouldn't be with me. She'll turn you against me—like she always does. Then you'll leave me. That's what fucking scares me."

He was right on the money. That was exactly how that would go.

"I know what she says to you—even when I'm not in the room. I know she'll never feel differently about me and what I do. We'll always be at odds with each other. And you picked her once—you'll do it again."

His dark eyes bored into my gaze, impatient for a response.

"I did pick her once...and I was miserable."

He sucked in a deep breath.

Those months had passed so quickly but so slowly at the same time. Even though Raven and I were free and had successfully liberated everyone from the camp, I'd had no reason to go on. There was no zest for life. My nights were sleepless. My heart was heavy. "But I won't pick her again."

His gaze turned stoic, like he didn't believe that.

"Because I won't have to. You'll do the right thing."

He closed his eyes and released a long, drawn-out breath. "Stop saying that shit—"

"You will."

His skin started to flush red again, but his anger didn't explode. "I won't let you go again, so I guess it doesn't matter."

"Yes, you will."

His eyes narrowed.

"You would never do that, Fender."

"You underestimate me—"

"I could walk out the front gate right now, and you'd let me go." I knew him better than he knew himself. I knew the real him—not this shadow.

His eyes drilled into my face, but he didn't refute me.

"You're forcing yourself to be something that you aren't. Aren't you tired?"

Silence.

"You've accomplished everything that you ever wanted. It's over—"

"I will consider your request." He dismissed the conversation by stepping away from me and moving into the sitting area. He opened a bottle of scotch, filled a glass, and then sat at the table to eat his dinner.

And that was the end of it.

TWENTY-TWO

FREEDOM

FENDER

We didn't speak through dinner and the rest of the evening.

But when we made love, all of that changed.

She slowly came back to me. Her nails dug into my back. Her kisses turned hard. She whispered her love to me. The last time we'd had a fight, I'd left, and we both could have died. She learned from that and didn't hold on to her anger.

I didn't either.

I got dressed and prepared to leave.

In my t-shirt, she sat at the edge of the bed, a mess from all the sex, but a beautiful mess. She watched my movements, her arms over her chest, dread in her eyes.

"I need to show you something."

She followed me downstairs. I led her through the foyer, behind the staircase, and down a hallway behind the kitchen. In a room was a bookshelf that took up the entire back wall.

"Pay attention." I walked over to the books on the shelf, specifically *War and Peace*, and tilted them back simultaneously. Then I went to the piano and hit the first white key.

The bookshelf turned just enough for someone to slide inside.

Her eyes widened. "The safe room..."

"Come on." I slipped inside and stepped into a square room made entirely of metal.

She looked around, seeing nothing but four walls.

There was a pad on the wall, and I hit the button.

The room started to move.

She jolted as we descended to the ground, looking around even though there were no windows to see the earth pass by. "It's an elevator..."

We made it to the bottom, and the doors opened.

I stepped into the concrete passageway. Guns and supplies lined the beginning of a long, dark tunnel. "This tunnel goes all the way to Paris. If the alarm ever goes off, don't hesitate. Run down here and join the staff. If the elevator isn't there, give it a second because it'll rise again."

She nodded her understanding.

"I'm sorry I didn't tell you before…" Gilbert might still be alive if I had. No one had ever tried to take me down at my residence, so it was a possibility I never seriously considered. My arrogance had cost lives.

We rose back in the elevator to the main room. The bookshelf was righted once again, and we walked to the foyer. My car was ready in the roundabout. I turned to her in front of the open doorway, my heart heavy because leaving her was the most painful thing I ever had to do.

Her arms were crossed over her chest, her eyes sad. "How long will you be gone?"

"Not sure."

"Is there a way we can talk?"

I never made personal phone calls while I was at the camp. We had satellite phones, but the reception was poor. Most of the conversations were just static. "No."

The disappointment was heavy. "Be careful, okay?"

"Always." My arms circled her petite body, and I brought her close to press a kiss to her forehead. She was more valuable than my money, my homes, my vault of jewels. She was the single most important thing in my life—and she had a beating heart that I had to protect. I'd never known love, not like this, and I hadn't felt love at all since the night I'd lost my family. She seemed to fix that—or at least put a gauze over the wound. "Je t'aime, *chérie*."

She pressed her forehead against my chest. "Je t'aime, mon fiancé."

I kissed her again because I loved the way that sounded on her perfect lips. I hugged her tighter, not wanting to let go, wanting to stay for just another moment. But I forced myself to pull away, forced myself to do what must be done.

But I did leave my heart behind—in her hands.

THE CAMP WAS EXACTLY as it should be.

The guards were always surprised by my unexpected visits, but never unprepared.

My horse was taken away, Nathan went to retrieve my dinner from the kitchen, and I silently walked beside Magnus as we entered my cabin. The second I was on the premises, I stopped thinking about Melanie and focused on the things that required my attention.

Magnus seemed to know I was in a bad mood because he said, "Talk tomorrow?"

"No." I pulled my sweaty shirt over my head and tossed it aside before I grabbed a bottle of water and my favorite scotch. I moved to the couch and took a seat, getting the water down before I started on the drink I really wanted.

Magnus noticed my unusual behavior but didn't comment on it. He took a seat.

We talked about securing the deal with the Colombians, if Alix was still being a bitch, other matters that required my attention. It was all business first—the reason I was there. I drank my scotch as we talked.

He didn't.

Guess he was more pussy-whipped than I was.

"I don't understand the risk you're taking. The risk doesn't outweigh current profits."

He resisted me at every step—and it was fucking annoying. "A business can't grow without risks."

"But we don't need to grow. We're already the biggest—"

"And we can be bigger." I flashed him a hard look. "When will you understand that, even if I had everything, it still wouldn't be enough."

Magnus finally backed off and rose to his feet, his mood soured by our disagreement. "Goodnight."

"No. I have something to say to you." This was the real reason I was in a foul mood.

He turned back and stared at me, a leaner and younger version of myself. We were two years apart, but sometimes that felt like a lifetime.

"Raven is free to leave the camp. Take her to Paris. Leave here there." My fingers rested on the top of my glass, anxious for another drink, but I'd already had plenty. That woman was the bane of my existence—and she fucking beat me.

Magnus couldn't recover from the shock. His open stare lingered.

"But if she pulls another stunt, comes back to this camp and starts shit, I will kill her." I took a drink. "Don't call my bluff. You won't be able to save her. Melanie won't either."

Magnus finally recovered from the surprise. "Thank you…"

"Keep your gratitude. Didn't do it for you."

He gave a slight nod in understanding. "You two made up."

"I asked her to marry me." I stared into the glass for a moment before I shifted my look to my brother, the only family I had in the world—until Melanie was my wife. Until she gave me children. Until she gave me a life that had been taken from me.

My brother didn't have an overt reaction, like he didn't know what to say.

"She said yes. But only if I released Raven."

Still nothing.

His reaction angered me, because he'd personally asked me to do this for him in the past. "I thought you would be more cheerful."

He shook his head slightly. "You wouldn't have to let Raven go if we ran this camp differently—"

"Melanie already tried. If I won't do it for her, why would I do it for you?" Now I understood his disappointment. He'd hoped that Melanie could leverage me to do more. But not even she could make me do the impossible—despite what she believed.

His eyes dropped for a moment.

"She said she would only marry me if I freed all the girls. I said no. Then she asked for her sister instead."

He gave a slight nod.

"What?"

"I'm just surprised that she made the request in the first place."

Annoyed, I looked away. "Don't be. You don't know her. And frankly, her sister doesn't either." Raven and Magnus had a low opinion of my woman, but in reality, she was the one who didn't give up. She was the one who kept trying to change me. Over and over.

Magnus remained quiet.

I knew he was hiding something from me. "What?"

He held my gaze without blinking, giving it to me straight like a man. "Melanie only came back to you to save Raven."

If Melanie hadn't confessed that to me already, his words would have caused a deep wound. But she came clean because she respected me, because she loved me, because she wanted to marry me and start that marriage off with complete honesty. But my brother's deception stung. "You kept this from me." His loyalties had never been so muddled until now—until Raven.

He continued to hold my gaze. "I didn't think you'd care. Didn't realize your feelings were so profound until now. Assumed this was just a physical relationship, infatuation, lust—"

"Have you ever seen me this way with a woman?"

He didn't answer.

"My feelings were profound the day I looked at her for the first time. Don't pretend you didn't know that."

Guilt moved into his eyes.

"But luckily for you, it doesn't matter. Whether she really wants to be with me or not, she's all I want."

Magnus gave a nod. "Then I'm happy for you."

I CROSSED the grounds and marched toward my brother's cabin.

It was sunset, the sky barely lit with a sea of orange and yellow. The heat immediately dimmed once evening had arrived. The torches were lit along the cabins, casting light to replace the fading sun.

I stopped at the door, stared at it for a while as if expecting it to open on its own. When that didn't happen, I pounded my closed knuckles against the wood before I stepped back.

Magnus opened the door a moment later. Barefoot and in his sweatpants, he looked at me quizzically because I never came to him. He always came to me. His hair was ruffled like he'd recently gotten out of the shower. He stepped out and shut the door behind him, silently asking what I wanted.

I nodded to the door. "I want to speak to her."

It took him a moment to understand the request. Once he did, his eyebrows furrowed. "Why—"

"That's my business. Not yours."

He immediately turned defensive, as if I were his enemy rather than his flesh and blood. He absent-mindedly positioned his body directly in front of the door, like that would be enough to stop me if I wanted her.

"It'll only take a moment."

"I can convey whatever message you wish to give—"

"Not the way I can."

His jaw clenched noticeably, his muscular arms tightening at the provocation.

"Bring her out here. Or I'll let myself inside."

He started to fume.

"If I were here to kill her, she would be dead already. Stop this guard-dog bullshit and step aside."

He clenched his jaw before he returned to the cabin and shut the door.

I waited.

And waited.

And fucking waited.

The door opened again. Magnus stepped out first.

She came next.

She was in a tank top and his sweatpants, her face plain and hideous. She had muscular arms from working in the camp for so long. Her hair was pulled back in a messy ponytail. She was so ordinary that I would probably forget what she looked like the second this conversation was over.

She didn't tremble in fear. She stood tall and proud—and faced me head on.

Magnus stayed.

I shifted my gaze to him. "Leave."

He resisted a moment. It took all his strength to force himself back inside the cabin and shut the door.

Her eyes never left my face. She sized me up the way I did with her. How could some ordinary woman cause me so much fucking grief? How could someone so ugly share the same blood as the most beautiful woman in the world? I stared at her just as hard as I stared at Melanie—but for a very different reason.

I stepped toward her.

She didn't step back. She didn't cower. She held her ground.

Annoyed me even more.

I stopped in front of her. "Let's get something straight—because Magnus is unable to deliver a simple fucking message."

Her eyes shifted back and forth as she looked into mine. Her breathing didn't change, like she wasn't the least bit scared of me.

"Melanie is twice the woman you'll ever be. You think you're brave for burning down this camp and releasing my prisoners, but where did that get you? Most of the prisoners were recaptured, and those who weren't were replaced with new ones, and you're still here—working for me."

Her breathing started to increase, probably in anger.

"You know what Melanie has done? She's saved your fucking life. The only reason you're breathing right now is because of her. No, not Magnus. Melanie. Because my allegiance to my brother's dick died the day he betrayed me—for you. Your sister made me promise to keep you alive, even after she broke her promise to me, and that's why there's air in your lungs this very second."

She breathed deeper and deeper, nostrils flaring with every exhale. "Why are you telling me this—"

"I talk. You listen."

Her eyes immediately lit up with flames. Flames from hell.

"Stop making her feel like shit. Stop making her cry. Stop making her feel like she's inferior to you—because she's not. You think you're better than she is? You're sleeping with the enemy too. He's guilty of shit you don't even know about. Get off your fucking high horse. She accepts Magnus. You know what else she said? She *likes* Magnus. Because he's there for you. Because he looks out for you. Because he's always preferred you to her." My voice rose and rose, echoing through the entire camp because I despised this woman with every fiber of my being. "She loves me—so you will accept that."

Fury exploded all over her face. "She doesn't love you—"

"Yes, she does." I didn't believe it just because Melanie told me. I believed it because I felt it. I fucking felt it every time she touched me, every time she looked at me, every time she pulled me deeper inside her. "Because I see who she really is—unlike you."

TWENTY-THREE

THE FATHER'S SINS

MELANIE

Every time he left, it was hard.

It was harder now.

The guards at the gate weren't enough to dim my fear. The location of the safe room wasn't enough either. Gilbert's dead body was forever ingrained in my mind. His pretentious voice still echoed in the hallways. His soul was probably still here, doing things for Fender without anyone knowing.

But Fender would return in the same condition as when he left.

And this time, my sister would come with him.

Gilbert knocked on the bedroom door before he poked his head inside. "Mademoiselle, you have visitors."

I gave him a blank stare because no one ever came to visit me. "Who?"

"Magnus and Raven."

I was on my feet instantly, eyes wide, excitement in my blood. "I'll...I'll be right down." I grabbed my heels and slipped them on before I fixed my hair in the mirror. Then I took the stairs, holding on to the rail so I wouldn't trip, and hurried to the parlor.

She was there—beside Magnus.

The work clothes were gone, replaced with a nice sundress with her hair done, looking just the way I remembered during the good times. I sat on the couch beside her, looking at her with the same deep look that she gave me.

She was free.

The stare continued. She gave me a slight smile, showing that same loving affection with her eyes that she always gave me—even when I was a pain in the ass.

My arms wrapped around her, and I embraced her for a long time, knowing that this journey was finally over. Neither one of us had to return to the camp. It was terrible that it lived on, but at least we'd escaped its clutches.

She pulled away and looked me over.

I looked at her, disagreeing with Fender so deeply. He spoke of my sister like she was unremarkable, but to me, she was the most exceptional woman who ever lived. I'd do anything to be more like her. "You look nice..."

A bit of disbelief moved into her gaze, but there was still a hint of gratitude that I'd said it. "Never as nice as you."

I shook my head slightly because I didn't believe that. Magnus didn't either, obviously. "Could you give us a moment?"

Magnus immediately rose to his feet to excuse himself.

Raven grabbed his wrist and tugged him back down. "I'm just going to tell him everything we say, so there's no point."

Magnus cooperated with the motions, taking his seat beside her once again, his arms on his knees, his eyes on the paintings on the wall. He had the same characteristics as his brother, the same physical mannerisms, but he wasn't quite so cold.

Raven stared at me for a while. "Magnus told me that you agreed to marry Fender in exchange for my freedom." Her eyes shifted back and forth as they regarded mine, the respect on the surface. "I really appreciate that. I do."

I dropped my gaze and stared at my hands in my lap. "I tried to get him to free the girls...but he wouldn't. At least he gave me you."

Raven gave a slight nod. "I'm glad that you tried. But I suspect his mind is so corroded and he doesn't understand how terrible he really is. He's lost all humanity..."

My initial instinct was to defend him, but I kept my mouth shut. I lifted my chin and looked at her, wishing I could describe who he really was. I wished I could convey the way he comforted Gilbert in his final moments. I wished I could share the way he made me feel, that I was better than the poor reputation I gave myself. I wished I could share the way he spoke of his family, the way he missed them even now. But I could never explain that in a way she would understand.

Her eyes glanced down at the large ring that was impossible to miss. "But you don't have to marry him."

It was so quiet that I could hear a hawk glide across the sky outside the window. My eyes narrowed on her face, failing to understand the words she spoke so clearly.

"Because I don't want to be free."

I should have known that my sister had a trick up her sleeve. "Raven, if you think you can destroy that camp from the inside, you're delusional. We tried to get rid of it and free all the prisoners, but that didn't work whatsoever. You need to let this go."

Raven shook her head. "That's not why. The only way that place is going to end is if Fender ends it...or he, himself, is ended."

I hoped that never happened—because I couldn't live without him. "Then I don't understand..."

Raven took a long time to answer, like she knew how crazy she sounded before she even said anything. "I can't live apart from him." Her voice came out as a whisper, like she didn't want Magnus to hear even though he was directly behind her, still staring at the painting on the wall.

I stared for a long time, realization slowly sinking in.

"Where he goes, that's where I go."

I was in utter disbelief. As much as I hated being apart from Fender, I had no desire to go back to that place. "But it's so terrible there."

With a sad look in her eyes, she nodded. "I know."

"And if you're in Paris, we can see each other all the time..."

"I know that too. But when Magnus goes to the camp, he's gone for a full month, and I just can't live with that kind of separation. All I'll be doing is waiting for him to come home."

I wanted to argue to get my way, but I didn't see an unselfish angle to take. If she were in Paris, we could get lunch, go sight-seeing, spend time together to make up for all the time we'd lost. If she went back to the camp, our time together would be very limited.

"So, you don't have to marry him. I'm not choosing to go to the camp to protect you. I'm going because I want to be there...with Magnus."

Magnus reached for the glass on the table and took a long drink, his expression harder than it was before. He never showed affection toward my sister, but he exuded it in his own way.

I didn't know what to say, because my sister basically told me this was the man she would marry. They stayed together—no matter what. She gave herself to him entirely...and I did the same to Fender.

Raven gave me a slight smile, like she was fulfilling her role as the protective big sister, saving me from a terrible fate. "You're off the hook."

How was I supposed to say this to her? How was I supposed to look her in the eye and confess the way I really felt? She made it very clear she would never understand, that she would never accept it. It would drill a permanent hole between us. Her low opinion of me would sink even lower. But as my fingers fidgeted with the ring on my left hand, I told the truth. "I'm going to marry him anyway."

The look on her face was heartbreaking. Shock. Confusion. Uncertainty. Her mind absorbed my words slowly, very slowly, and once there was nothing left to do but accept my response, her eyes looked empty. "Why...?"

I dropped my gaze because I was ashamed, too ashamed to look my sister in the eye. "The same reason you want to be at the camp with Magnus."

"No..."

Like a child who'd broken the rules, I kept my head down. I promised a lifetime to the man of this palace, and this moment should be a happy one between two sisters, but it was a nightmare. There was no screaming in joy. No wedding plans. No hugs. No tears. No mention of Mom...

Raven grappled with the words about to come out of her mouth, like she didn't know how to speak because she'd never expected to say those words. "How can you feel that way for the man who subjugates innocent people to a lifetime of imprisonment, and then a departure from life with a cruel execution? How...? Melanie, ignore the diamonds and the gowns. I know you're scared to be on your own, but give yourself more credit than that. You can do it. You don't need him."

I kept my eyes on my hands. "It's not like that." It was nice to be taken care of, to have a man provide for me, protect me, give me a life I'd never thought possible. But that wasn't the reason I'd fallen in love with him. "It's not about the money and the security..."

"What is it? The sex?"

It was the best I'd ever had, but it wasn't that either. "No."

"Then what?" Her voice started to rise, unable to keep her anger in check.

I inhaled a deep breath, wishing I could show her a reel of all the quiet moments we shared. I wished I could show her who he really was. "I know he's responsible for a lot of terrible things, but he's more than that. He's just so hurt by the terrible things he's seen that he struggles to feel empathy and compassion for others—"

"Then *how* could you possibly care for a man who feels nothing for others?" Raven's eyes were big and raging, full of sheer disappointment.

"Because I believe he can change. I believe he can come back to the right side. I believe, in enough time, he will be who he used to be... He's just not there yet." I believed it with my whole heart. With every passing day, he softened, dropped his guard, cared more about a life with me than the work on his desk. He wanted a family. How could a man want a family if he was really that dead inside? He was becoming who he used to be, a man that I'd never met.

"Even if that turns out to be true, it doesn't change what he's already done. He's ordered his men to execute the weakest worker every week to keep the rest of them working like bees in a hive. He's done that for *years*, Melanie." Her voice rose higher and higher, her anger getting the best of her. "He may not be the one with the knife or the rope, but he's the one with the blood on his hands. How the fuck do you feel anything for that monster?"

Magnus placed his hand on her thigh, silently trying to calm her.

I'd barely said a few words to Magnus, but there was a connection between us, because he was the only person who understood how I felt. He loved his brother too. He was loyal to his brother, no matter what. I dropped my chin again, eyes slowly filling with tears. "That's a bit hypocritical, don't you think?"

Venom hissed from her mouth like a snake. "My man is *nothing* like yours." She forced her voice to steady, but her rage was making her red in the face. "He's tried to stop Fender many times. He's tried to convince him to run the camp in a different way. He's tried to reason with him. They are *not* the same."

The moisture toppled over my lashes and dripped straight down my cheeks. "I know I can change him. I can..."

"You're still going to marry him without knowing for sure?"

My answer was immediate. "Yes...because I have faith in him."

"Or is it because you know you have no choice?" Raven snapped. "Because, if a man forces you to marry him, that's not love. That's cruelty."

"He's not forcing me." I lifted my chin and wiped away my tears. "He's never forced me to do anything. I can leave this place whenever I want. I stay because I want to stay. I'm telling you, he's not the barbarian you know him as." He'd had all the power that first night in my cabin. He could have forced me to do anything. And even afterward, he still had all the power, but not once did he abuse it. He made me feel safer than I'd ever been my whole life. A man had never given me as much respect as he gave me. He was the man of the house, the boss, the dictator, but he reported to one person—me.

Raven continued to shout at me. "I don't care how you know him when you're living in this mansion and life is good! He chooses to execute innocent people. *Period.* Some of those women could be your friends. One of those women could've been me. The only reason why it wasn't is because Magnus saved me. Let *that* sink in."

I inhaled a deep breath, more tears falling down my cheeks. "I understand...I do. I feel both things at once. I hate him for the things he's done, but I've also fallen in love with the other side of him. You have no idea how ashamed I feel right now, feeling you looking at me like that, knowing you're right and I'm wrong. But I also can't change the way I feel, because I've never felt this way about a man in my life."

Raven had no sympathy whatsoever. "You're too young to know what real love is. You've barely had a long-term relationship with any man in your life. You've just been traumatized by what you've been through, and you found a man who can protect you against all that. Stockholm syndrome. It's not real."

Magnus gripped her thigh. "Ma petite amie—"

"Stay out of this." Raven didn't look at him.

He didn't get a word in, but I appreciated the fact that he tried. He was on my side. I knew he was. "Raven..." I wiped away my tears with my fingertips and breathed until

I was calm enough to speak. "I know it's wrong...I do. If I could just not feel this way, I would. I know Magnus and Fender are totally different people, but how are you going to be with a man who continually works at the camp? Maybe he doesn't like it, but he still participates. Fender doesn't like it either, but he feels like he has no other choice. Why can you be with Magnus, but I can't be with Fender? Magnus has never actually tried to stop anything." I didn't mean to throw him under the bus, but I viewed the brothers as the same person. They were both good men doing evil things because they were still in survival mode, even though they'd made it back on their feet a long time ago.

Raven's gaze turned cold. "He saved us, didn't he?"

Magnus turned his gaze on me, looking past Raven's head. "I will stop it."

My eyes focused on him, the only person who understood exactly how I felt.

He broke contact and looked at the wall again. "I don't know how, but I will."

Raven inhaled a deep breath, and a look of pride came over her face.

Magnus spoke again. "But I understand, Melanie."

My eyes slowly softened, and I wanted to reach for his hand, my lifeline. When I wasn't in the room and Raven said how terrible I was as a person, he would be there to defend me, to ask Raven to have compassion rather than hate.

Raven looked at him, unsure of the meaning of his words.

He continued. "Fender is a good man. He's loyal like no man I've ever known. He's strong, refusing to break for anyone. He'd cut off his own arm and give it to somebody he cared about if that's what made them happy. He's just hurt by what happened to us, and somehow having all the money in the world will make our father pay for what he did to our family. Hurt people hurt people...and Fender is so traumatized by what he had to witness in our childhood home that he's numb to the pain and suffering. It doesn't justify what he's done. But he's not himself. He hasn't really been himself since that night. I believe he can see reason and change. I do. Yes, Melanie, I understand. I hate him for what he's done...but I still love him."

***

MY CONVERSATION with my sister haunted me every single moment of every single day.

Until Fender came home.

I spotted his car at the gate, and I ran downstairs to the foyer to meet him when he pulled up. I stepped outside onto the steps and watched his powerful car circle the roundabout and park at the curb.

He stepped out, dressed in all black, black boots on his feet. He shut the door and stared at me for a moment before he came around the back of the car, the valet taking the seat he'd just vacated and driving off.

With that intense stare, he walked up to me, his gaze piercing my flesh.

My arms immediately circled his neck, and I pressed my cheek to his chest, inhaling the scent that had started to fade on the sheets, feeling the warmth that was hotter than the summer sun. I closed my eyes as I held on.

His powerful arms circled my body, holding me tight, and he rested his chin on my forehead, one hand digging into my hair. He held me that way without saying anything, his breathing steady and slow, peaceful.

He dipped his chin and pressed a kiss to my head. "You've never done this before."

I pulled back so I could meet his gaze, not understanding the meaning of his words.

A slight smile moved on to his lips. It was such a handsome look on him. It made him soft in the sexiest way. Eroded a decade off his lifespan, a glimmer of the happy boy he used to be. "Greeted me."

"Well...I missed you."

His smile continued, his hand moving up my cheek and pushing my hair back. "I missed you too, *chérie*."

THE EVENING WAS SPENT in our bedroom, me on top, with his back against the headboard, his hands squeezing my hips, his fingers kneading my ass. My hands planted against his chest, the band of my ring leaving a mark when I pulled away. Again and again, it happened, our final time ending with him on top of me, his narrow hips between my thighs, fucking me like he'd been gone for months rather than weeks.

But once it was over, the sadness returned.

The heat of the moment drove away the coldness in my heart. His kisses made me feel loved when I felt unworthy of his love. His desire made me feel like the most beautiful woman in the world when I was the ugliest—at least on the inside.

Gilbert left a late dinner outside the door, so I set the dining table and we sat together.

Fender normally showered the instant he came home, but I'd demanded his attention to the exclusion of everything else. We sat across from each other, me in his t-shirt, him in his boxers, and ate in silence.

My eyes were down on my food, and I didn't ask him how his trip was. My mind was elsewhere.

Like always, he read my mood like words projected on the wall behind me. "What is it?"

I lifted my eyes at his question.

He chewed his food as he stared at me across the table, his massive shoulders strong, his chest hard like stone. His jawline was covered with hair because he didn't shave as often when he was at the camp.

"Magnus and Raven came by a few days ago..."

"I know. Is that not what you wanted?"

"No, it is," I said quickly. "I just... Never mind."

His eyes were instantly hostile, pressuring me for an answer.

"I told her I agreed to marry you...and she wasn't happy about that."

His mood darkened even further. Invisible rain clouds appeared over him, making the bedroom feel like winter instead of summer. "You're a grown woman, Melanie. You need to stop caring what that hypocrite thinks. She doesn't belong on the pedestal where you've placed her."

"She's my sister..."

"Magnus is well aware that I don't care for her. You think I'd ever intervene?"

I dropped my gaze.

"The only people who see the world in black-and-white are people who don't understand how the world really works. They walk down a street in Paris and only notice the couples admiring the Eiffel Tower, the little coffee shops and bistros. They don't see the president having dinner with me, the most powerful drug kingpin in Europe. They don't see the Chasseurs in the catacombs beneath the streets. They don't see reality because they have no idea what reality even looks like. That's your sister. She thinks she's a hero. She thinks she's a saint. But she's an idiot casting judgment on things she doesn't understand. She's spent a few months in the camp, and if she thinks that's horrible, she doesn't know the half of it. If she had to survive what Magnus and I have survived, she would shut her fucking mouth. She doesn't understand—and she should be grateful she doesn't."

I suspected Magnus had already told her about that night—and it didn't change anything.

He watched me for a while, his anger slowly fading into disappointment. "Does that change your answer?" His voice dropped a few decibels, growing quiet but deep. He immediately raised his guard, preparing for me to choose her over him, to leave him once again.

I shook my head. "I can't live without you." I didn't play games. I didn't pretend that he wasn't the love of my life. I didn't pretend that this relationship was okay, but I also didn't pretend it wasn't the best thing that ever happened to me.

The look he wore was indescribable, a mix of surprise and love so deep it actually pained him. His stare lingered for a long time, his dinner now forgotten because my devotion filled his empty stomach.

"Can you live without me...?"

After a long stare, he shook his head. "If I ever lost you, I'd put a knife to my throat and take my life." Sincerity was in his eyes, that same look he'd given me since our first night together. His love had only deepened, had grown to epic proportions. "Because I'd rather die than live without you."

I had a love no one else did. I could never throw that away. I could never walk away and hope to find a man who could hold a candle to this one. So that left me with one choice. "If that's how you really feel, I want you to do something for me."

"Anything." He leaned forward, his arms resting on the table, his plate of cold food in front of him.

"Release the girls."

Slowly, his eyes turned angry, walking right into the trap I'd laid.

"I need you to do this."

"My answer will not change, *chérie*." He kept his voice low, but his anger was audible.

"Yes, it will."

He clenched his jaw and shook his head.

"You can still run that camp. Just do it differently—"

"Don't tell me how to run my business."

"It's not a business. It's slavery." Even though he kept his voice low and calm, I didn't. My words came out harsh and a little hysterical.

He clenched his jaw again. "I just got home. Really don't want to do this right now."

"I *never* want to do this. But I have to, Fender."

He licked his bottom lip before he chewed on the inside of his cheek, his eyes dropping to his plate. It was a testament to our relationship that he didn't scream and flip the table over. He was calm, as calm as he could possibly be.

"You said you want to have a family?"

His eyes immediately darted back to mine.

"Sons...daughters...?"

"Yes."

"Why?"

His eyes narrowed. "I must continue the family line."

"You have Magnus."

"He's not a count. I am."

"It's still your family line. And that's not the reason."

His arms flexed on the table, as if I'd just entered dangerous territory.

"You want to have a family to replace what you lost. You love me, and you want to grow that love into little people. You want this big house to be filled with happiness and laughter." I knew Fender's heart. I knew his desire to have a family had nothing to do with his lineage.

He didn't refute the assumption.

"You're going to go to the camp every couple weeks and then come home like nothing happened? What will you do when your daughter finds out what you do to other women? Can you live with that?"

Dead silence.

"Fender—"

"Whether I stop tomorrow or never stop, the blood is still on my hands. I can't be redeemed. I can't be forgiven. So, it makes no difference. I did what I had to do to survive, and no, I have no regrets about that. I accept the consequences of my actions when I'm forced to face them, whether that's in this life or the next."

I shook my head. "I think you can be redeemed—"

"There's no coming back after that. There is no justification I can possibly make to support my actions. I knew what I was doing when I did it. I wasn't under duress. I wasn't confused. I only cared about getting what I wanted to the exclusion of everything else. I don't deserve to be forgiven. Not now. Not ever. So, there is literally no point in stopping my actions now. When I get to the pearly gates, I will go down below for eternity. Nothing I do will change that now."

My eyes started to water, imagining his fate, even if he deserved it. "I can't go to heaven without you."

He dropped his gaze.

"So, you have to try."

He kept his eyes on his plate.

"You can't change the past. But you can change the future. You can save so many people..."

"This conversation is over." He lifted his chin and looked at me, his eyes cold and lifeless.

"It's not over. Do this for me—"

"No."

"Fender—"

His voice grew louder. "The same blood that ran in my father's veins runs in mine. I'm evil—down to the bone. There is no hope for me."

Tears splashed down my cheeks. "That's not true—"

"Don't make me leave. Because despite how furious I am right now, I still want to stay with you. I never want to march out of here and leave you alone. I never want to abandon you again. So, drop it now—so I can stay."

TWENTY-FOUR
IT'S JUST BUSINESS

FENDER

She was on my chest, her arm tucked around my waist, her leg on top of my thigh.

I held her against me, one arm around the deep curve in her back with my hand on her stomach. My fingertips grazed her shoulder lightly, feeling the skin that felt identical to the rose petals that had been on the bed the night I'd asked her to marry me.

Conversations were nonexistent. We spent time apart. But we came together every night and loved each other like there was nothing wedged between us. She still wore her ring. She was still mine.

I would always be hers.

Loving *Chérie* was like living with my heart outside my body.

It was always vulnerable. It always ached.

I kissed her before I slid out of bed.

She propped herself up and watched me go with disappointment in her eyes. She hated my actions. She hated my business. But she still loved me anyway. She still showed it in her eyes every time she looked at me.

That was how I knew this was real.

"Shower." I leaned down and kissed her before I stepped into the bathroom. Warm water washed down my body, flashbacks entering my mind whenever I wasn't actively doing something.

I remembered the way I'd killed my father.

Brutal. Cruel. Vengeful.

That was exactly how I would go someday.

My sins would catch up with me.

And then *Chérie* would have to live without me. Unprotected. Unhappy. Widowed.

I would never see her again—because I was going downstairs, and she was going upstairs.

When I stepped out of the bathroom, Gilbert greeted me. "Magnus is here to see you."

I scanned the bedroom, no sight of Melanie.

He read my look. "She's speaking with him downstairs."

I pulled on my sweatpants then made my way downstairs into the parlor.

Melanie sat across from him, the two in deep conversation.

I approached and looked down at Melanie, silently telling her to dismiss herself.

She read that look and excused herself.

I watched her walk away before I took the vacated spot and sat across from my brother. "My fiancée tells me her sister isn't too happy about the news." The hostility was out in the open, because yet again, that bitch was sabotaging my life.

Magnus wore a stoic expression, in jeans and a gray shirt, his hands together between his thighs. "Can you blame her?"

My eyes narrowed at the insult. "I'm richer than the devil, I'm good-looking, I granted her freedom. Yes. I can blame her." I grabbed the glass of wine Gilbert had provided and took a drink.

My brother wasn't as restrained as he usually was. He spoke his mind, like he had something important to say. "Raven isn't impressed by money. And she doesn't want her freedom." Pride was noticeable not just in his eyes, but in the sound of his voice. "She wants to be with me wherever I go."

I relaxed into the couch, my arm resting over the back with the wineglass still in my grasp. If he wanted to be proud of the loyalty he'd acquired from a woman no other man would want, that was his prerogative. Seconds of intense eye contact transpired before my eyes narrowed slightly. "Isn't that romantic?" I brought the glass to my lips and took another drink. "If the bitch wants to work, let her."

Magnus immediately turned angry. "Don't do that."

"What?" I knew what, but I asked anyway. Just needed to remind him that his woman was forever beneath mine.

"You know exactly what, Fender. I think Melanie is dumb as a dog, but you don't hear me saying that."

I didn't appreciate the insult, but I didn't respond to it because I was the one who'd made the first attack. It was pointless anyway, because he was wrong. They were both wrong about every assumption they made about *Chérie*. I returned the wineglass to the table. "Sounds like this is getting serious..."

He ignored my sarcasm and held my gaze.

I let the tension go. "I guess I'm gonna have to learn to tolerate her, aren't I?"

"She's more than tolerable." That pride was back.

"I disagree. And I'll always disagree." We'd leave it at that.

After a tense silence, Magnus spoke. "When's the wedding?"

"Whenever she gets a dress, I guess. We aren't having a big ridiculous wedding. We'll probably get married out on the lawn."

"I expected you to throw a big party."

Our wedding was just about us. No one else. I didn't want to have to entertain guests with conversations I didn't care about. I wanted all my attention on *Chérie*. "She doesn't know any of those people. Prefers it just be us...and the two of you."

He didn't respond to the invitation.

"What do you want?" I grew impatient. "I assume you have something else in mind besides discussing my wedding?"

He leaned back into the couch with his knees apart, regarding me with a steely gaze. "It's time to change things, Fender." He didn't specify, but he didn't need to. It had always been a source of tension between us, and now with the girls in our lives, it came more frequently.

My gaze immediately turned cold. I'd just had to deal with this shit from Melanie a few nights ago, and now my brother came all the way to my residence just to mention it for the millionth time.

"Your fiancée used to be a prisoner there. Does that not change how you feel?"

I drank the wine. "I know I've made that up to her."

"And what about the rest of the girls?" He was more aggressive than he used to be, like he wasn't leaving that couch until he got what he wanted.

Never gonna happen. I released a low and drawn-out sigh, fighting to keep my patience with him. "We've discussed this before, Magnus. If there was another way, I would do it. There's not."

He'd been waiting for that answer because he already had a rebuttal. "There's always another way. I will personally see to the project. I will personally vet every single person we hire. I will make sure they're loyal."

"There's no way to be completely certain of hired help. The girls that we have are completely certain—because they'll never leave."

His fingers automatically tightened into a fist of pure frustration. "You've accomplished everything that you wanted. You have the money, you have the woman—now live your life. Stop living in the past. Stop trying to prove something to our decomposed corpse of a father. There is no reason to continue carrying on this way."

The mention of that coward made me look away, because I still carried so much regret from that night. Magnus was the only one I'd managed to save. If I'd gotten there sooner, it could have been two instead of one. The money and the power did soothe my wounds, even now, because I would think about it often, think about everything I'd accomplished despite the odds stacked against me. I did what our father couldn't. He pissed away our wealth and never bothered to try to earn it back. I did. Alone. "I've heard your concerns before. The only reason you are vocal once again is because that woman has a grip on your spine and she's twisting it."

"I'm glad she's twisting it. Your fiancée wants the same. How do you expect to have a life with her when she doesn't respect what you're doing?"

I pictured a long life with her, with four kids, her beauty still prevalent even as she aged. Men in my circle always took mistresses when their wives became too old, but I never would. She was more than enough for me. But I imagined through the years, this conversation would rise again...and again. "It's just business."

"But it's not *just* business. It's lives, Fender." His voice rose with his anger, trying to knock some sense into me. "I know you're better than this."

Every time he said that, it pissed me off. He claimed to see the good through the bad, but there was no shred of goodness anywhere inside me. My humanity died the moment I watched my father try to gun down his two remaining sons. "Sorry to disappoint you, but I'm not." I suddenly sat forward with my arms resting on the insides of my thighs. I looked him dead in the eye and hoped he would finally understand. "Our father murdered our family without any hesitation. He was a coward and took their lives in their sleep. He didn't kill himself instead of claiming the lives of innocent people. And you know what? I'm just like him. The evil that ran in his veins runs in mine." I spoke the truth, and it somehow set me free but also pulled me deeper under. I wasn't proud to say it, to be honest with myself and my brother, who still looked up to me to this day.

Magnus looked at me differently, a gentle softness coming into his eyes, a look that he gave Raven, not me. "That's not true." He spoke with confidence, like there was no doubt in his mind he was right, when he was actually dead wrong.

"Yes, it is. When you see shit like that, you never recover. I'm not human anymore. I don't care about anyone or anything. And it's much easier that way."

He shook his head. "That's not true. You asked a woman to marry you because you love her. You would take a knife in the chest for me because I'm your brother. It's hard to carry the weight of the past on your shoulders, but don't let it define you. You still have a soul. I know you do."

As much as I wanted to believe that, I couldn't. "I've already done what I've done. If there's a heaven and hell, you know which one I'm going to. I'm damned, and nothing I do now will change that." I had been raised in a religious family, but my connection to God died that night. If He existed, He wouldn't have allowed my father to take the lives of the people I loved. He wouldn't have let us starve on the street and sleep in the rain. He wouldn't have driven us to this savage existence. It was the devil that did all of that. It was the devil that turned me evil.

Magnus's breathing deepened as the silence passed, like my words actually pained him, just the way they pained Melanie. For whatever reason, I had two people who loved me, when I didn't deserve either one. "I believe all people can be redeemed. All people can earn redemption. You just have to try."

I considered his words but didn't believe them. "You can be redeemed, Magnus. Your soul is still whole." He didn't have to witness what I did. If he had, he would be just like me, and I was grateful he wasn't just like me. "You're still innocent. Me...it's too late for me, and we both know it. May as well make as much money as I can and enjoy spending it all while I'm still here." I set down the wineglass in dismissal, because this conversation was over as far as I was concerned. I rose to my feet.

He did the same. "Fender."

With a clenched jaw, I wished this conversation would just end. My brother's optimistic belief only made my damnation worse. It was times like these when I wished I were dead, that someone would just pull the trigger and put me where I belonged—in the ground.

He shook his head as he looked at me. "We need to free those girls. Period." His look was full of pity, like he actually felt bad for me.

He shouldn't.

"We can't do this anymore."

I remained hostile. Conversation was over.

"You need to stop this. Now." He kept prodding and prodding. Pushing and pushing. Believing when there was no reason to believe.

I stared him down, furious. "Or what?"

His eyes narrowed at my choice of words.

"You going to kill me?" I took a step closer to him, unleashing the silent challenge. He needed to stay the fuck out of my way and shut his goddamn mouth.

His gaze immediately smoldered in rage at the insinuation. For whatever reason, my brother loved me. Loved me despite what I did. Loved me despite the fact that I didn't deserve it. "No. I'm not our father."

My anger sheathed, touched by what he said.

"But this will happen whether you like it or not. I know there's still humanity inside you. I know you still have a chance. I just hope you find the strength to join me... instead of resisting me."

I KEPT to myself for the next few days.

Worked in my office. Went on distribution checks. Slept beside her every night without really being present.

She knew my thoughts were heavy but didn't ask about them.

I sat behind my desk and looked at my computer, but I didn't read a single word because my mind was elsewhere. Magnus was at the forefront of my mind, a concern I'd never thought I would have. He'd never challenged me like that. Never disobeyed an order. Never deviated from the path.

Did he mean what he said?

Or had he said it in anger?

"Everything okay?"

My eyes shifted to Melanie on the couch.

"You make that face when you're upset, and you've had that face for days now."

I knew her better than she knew herself. And apparently, she knew me in the same way. I closed my laptop and sat across from her on the other couch. My hand moved through my short hair then down the back of my neck, massaging the tension in the muscles.

"What did Magnus say to you?" she whispered.

I dropped my hand and didn't give an answer.

But she already knew. "Fender—"

"My relationship with my brother has never been strained like this. Even when we were sleeping beside a dumpster, it was never this bad. We robbed innocent people together and never questioned it. And now...I feel like I've lost him."

Her eyes softened like wilted flowers.

"It's the one thing I thought I would never lose."

"You could never lose him," she said gently. "But he wouldn't be a good brother if he weren't pushing you to be better than what you are now."

I looked away.

"You may believe in different things, but your loyalty to each other will never die."

She hadn't heard the conversation. She hadn't felt the shift under my feet. She hadn't heard the change in his tone.

"Isn't your relationship with your brother more important than this?" she whispered.

I looked at her again.

"Isn't your existing family more important than the one you lost?"

Silence.

"Remember, it's not just Magnus anymore. It's me. And as much as you don't want it to be...it's Raven too. We're a family now. Let the past go. Embrace the future—with us." She pleaded with her eyes, begged me to do what I was incapable of doing.

My phone vibrated in my pocket, but I ignored it.

"It's never too late to do the right thing."

I looked away, seriously considering her words. My father was decomposed somewhere in the ocean. If his remains were found, they would never be identified. He tried to wipe us out of existence, but we survived, and now he was the one forgotten. My surname was powerful. My lineage was preserved. I got revenge for us. And I could continue to make that family grow...with the woman I loved.

My phone rang again.

This time, I didn't ignore it. I sighed and dug my phone out of my pocket. "Quoi?"

Nathan spoke over the line. "Magnus a arrêté la Neige Rouge."

In silence, I processed the words he'd just said to me.

"Quels sont vos ordres?"

I felt so much rage. It started in my stomach then exploded everywhere. I pictured my brother in my mind, pictured him betraying everything I'd worked toward. He made his claim, and I was foolish for calling his bluff. It wasn't his actions that infuriated me. It was his disloyalty. He'd betrayed me several times, and I forgave him because he was my kin. But now, he spat on my mercy. "Je suis en route." I hung up.

Melanie's eyes were wide because she knew something had happened. "What's going on?"

I shoved the phone into my pocket and rose to my feet. "Magnus banned the Red Snow. And now I'm going to the camp to kill him."

THE ANGER NEVER FADED.

It was high the entire drive, the whole horse ride.

Melanie tried to talk me out of my decision, but her words fell on deaf ears. This level of fury was the only thing that could make me forget her existence. It was as if she wasn't there at all. Her tears, her pleas, her kisses, literally meant nothing to me.

There was only one thing I cared about.

Magnus.

I rode into the camp and dropped down from my horse. The reins were thrown to one of the guards. My boots hit the dirt, and my knife was suddenly heavy in my pocket. When I set eyes on him, I wasn't sure what I would do.

If I would slit his throat right on the spot.

Or stab him in the gut and watch him bleed to death.

Magnus emerged from behind a cabin—and walked right toward me.

With his head held high and a strong posture that lacked apology, he approached me. Eyes cold like winter, shoulders tense in preparation for a fight, a jaw so tight that it was obvious he was clenching his teeth.

The men watched.

Magnus stopped in front of me, waiting for his fate, ready to accept the consequences of his actions.

There was so much rage that I couldn't suppress it. It erupted over my features, made my teeth hurt because they ground together like pepper in a grinder. My eyes were so wide with fury that the sockets actually hurt. He hadn't just betrayed me. He'd humiliated me. Again.

And I was done being humiliated.

He held my gaze, arms by his sides, and waited.

I wanted to reach for that knife and slice his throat right then and there. Watch him collapse. Watch him grip his throat and gasp for the air that would never reach his lungs. But I didn't.

I couldn't. "If you want to have children someday, don't fuck with me." I would castrate his remaining testicle right then and there if it wouldn't make him sterile. But I'd already taken one, and taking another would affect my lineage as well as his. The only reason I had an ounce of mercy was because of the blood that ran in his veins.

There was no apology.

He didn't drop his gaze like the last time he'd betrayed me.

He had the audacity not to look ashamed.

He stared at me head on and spoke words I never thought he'd say. "You don't want to fuck with me either, brother."

I inhaled a sharp breath, his words audible for everyone to hear.

Couldn't believe it.

He'd crossed a line.

I had to kill him.

Had to.

I would lose all the respect of my men if I didn't.

He needed to be forced to the ground so I could machete his fucking head off the way I did to the Renaldi brothers.

But I didn't.

And if I didn't walk away right now, I might.

I walked past him—even though it was the hardest thing I'd ever had to do.

Magnus never came to my cabin.

He didn't approach me at all.

There was no apology. No groveling. No shame.

I'd given him more time, but it was becoming very clear to me that he wouldn't cave.

He'd humiliated me so deeply that I couldn't show my face to my men, not unless I had a response to clean the stain that he'd forced on me. The power had been taken from me, which had never happened in my adult life before I gave it to Melanie. But Magnus stripped it from me.

Fucking took it.

I had to do something.

I left my cabin and marched to the clearing. It wasn't Friday, but I didn't need it to be Friday to do what I was about to do. "Alix, pick the weakest three."

Alix turned to me, his face covered by a hood, but his expression somehow visible.

"Now."

He didn't hesitate before he left to change in his cabin.

Nathan lit the torches around the clearing, the sun disappearing over the horizon the moment the last one was lit.

The women all knew what the torches meant.

Red Snow.

Alix returned, in his executioner gear, ready to claim the lives of three people.

One by one, he grabbed them.

They screamed. They begged. They cried.

I felt nothing.

I felt nothing after my own blood betrayed me.

The one person I trusted more than anyone stabbed me in the fucking back.

Magnus must have heard the screams because he came running, heading right for Alix. "What the fuck are you doing? I made my stance on this perfectly clear."

Alix turned around and left the women on the ground. The mask covered the bottom half of his face, but the shine in his eyes showed his hidden smile. "I don't take orders from you, asshole."

I stepped behind Magnus and waited for him to turn around.

Magnus pulled out his knife from his pocket and held it at the ready. "Let them go, or I'll cut off your balls, your lips, and your nose."

Alix wasn't scared because he had a more formidable foe on his side. He looked behind Magnus, right at me.

My brother stilled—because he knew.

He slowly turned around and met my look, a hint of surprise there, as if he actually believed there was a chance Alix was the one behind this. His faith infuriated me.

My concentrated stare was full of anger and disappointment. The betrayal stung—and it would always sting. Magnus had forced me to do this because I had no other option. "Because of your foolishness, I will take three lives instead of one. The women can thank you for that."

He shook his head slightly, still in disbelief. The women and guards stared at us as the torches flickered. His eyes remained on me as if there was no one else there, and when he spoke, it was just for me to hear. "You're better than this."

Nothing would dim my anger. Nothing. "Sorry to disappoint you, *brother*."

He flinched at my cruelty. "It doesn't have to be this way."

"Yes, it does." I looked past him and nodded at Alix, telling him to continue with the butchering.

With lightning speed, Magnus punched Alix so hard in the back of the head that he fell to the ground and didn't get up again. There must have been so much adrenaline in his veins to numb the pain, because his knuckles slammed into the hardest skull I'd ever seen. He turned back to me and stared me down, now as his enemy.

The two other guards standing with the women didn't move forward, having seen their enormous comrade collapse on the ground from a single hit.

Magnus held his ground and didn't back down. "I'm not going to let this happen."

He officially severed all loyalty to me. I was the one who saved his life. He wouldn't even be here right now if it weren't for me. But he seemed to have forgotten that. He seemed to have forgotten the night I got jumped trying to get enough money to get him to the doctor when he was sick. "You're weak."

"And you're deranged."

"Step aside, Magnus. I mean it." The threat was unmistakable. It was a showdown—and I would come out the victor.

"Or what?" he challenged. "You're going to kill me?" He echoed the same question I'd asked of him, calling my bluff publicly, saying it loudly so everyone could hear. He put me on the spot, pushed me to the brink.

My anger increased tenfold. I'd never wanted to kill someone I loved, but now I actually wanted to. I wanted to bury him in the graveyard where our family rested in eternal peace. He betrayed me—so he was dead to me anyway.

"The only way you're gonna stop me is by killing me. So, I suggest you pull out your knife and do it."

The line was drawn in the sand.

He left me no choice.

I had to do it.

All eyes were on me.

It was so quiet that the torches sounded like an inferno.

To do nothing would permanently humiliate me. It would damage my power. It would ruin everything I'd built.

But all I did was stare.

He knew I couldn't do it. He fucking knew it. "We can do this another way. I promise you."

My eyes remained focused with hatred.

He stepped closer to me, lowering his voice. "Don't be like Father. Be like Mother."

The mention of her was a wound that no one could see. Because, of everyone I'd lost, I missed her the most. Croissants on Christmas morning. The sight of her in the first row at my symphony concerts. Listening to her sing as she drove us to school in the morning. She was the most innocent person who'd ever lived—and she was murdered.

Magnus must have known he'd hit me hard because he pressed harder. "Let's stop disappointing her more than we already have. Come on, Fender."

I refused to be swayed. I refused to give up my hatred. My vengeance was all I had left. "We've already talked about this. It's too late."

He shook his head. "It's never too late. Stop this."

The silence lasted forever. I didn't pull out my weapon or order the guards to continue the slaughter. I didn't move against him either. I didn't kill him where he stood. With a defeated voice, I spoke. "You win, Magnus."

Magnus couldn't control his reaction. Relief rippled across his face like a pond once a stone had been thrown into it. Affection came soon afterward.

I shattered it. "For now. When your rotation is finished, you'll be discharged from your service. You will never return here—and I will run this camp as I see fit."

His eyes fell as a new level of disappointment hit him like a ton of bricks.

"You called my bluff and won." I nodded to the guards to release the crying women and put out the torches. I'd allowed my brother to humiliate me publicly because killing him was something I just couldn't do. So, I had to do something else instead. Something deep. Something permanent. "I won't kill you. But we aren't brothers anymore. When you leave...I don't want to see you again."

Hurt moved into his features, as if what I said was just as bad as a knife to his stomach. Now he was the one who looked betrayed. I didn't take his life, but I took our relationship—and that was just as bad.

I spoke to my brother one last time in this life. "You're dead to me."

DAYS PASSED.

Once that final conversation happened, I didn't think about my brother again.

He didn't exist.

When he left the camp, it would be over.

I wouldn't have a brother anymore.

My decision spared some of my humiliation, but not nearly enough. And that wasn't the only reason why I did it.

I did it because I wanted to.

I watched the TV in the dark, my thoughts drifting to Melanie. Now that my brother had been exiled from my life, it would complicate my relationship with her. She'd want to see her sister, and I wouldn't be there in order to avoid Magnus. But she wouldn't leave me.

I knew that.

She was the only family I would have left.

Magnus's voice was audible on the other side of the door, talking to Eric. He overpowered Eric and entered the cabin, sharp hostility in his eyes. His anger hadn't abated over the course of the last few days.

Neither had mine.

I turned off the TV and stared him down.

He stared back.

"Say what you want to say so you can leave."

His eyes narrowed at my coldness. "I've never been disloyal to you—"

"Bullshit."

He stepped closer. "I haven't. I would take a knife for you in a heartbeat. I would hang for your crimes. I would do anything for you—"

"Clearly not."

His hands tightened into fists before he dropped into the chair across from me. "The reason this camp has been untouched is because I'm here. I'm your eyes and ears when you're elsewhere. You trust me, and without me, this place will go to shit. You fucking know it."

"And it hasn't already?" I gave him a cold look.

"No. It's being remodeled, which we needed—"

"Wasn't it remodeled when your little cunt burned it to the ground?"

His eyes immediately flashed in anger. "Let's not forget that your fiancée burned it down too. Let's not forget that she killed the executioner. The woman you've vowed to love your entire life feels the same way I do. You're the only one who feels otherwise. So, stop being stubborn."

I grabbed my scotch and took a drink. "It has nothing to do with stubbornness."

"It has everything to do with it. I'm not leaving my post. I will continue to work here since I need to watch your back because no one else will do it. I have no problem with what we do for a living. I feel no remorse for putting drugs on the street. I feel no remorse for killing men who deserve death. But I can't do it at the expense of the innocent—not anymore."

"That's only been a concern to you since your dick got wet."

"Fuck you. It's always been a concern to me. But I admit loving a prisoner has definitely put me over the edge."

I would never understand his fascination. She wasn't worthy of love.

"Fender, we just need to change this aspect of the camp. That's all."

"We've talked about this. It doesn't work—"

"Then we make it work."

I shook my head slightly. "If it were feasible, I would do it. I won't sit here and say the killing of those girls is justified. It's wrong. Irrevocably wrong. But I have other priorities that are more important to me."

Magnus shook his head. "There is no priority more important than innocent lives."

I looked away, annoyed with this conversation.

"I'm not gonna let this go, Fender. You can banish me from the camp, but I'm going to get back in here just the way I got into your cabin."

I turned back to him, eyes narrowed. "Are you threatening me?"

He held my gaze without flinching. "I'm warning you."

"Sounds like the same thing to me."

"Trust me, you would know if I were threatening you."

I shook my head. "Don't make me do it when I don't want to."

"But you *do* want to stop killing the girls."

"No, I'm not talking about that." Both of my hands tightened into fists. "I'm talking about *you*. If you keep opposing me, you'll leave me no choice. Don't put me in that position."

Magnus inhaled a slow breath.

"Take the girl, and go live your life. Don't interfere with mine."

His eyes narrowed in anger. "Fender, why won't you even try?"

I grabbed my glass again and drank every single drop left. "Because I don't want to take the risk. I'll never forget how it feels to be powerless, to dig in a garbage can for food, to be at the mercy of someone bigger and stronger than you. I hate what we do to those girls as much as you do. But there is no other way. I care a lot more about my power than their lives. Yes, that means I'll be damned, but we both know I was damned a long time ago." I rose to my feet and left the sitting area. "I'm not having this conversation anymore. I made my choice, and you've clearly made yours. Come back to the camp, and I'll do what I have to...and I guess you'll do what you have to."

MELANIE

I watched his car pull around.

It was a warm summer evening. The sun had just dipped behind the horizon, casting the sky in a beautiful array of colors. Butterflies were visible above the garden. The smooth sounds of the fountain were the background, gentle music to this beautiful and historic place.

But my heart hadn't felt peace since he'd left.

He'd threatened to kill Magnus, and there was nothing I could do to stop it. I couldn't warn Raven. I just had to have faith that his love was stronger than his fury.

He left the car behind and marched to me.

Livid.

His eyes were dark. His arms swung by his sides. His jaw was tight.

My heart started to race in fear.

Instead of walking up to me, he maneuvered around me, ignoring me just the way he had before he left.

I went after him. "What happened?"

He continued to ignore me.

"Fender." I grabbed his wrist and stopped him before he moved to the steps. "Don't ignore me."

He released a loud sigh before he turned back to me, not a drop of love in his eyes.

"It's me." I gently pulled him closer, wanting an embrace after his long absence. I rose on my tiptoes and cupped his face, pressing a kiss to his tight lips.

He was unresponsive.

I kissed the corner of his mouth several times, bringing us close together, enveloping him as an antidote to his rage.

His hands moved to my waist.

His lips moved to mine.

Slowly, he came back to me, surrounding me in his strong embrace, smothering me with the love that I'd missed. His chin rested on my head as he held me in the foyer, his fingers lightly playing with my hair at my spine.

Once the man I loved was back, I pulled away and looked into his face, desperate for the answer I'd asked for.

His eyes were locked on to mine. "I didn't kill him."

I didn't realize I was holding my breath until it slowly left my lungs.

"But we aren't brothers anymore. He's exiled from the camp—as well as my life."

HE WAS quiet for the rest of the night.

Our lovemaking wasn't the same.

He wasn't present.

It was quick and to the point, getting us both off so he could move on, just like in the mornings.

He lay on his side of the bed, his eyes on the open window, his arm underneath his head.

"You want to talk about it?"

He was still as stone, like he didn't hear the question. "No."

I propped myself up on my elbow beside him, my fingers gliding over his chest. I hoped this was the precursor to change, that his brother's bold move would force him to alter his business practices. There would be resistance, but it would fade.

"Magnus humiliated me in front of my men." He said he didn't want to talk, but yet, he spoke.

I was silent, not wanting to impede his momentum.

"He called my bluff. Exiling him was the only option I had to spare my dignity and spare his life."

My fingers traced his muscles, hoping for more.

Nothing came.

"He's just trying to do the right thing, Fender. You know that." It was a stupid thing to say, a perfect way to provoke his rage.

But he remained subdued. As if he knew. He'd always known. "Our bond is more important than the blood of innocent people. I'd assumed he felt the same way. Guess not."

"No reason you can't have both."

His empty eyes remained on the window, looking into the darkness. "He betrayed me. I forgave him. Then he does this..."

"He chose to do the right thing over you. But if you want to preserve your relationship, you need to choose the right thing, too. Then there is no betrayal. There's nothing more important than family. I know how much you love your brother."

He remained lifeless.

"You can't be angry with him for doing what should have been done a long time ago." It didn't make sense, and Fender was too intelligent not to understand that. "So, what is the real reason you would cut him out of your life?"

He remained quiet.

I kept my silence, hoping he just needed more time to form his thoughts.

"The last time I dropped my guard, my father butchered my family. If my brother is standing behind me, I never look because I don't need to. He has my back—through and through. With my brother, I'm never anything short of honest, sharing every thought that comes into my mind. My guard has never been raised. And then he does all these things...and now my guard is up. It's a shitty feeling."

"Magnus would never hurt you. He would have resorted to that already if that were his intention. It's not. He's always had your back—even now. He's just ready to move on from your past quicker than you are. It's not personal."

Fender didn't look at me. His eyes remained focused, replaying conversations that I never witnessed. "Did you get your dress?"

The change in subject threw me off for a moment. "My wedding dress?"

"Yes."

"Yeah...it was dropped off yesterday." It had been custom made by Valentino, and the designer had come to take my measurements and create the dress for me. When it was delivered, I'd nearly cried. Never in my life had I thought I'd wear a dress like that.

He turned his head and looked at me. "Marry me tomorrow." His dark eyes bored into mine, like my only answer could be yes. The conversation about his brother was already old news.

"Yes—if Magnus and Raven are there."

Disappointment flashed in his gaze. "It's about us. Not them—"

"I'm not getting married without my sister there. And I'm not letting you get married without your brother."

He inhaled an agitated breath. "That's not going to happen, *chérie*—"

"Then you're not going to marry me."

His eyes shifted back and forth as he looked into mine, hostile.

"Marriage is about doing the right thing for the other person—always. You'd regret not having your brother there. So, we'll wait until you're ready."

———

IT WAS TENSE BETWEEN US.

Fender was a man of few words, but those words were even rarer now.

He was angry with me, but there was no amount of anger that would drive us apart. He remained by my side day and night. He made love to me like he meant it. But there was noticeable distance between us throughout the day.

I stood by my decision—and I wouldn't change it.

We sat together at the dining table in our bedroom, eating in silence. He didn't reach for the scotch, though he clearly wanted to, respecting my wishes even when our relationship was strained.

There was nothing he wanted more than to me marry me.

Denying him was the best way to infuriate him.

A commotion sounded downstairs. Distant voices. Then Magnus's loud voice reached us all the way upstairs because he screamed in duress. "Fender! Get your ass down here now!"

Fender moved so fast I barely processed what happened. He was out of his chair and at the door to the bedroom. He shouted back, just as heated, "Fuck off!" I'd never heard him yell with so much rage, project his voice so loudly.

It made me realize that even when he was angry with me, he was gentle. That even at our worst, he still showed me respect. I got out of my chair and pulled on a dress as Fender headed down the hallway to the stairs. It was my opportunity to smooth this over. Even an opportunity to convince Fender to change his mind.

Magnus screamed again. "Napoleon took the camp, and I'm the only survivor. So, get your motherfucking ass down here now."

My dress was on, but I stilled. I knew exactly who Napoleon was. Fender had mentioned him a few times. I'd met him at a couple events. He was a new partner in Fender's distribution network.

Magnus yelled again, lower this time because Fender must be at the top of the stairs. "He hit the camp with men and guns. Defeated us within an hour. He kept the prisoners and executed the guards. Raven and I escaped on horseback."

"Oh thank god…" My hand gripped my chest, and I left the bedroom.

Fender's footsteps sounded as he headed down the stairs. When he spoke, his tone was totally different. Calm. "This all just happened?"

Magnus's voice mirrored his. "About eight hours ago. We got to my motorcycle at the house and drove straight here."

I made it to the top of the stairs and looked at the three of them. Raven was in her work attire, standing slightly behind Magnus as she looked at Fender.

Fender didn't know how to contain his anger, so he turned away and ran his hands over the stubble of his jawline. One hand was on his hip, and he paced in the entryway, his bare feet striking the tile with his movements.

I regarded my sister for a long time, feeling so much relief at the sight of her unharmed. It didn't matter if every interaction we had resulted in fights and tears. Every time I saw her, it filled my heart with so much love. I moved down the stairs quickly and beelined straight for her. My arms encircled her, and I gripped her hard, felt her clutch me in return. "Are you okay?" I squeezed her, never wanting to let go.

"I'm fine," she answered. "Just a bit overwhelmed. But I'll get over it." When she pulled back and looked at me, there was nothing but pure love there too. She didn't agree with my decisions or who I loved, but that would never change the way she felt for me. Ever.

Fender continued to pace like he didn't know what else to do. "How did he know where the camp was?" It was the first time he'd ever looked panicked. Calmly panicked. Moving and shifting as if staying still were impossible.

Magnus's eyes followed his movements. "I think he followed you."

He faced the opposite wall, his hands on his hips, his breathing increasing. The fury was starting to grow, beginning with a small fire and rising into an inferno. Invisible smoke left his nostrils. Rage exuded from his entire presence. So angry, he couldn't even look at his brother.

Magnus shook his head slightly as he stared at Fender's back. "One by one, they executed each one of us. I was with Alix, Eric, and Nathan while they were shot in the skull. I don't feel bad for what happened to them, but they didn't deserve that either." He turned angry himself, his voice full of furious accusation. "Your men died because you failed to listen to me."

Fender stilled.

Magnus spoke with heated emotion, like he needed to get it out for his own sake. "And the only reason I'm alive now is because Raven saved me. I was on my knees in the dirt, the last one to get a bullet in my head, but she shot him first."

There was a long stretch of silence.

I looked at Raven, surprised but also not.

Fender remained still, his back no longer rising and falling with his deep breathing.

Then he slowly turned around.

He didn't look at Magnus.

He looked at Raven.

For a very long time.

He was still angry, still furious, but there was something else there now.

Raven held his gaze and didn't blink.

Neither did he.

He stared at her the way he stared at me, like a few seconds weren't enough to absorb what he wanted to see.

Magnus spoke again, pride in his voice. "I am the sole survivor because of her."

Fender didn't say a word as he stared, but he didn't need to.

The look said it all.

FENDER

I sat across from my brother in the parlor. Minutes passed even though we didn't have them to waste. The door was closed, so we were alone, but I felt Raven's presence outside, registered her in a different way from before.

As an ally.

It was hard to look at my brother. Not because of anger, resentment, or anything that I'd felt for the last few days.

But because I was ashamed. "You were right, and I didn't listen."

Magnus stared at me stoically, without a hint of gloating. There was actually pity there—even though he was the one who'd almost died.

Because of my stupidity. "Now the camp is lost."

He still said nothing. Didn't say I told you so. Didn't even seem angry with me.

I rubbed my palms together as I considered our next move. "We have to take it back."

Now he had a reaction. "Why?"

"Because we can't let him get away with that, Magnus. We don't let someone make a fool out of us."

Now his fury emerged. "You mean, make a fool out of *you*."

I swallowed the insult like a man. A big pill without water. "We still have to do something. We have to take that camp back. We can't just let them overrun our business like this."

Magnus cocked his eyebrow and released words dripping in sarcasm. "So, after all this...you still care about money?" He shook his head in disbelief. "Fender, you need to let it go."

Unable to remain subdued, I lashed out like a knife at his throat. "This man killed all my men and almost killed my brother. Do you think I'm gonna let that go?" We were the same man, but we rarely agreed on anything anymore. That man tried to execute someone I loved, so no, I was not letting that shit go.

"Do you want to take the camp back for revenge? Or do you want to take it back so you can run business like usual?"

I gave no answer—because I wasn't sure of the answer anymore.

The disappointment he gave me was brutal, like his opinion of me somehow sank even lower. "If your answer is the second one, or both, don't expect me to help you."

I massaged my knuckles because they suddenly felt broken.

"I will only help you if you run the camp differently. You set the girls free and hire people to do the labor. If we can't come to an agreement on that, I'll walk away."

I stared at him in silence, knowing it wasn't a bluff. Everything had changed now, and for the first time, I was starting to truly understand the error of my ways. My arrogance had made me complacent. My insatiable revenge had made me stupid. My obsession with the past had compromised my future. I'd lost Gilbert. I could have lost the love of my life as well. And to top it off...I'd almost lost the man across from me—a man I would die for.

"We do it my way. Or we don't do it at all."

I chewed the inside of my cheek and gave a slight nod. "Well, my way obviously doesn't work..." I admitted, defeated. I raised the white flag of surrender and let it blow in the breeze. My reign had come to a halt—and it had been a long time coming.

Now, he looked at me the way he used to, showing the same pride he showed in Raven.

That soothed the pain a bit. "And if we do nothing, those girls will never be free. They'll continue to be prisoners, just changing owners." I dropped my chin and stared at my hands for a while. "I'm not sure if I'm fit for the drug business anymore anyway. I let greed get the best of me. I almost lost the most important thing that matters to me—you." I lifted my gaze and looked at my brother, feeling the emotion start to bubble in my chest but never make it up my throat. Those nights on the streets. Those dumpster dives. Those moments when we only had each other. Despite the pain and suffering we'd experienced, those memories meant the world to me. "I want revenge for what Napoleon has done. He humiliated me. He took what's mine. He killed my men. And then he touched my brother. I want him dead."

With soft eyes, he nodded in agreement.

"And if I rescue those women...maybe our mother won't hate me so much, won't be so disappointed in the monster I've become." Ever since Melanie had come into my life, I'd tried not to think about our mother. Once my actions were accounted for, the guilt gnawed at me. She wouldn't be proud of the wealth I'd reclaimed for our family—because of the way I'd done it. It felt like an insult to her memory. I'd cared so much about getting revenge against our father that I'd stopped caring about honoring our mother's memory.

His voice came out as a whisper. "She doesn't hate you, Fender."

"She should. I became a worse version of our father. I became everything that I hate."

He was quiet for a while, regarding me with brotherly affection. "So, you're with me?"

I watched him, seeing a man I admired, seeing someone I should have aspired to. He'd always looked up to me because I was older, because I was the reason we'd survived on the streets. But he was the one I should have admired—because he'd always retained his humanity. "You know I'm always with you, brother." I shared my thoughts in my silence, shared the way I felt about him without words, because we'd never exchanged words like that. It was better left unspoken—because love couldn't really be described in words anyway. "I guess that means I'm about to retire." I shrugged off the intense moment and changed the subject. "What do people do in retirement?"

He gave a slight smile. "No idea. Have a couple kids? Go on trips? You're asking the wrong person."

"Well, what are you going to do?"

He shrugged. "I haven't thought about it."

"I guess we get old...and fat."

Magnus released a short laugh, the joke making him look like a teenager again. "I don't think the girls will stick around if we let that happen."

The happiness on his face made me smile, because these moments had been so rare for the last decade. In fact, I wasn't sure if they'd ever happened at all. It was all business and nothing else. I'd cared so much about building wealth that I'd neglected the one relationship I actually valued. Now he had someone who valued him the way I should have valued him. "You've got a good woman, Magnus. She's earned my respect."

His smile disappeared, his look turning serious once again. Visibly touched, he stared for a while, like my approval meant the world to him, when it shouldn't matter at all. "Thanks. Means a lot to me."

Everything changed the moment I knew what Raven had done. She was there for my brother when I wasn't. She saved his life when my negligence would have gotten him killed. The only reason he was in front of me now was because of her bravery, her devotion, and her love. I wished I could take back every insult I'd given her, whether it was to her face or behind her back. She didn't deserve it. Whether they stayed together or not, I would always look after her, always be there for her for anything she needed. Forever. "I owe her my life...since she saved yours."

WE LAID OUT OUR PLANS. Made some calls. Prepared for an attack that would wipe them out for good. With men and guns, we would approach the camp from the rear, kill the new guards in their sleep.

They wouldn't expect a retaliation so quickly, so we had the element of surprise.

We returned to the girls who were still in the foyer together, sitting side by side with their hands clasped together.

When Raven noticed Magnus approach, she rose to her feet, ready to listen to whatever he said.

"We're going to hit the camp tomorrow night." He spoke to her plainly and didn't mince his words because she could handle it.

Melanie came up to me, but her eyes were on Magnus as she listened.

"And then what?" Raven shifted her gaze to me for a brief moment before she looked at him again.

"We'll talk when we get home. Come on." He moved to the front door, gave me a goodbye nod, and then walked out.

Raven followed.

I watched her go, my heartbeat loud in my ears.

Melanie stared at me, like she knew what I was thinking.

I walked out of the foyer and followed them.

Magnus was around the front of one of my cars, ready to open the driver's door.

Raven's back was to me.

I walked down to the middle step. "Raven."

She stilled at the sound of my voice.

Magnus watched me before he shifted his gaze to her. Then he gave her a slight nod.

She slowly turned around and regarded me. War was still on her face. She didn't like me, and she would never like me.

Fair enough.

But she closed the door and moved up the steps until she was closer to me but still at least six feet back.

The last time I'd spoken to her in private, I was vicious. I'd treated her like a dog. I didn't do that now.

Magnus got into the car and shut the door, giving us privacy. He was no longer protective.

Because I would die for this woman in a heartbeat.

Her hostile eyes shifted back and forth as she looked at me, waited for me to say words that were long overdue.

"Thank you."

Her eyes dimmed slightly.

"I couldn't live without him."

"I didn't do it for you." She kept her voice even despite all the rage she felt for me. It was difficult for her just to be near me because her disdain was so heavy.

"I know why you did it. And I'm glad that's the reason." He had a loyal woman who would take a bullet for him the way

I would. Couldn't ask for anything more. "I'm yours for life. Whatever you need—"

"I want the girls to be free." Her eyes darkened at the request, furious, like she expected my answer to be no.

"I already said yes, but I didn't do it for you."

She sucked in a sharp breath, her eyes automatically welling up with tears of relief.

"My offer remains. You saved his life—mine is yours to claim."

Her wet eyes took me in, shifting back and forth quickly. "Why?"

"Because you saved his life—"

"No. Why did you agree to free the girls? Magnus?"

It was for a lot of reasons, but I didn't care to explain. "Because it was time. Time for us all to move on."

Her fury remained, like that answer wasn't good enough.

"I'm sorry—for everything." I never apologized to anyone, so she had no idea how heavy that sentiment was.

It clearly meant nothing to her because she got in the car without looking back.

Magnus started the car, and they drove away.

I watched them go then heard the sound of heels approaching.

Melanie came to my side, her arm sliding through mine. "My sister has a long memory..."

I watched the car until the taillights disappeared. "I don't expect her to care about a word I said. But I had to say it anyway. She has every right to hate me for the rest of her life. Wouldn't expect anything less from her."

"What's happening?"

I turned to look at her. "We're taking back the camp."

"As in, your men are?" Fear danced on the surface of her eyes, wishing for an answer I wouldn't give.

"Yes. Along with Magnus and me."

"No..." Her hand released my arm as she stepped back.

"*Chérie*—"

"They killed everyone at the camp. I don't want you going back there—"

"I have to."

"Send someone else—"

"*Chérie.*"

Her eyes watered as she shook her head.

"*Chérie.*" My hand cupped her face, trying to calm her with my confidence. "I have to do this."

"Why?" She turned her cheek into my hand, wanting the callused fingertips for comfort.

"Because I'm the best. So is Magnus."

"I can't live without you..."

"I can't live without you either, *chérie*. I'll come back."

Tears that sparkled like diamonds dripped down her cheeks.

"Nothing will stop me from coming back to you. I will marry you. I will have a family with you. We will live the rest of our lives together—in peace and quiet." I didn't know who I was without my business, but looking at her told me who I would become. Husband. Father. Brother. We would be everything that I'd lost.

"Peace?" she whispered.

I nodded. "We're taking back the camp for vengeance—and freedom."

Realization came into her eyes. "You're...you're letting them go?"

"Yes."

She cupped her face and stepped back, the revelation hitting her in a way she could barely handle. More tears came. Her breathing skyrocketed. An emotional crescendo washed over her, breaking her in two. "Oh my god..." The look she gave me was unique, special, never seen before. "I knew it...I knew you would." She dropped her hands from her face and moved into me, gripping me as tightly as if she hung from a cliff. "I always knew."

THE NIGHT WAS SPENT with her in my arms.

She kissed me in a way she never had before.

Made love to me in a way she never had before.

Our relationship had always been intense and passionate, but it was much deeper now, much bolder.

She'd fallen more in love with me.

She'd never be able to give me that final piece of her, not when I continued to do something she detested. But once she allowed herself to, that small piece was heavier than all the rest.

If I'd known, I would have done it much sooner.

She was everything to me. It was hard to believe that she hadn't always been a part of me, that this powerful connection was recent. My memory played tricks on me, and sometimes I thought she had been in the dumpster with my brother and me. That she was right there with me the night my family died. The connection between us seemed to disobey the laws of physics—because time didn't apply to us the way it did with everyone else.

When the sun came up the next morning, everything changed.

She knew I'd depart that afternoon, and she couldn't keep it together.

I was a soldier going off to war—and she was afraid I would leave her widowed.

Tears would come unexpectedly. Panic attacks would strike her and make her hyperventilate. All I could do was kiss her to calm her down, but another round came again...and again.

"*Chérie*." My thumbs brushed away her tears as she sat beside me on the couch, her face puffy and red. She'd taken a few painkillers because the tears had brought on a headache she couldn't defeat. "What happened when you were trapped in that bedroom with Gilbert?"

Her bottom lip trembled as she looked at me.

"I defeated them all—by myself. Nothing stopped me from getting to you. I was outnumbered ten to one. That made no difference. The same will happen tonight. I will slaughter them all, free the girls, and come back to you."

She nodded slightly. "I just don't understand why you can't send someone else, pay them whatever they want."

My thumbs continued to brush away her tears. "Because I'm the one who did this. I started the camp. I ignored Magnus and got all my men killed. I'm responsible for everything—and I will fix it. I'm not a coward."

"I know you aren't. But you should stay...for me."

I shook my head. "Magnus would never stay. And I can't let him go in alone. I need to be there to watch his back."

"He doesn't need you—"

"Doesn't matter. Where he goes, I go. You understand that better than anybody."

She gave a bigger nod through her tears, thinking of her sister.

"I'm going to leave you with Raven at Magnus's house. You'll be safe there if I don't—"

"Don't fucking say that." Tears poured down her cheeks. "I don't...I don't want to hear that."

It always hurt to watch her cry, but it hurt even more to see her like this. It was almost enough to make me back out so I could stay there with her.

Almost.

***

WE ARRIVED AT THE APARTMENT.

She would normally take in the beautiful scenery with a mesmerized gaze.

But right now, she was too delirious to care about anything.

We took the elevator to the main floor and stepped inside.

Magnus and Raven were heard speaking, saying their goodbyes.

Raven sounded identical to Melanie when she spoke to him, tears in her throat. "I never thought I would have a man like this. I just got you...I'm not ready to let you go. You're supposed to be my husband. We're supposed to make babies. Please don't take that away from me."

Melanie had stopped crying, but she was clearly on the brink of doing it again. With her hand in mine, she let me guide her forward, Magnus and Raven appearing through the main sitting room.

My brother and I stared at each other.

Melanie and Raven did the same.

Magnus turned to Raven, ready to say his final goodbye.

With wet eyes, Raven stared at him, unable to speak because it hurt so much.

Magnus moved to her, cupped her face, and kissed her.

She clutched him tightly. "I love you."

Magnus let her hold on to him as long as she needed before he turned away. "I love you too." He moved past me and approached the elevator, purposely not turning back to Raven, like it was too hard to look at her again.

I stared at Melanie, hating to abandon her when she was in distress. There was nothing I could say to make this better, not when I'd already said everything I could a million times. There was only one thing that I should say a million times. "Je t'aime, *chérie*."

Her eyes watered, but she didn't say it back, like if she didn't say it, I would never leave.

I turned away, knowing she would never say it if it kept me there.

She grabbed my wrist and pulled me back, moving into my chest as she gripped me so hard that twenty men couldn't pull her off me. "Je t'aime..."

I pressed a kiss to her forehead then forced myself to leave her behind.

To walk out with my brother.

To know that there was a chance I might never return.

We stepped into the elevator and waited for the doors to close.

The girls held on to each other, side by side, their hands coming together in solidarity of their pain.

Magnus couldn't look. His eyes remained on the floor.

The doors closed.

Magnus released the breath he was holding and lifted his chin, his hands in the pockets of his jeans.

My hand went to his shoulder. "It'll be over soon, brother."

WE INFILTRATED THE CAMP.

The men made it over the wall, and we spread out.

But then the alarm rang.

Not sure who saw us, but it didn't matter.

They would all be dead soon anyway.

I broke in to the first cabin. The men were half asleep in their bunks, hearing the alarm but not quite awake enough to respond to it. But when they saw my silhouette in the darkness, they screamed.

"Shoot him!"

My knife slid into his throat, killing him instantly. The man beside him got up to run, but I slammed the butt of my knife into his head, knocking him out instantly. Shouts sounded, and the men fumbled for their guns in the darkness, too disoriented to do anything before I got to them. They were both down in seconds.

Off to the next cabin.

The next row of cabins was for the girls, so I kicked down each door so they could run if a fire started.

When the door smashed in, they all screamed.

"Stay where you are. You'll be free in a few moments."

Maybe they recognized me in the darkness. Maybe they didn't. But none of them moved.

Men ran out of their cabins in response to the assault. Gunfire pierced the darkness once it had become an all-out war. Men collapsed to the ground on both sides, mowed down by the spray of bullets. I hid behind a cabin when one of their men ran out, and I stabbed him right between the ribs and watched him collapse. His comrade ran back, knowing I was out there.

I chased him down and slit his throat.

Blood was all over me.

The screaming continued.

Women screamed too, having no idea if they would be slaughtered or freed.

My eyes immediately scanned for Magnus, making sure that he was okay, that he was enjoying this killing spree as much as I was.

Didn't see him anywhere.

I ran across the clearing, making it to the next cabin before the bullets meant for me hit their mark. They struck the wooden cabin, making the girls inside scream. I counted the bullets and ran to the next building as they reloaded. Farther and farther I went, killing the men I came across, searching the area where Magnus was supposed to be.

Then I saw him.

Napoleon.

Napoleon slammed his cane into Magnus's skull, making him too disoriented to fight. Both on the ground and fighting to the death.

This was happening because of me.

Because I didn't fucking listen.

I sprinted, and instead of holding my silence to give me the element of surprise, I screamed. "Magnus!" He needed to know that I was coming, to keep fighting because I would be there in two seconds. "Get the fuck off him!" Rage like I'd never known hit me so fucking hard, gave me adrenaline I'd never experienced before. My brother was bloody and bruised, seconds away from death if I didn't get there in time.

Magnus had the strength to kick Napoleon away, to extend his life long enough for me to get there.

I slid to my knees and pulled out my knife, moving over Magnus to protect him before I slaughtered this motherfucker.

But he was quicker.

He spun backward, his hidden knife at the ready, and hit me dead in the center of my stomach.

I'd never been stabbed. Hardly been nicked. The air left my lungs. My body shut down. The fight left me even though I didn't feel an ounce of pain. The last thing I did before I collapsed was share a look with Magnus.

Napoleon's voice was full of victory. "Two-for-one special."

Then I hit the earth.

My brother's scream split the night. "*No!*"

I lay there on my back, my heart racing, the blood pooling around me.

I couldn't even talk, I was so stunned. All I could do was think.

Win, Magnus.

I could only stare at the sky, look at the stars that watched me fade away. The sounds of fighting were right next to me, Napoleon and Magnus both grunting and crawling in the dirt, fighting to be the victor.

I couldn't watch.

Come on, brother.

I couldn't watch my brother die.

My faith had died the night my mother was killed. But in that moment, I prayed. Not to God, but to her. *Mom, please. Help him.*

My brother's victory scream tore through the air. "Die, motherfucker!" He slammed something down on Napoleon over and over again, grunting with every hit, blood spraying everywhere.

I closed my eyes in relief, knowing she was still here. *Thank you.*

Magnus took a few deep breaths before he crawled to me, his face appearing in my vision, caked in blood that wasn't his. "Fender!" His eyes shifted to the knife that was still stuck inside me. "I'm here." His eyes lingered on the knife for a long time, his eyes falling in pain. "You're going to be alright..." His look gave him away like it always did. He looked over his shoulder and shouted for help. "I need a medic! Satellite phone! Get over here!"

I knew my fate before he said a word.

But at least it was me and not him.

I could live with that.

I could die with that.

I shifted my gaze away from his voice and looked at the night sky. There were sounds of distant fighting, the gunshots becoming fewer and further in between. I knew we'd won the battle without having to see it myself. The stars shone down on me, ready to claim my soul and deliver it where it belonged.

It was stupid to hope I would end up anywhere besides hell, but I hoped I would see my mother again. "No, I'm not going to be alright." I looked at my brother again, watching him do his best to remain as calm as possible, to bottle his true emotions as well as he could. "But thanks for lying."

Magnus pulled his shirt over his head then grabbed the hilt of the knife. Without preamble, he yanked it out.

I immediately gasped in pain, feeling everything now that the adrenaline was gone.

"I need a few guys. Now!" He wrapped the shirt around my wound and applied pressure. "Fender, you can get through this. I need you to stay with me, alright?" Uncontrollable tears formed in his eyes, the distress inching into his features when he realized how deep the knife went. He breathed harder and harder, forced to watch me die, the blood dripping past his palms because there was nothing he could do to stop it.

I wished I were already dead so he wouldn't have to go through this. "Magnus."

He ignored me and took the bandages from the medic to apply to my stomach, shouting out orders. "Call our pilot. Tell him to bring the chopper now. Fender needs to get to the hospital."

Men stepped away to follow his orders.

There was no reason I should still be alive right now. The knife had been ten inches. It stabbed me all the way through, sliced through the organs in the way, the internal bleeding worse than the external wound.

But I knew why I was still there.

She kept me there—so I could say goodbye.

My voice came again, weaker. "Magnus."

Magnus wouldn't look at me. He couldn't. He knew this was it, but he couldn't face it.

I didn't have much time. I was growing weaker by the second. I placed my hand on his, soaking his hand with my blood. "I deserve this."

He shook his head, still not looking at me, sniffing back the tears that emerged. "Stop it."

"You know I deserve this. The girls are free, and I'll be dead. That's how it should be."

His bottom lip trembled as the tears streaked down his cheeks. "You aren't going to die! Stop it!"

I squeezed his hand. "Brother."

He breathed harder and harder, the pain too difficult to face. "Please don't..."

"Look at me."

He wouldn't.

"Magnus."

Finally, he did. Eyes identical to mine pierced into my soul. His emotions rose, his eyes wet and reflecting the light of the torches around us. His hand remained pressed to my wound as he continued to try to save me, even though it was pointless.

He knew it.

I knew it.

I gripped his hand, prepared to say my last words. "You were the man I could never be but always wanted to be. You said I was the one you looked up to, but it was always the other way around. You're a good brother...and I love you." I'd never said those words to him in our lifetime, except when we were little boys, but I said them now.

He breathed through his tears, his features mushed together in anguish. "I love you, brother."

I squeezed his hand again. "Tell Melanie...nothing would've made me happier than to see her in that white dress and make her my wife. Tell her to forgive me...but I did what I had to do. And I would do it again...even if I knew what would happen." My heart broke for Melanie, that I had to leave her behind, but I was grateful I had been there to keep my brother alive. It was always my job to protect him—and I didn't fail.

He nodded.

My eyes blinked a few times, the image of my brother's face and the stars fading further and further.

Then it went dark.

TWENTY-SEVEN

TEN-INCH BLADE

MELANIE

Raven and I sat beside each other on the couch.

The windows showed the darkness outside.

We both waited for sunrise, both looked at the clock over and over, wishing time would pass in the blink of an eye.

Neither one of us spoke, too upset to talk about anything.

I'd thought my time at the camp was torture. I'd thought being apart from Raven was torture.

No. It was this.

If he didn't come back...I wouldn't know what to do.

"There's something I need to tell you..." It was the first time she'd spoken since the men had left.

My head turned her away, seeing her pale-as-snow skin, seeing the stress discolor her eyes.

"When I was at the camp, Alix had it in for me. He was determined to get me, no matter the cost."

I wasn't sure if I wanted to hear this. "Raven..."

"Magnus always protected me, but they pinned him down so there was nothing he could do. Alix yanked me from the cabin, stripped me naked, and dragged me across the ground by the hair..."

"Oh god." I cupped my mouth, my eyes closing to shut out the imagery she painted for me.

Raven continued with a calm voice, as if she felt no emotion whatsoever. "It didn't happen—because Fender stopped it."

My eyes opened, and my hands slowly fell from my mouth.

"He'd just arrived at the camp. That was why Fender was out there to see it." She inhaled a deep breath then looked at me. "He told Magnus that he did it for him, but Magnus doesn't believe him. He thinks he did it for you."

I knew he'd done it for me.

"Just wanted you to know that...because he obviously didn't tell you."

I shook my head. "No, he didn't."

She looked forward again.

"Does this mean...I have your blessing?"

She stared at the clock, her face devoid of emotion. Seconds trickled by until they turned into a full minute. "You can have anyone you want, Melanie. There are better men than him."

I swallowed my disappointment with a dry throat. "He's freeing the girls now."

"Doesn't excuse the fact that he enslaved them in the first place—"

"Raven." I inhaled a deep breath, feeling the pain in every corner of my body. "I'm going to marry him whether I have your blessing or not."

She turned to look at me, equally disappointed.

"I know him in a way you never will. I believe he's a good man...who just lost his way. You've seen glimpses of his goodness yourself."

"If Magnus hadn't stopped him, he was going to hang three girls at once."

I shook my head. "He wouldn't have gone through with it. I believe that with all my heart."

She looked forward again, her eyes down. "Perhaps he won't come back...and that will fix the situation."

I inhaled a sharp breath as my eyes drilled into her cheek, flames rising from wet firewood. "How dare you say that to me." Tears welled in my eyes because it hurt so damn much.

She wouldn't look at me. Her eyes remained down. There was no apology. No justification for the horrible thing she said.

Her presence had given me comfort, but now, it just made me sick to my stomach. It was the first time I truly wanted nothing to do with her. I rose from the couch and moved into the other room—because I'd rather suffer in silence than sit beside her a moment longer.

HOURS LATER, the quiet sound of the elevator reached my ears. The gears shifted, and the distant hum of machinery was unmistakable. "Fender..." I left the room and entered the main sitting area where I'd left Raven.

She must have heard it too because she was on her feet and heading to the same hallway.

We stopped in front of the elevator, waiting for it to open and reveal our men.

The door slid open, revealing a tall brunette.

The disappointment was heavy to swallow, because I could picture Fender standing there, a slight smile on his face. He would walk up to me and say, "Let's go home, *chérie*." It all happened in the blink of an eye, my imagination running wild.

This stranger was a slap in the face.

Raven knew her. "Miranda? What are you doing here?"

"Who is she?" I asked.

Raven ignored me and stepped forward.

Miranda entered the apartment in professional attire, heels clacking against the hardwood floor. "Magnus requested I take you two to the hospital."

"The...the hospital?" My hand immediately went to my throat, the tears starting from deep inside my body, the anxiety infecting my body like a deadly disease. If Magnus had made the call, that meant he wasn't the one in the hospital. "Fender..."

Raven turned to me, as if she'd drawn the same conclusion.

Miranda kept her calm composure. "Ready to go?"

"Is he okay?" I choked on a sob and cupped my mouth to make it stop. "Please tell me he's okay..."

She scratched the side of her neck and looked down. "Magnus didn't give me any information. He just told me to bring you two to him."

"Is Magnus okay?" Raven asked.

Miranda nodded.

I stepped back, the heat flushing my body and making me dizzy. I backed up into a wall and stopped, my hand back over my mouth, my eyes on the floor, hyperventilating on the spot.

Raven placed her hand on my shoulder. "Melanie, we don't know anything—"

"Fender wouldn't need the hospital unless it was really bad..." He was bulletproof. He was the strongest man I'd ever met. Whatever happened was serious.

"Melanie—"

"This is what you wanted, isn't it?" I threw her arm off my body. "Congratulations."

She cowered at my viciousness, her eyes turning guarded and hurt at the same time. Her hand was in the air, and it slowly lowered back to her side as she watched me come apart, watched me experience agony and rage at the same time.

"I take it back, okay?"

"You won't forgive Fender for anything, so don't expect me to forgive you for wishing such a terrible thing. That man is my whole world..." Sobs racked me, made me move to the other wall. "He loves me for who I am—unlike you. He makes me happy. He makes me feel good about myself."

Raven watched me, her eyes softening. "I'm sorry, okay?"

"I don't give a shit if you're sorry." I threw down my arms. "If he dies..." I shook my head. "I'll never forgive you. I'll never forgive you for wishing that misery on me. I'll never forgive you for wishing me to be alone for the rest of my life."

Raven stared at me for a long time, her eyes falling to the ground. "I didn't realize you felt this way—"

"Because you didn't listen. You always assume I'm too stupid to know what I want. Well, he doesn't think I'm stupid. He doesn't think I'm dull. He doesn't think I'm as weak and pathetic as you describe me."

"Melanie, I don't think you're stupid—"

"Yes, you do. Don't lie."

She winced.

"And that's fine. Because he thinks the world of me—and that's all I need."

MIRANDA TOOK us to the hospital.

We went to the ER and found Magnus in the waiting room.

The second Raven saw him, she sprinted to him.

He got to his feet and caught her at the perfect moment, his arms locking around her, his lips kissing her as she kissed him. His hand cupped the back of her head, and he closed his eyes as he held her.

I looked around.

Fender wasn't there.

I started to cry because my worst fear was coming true.

"Oh god..."

Watching them love each other only reminded me of what I had—and what I might lose. You never really appreciated something until it was gone. Fender was by my side nearly all the time, and I'd give anything to go back in time and experience one of those quiet moments, the two of us in comfortable silence in his office, watching TV on the couch, lying in bed together.

I couldn't lose that.

Magnus and Raven broke apart. Magnus looked at me, pain in his eyes, and then stepped toward me.

No.

I couldn't handle this.

I was already crying, looking at him expectantly, hoping for the best news possible.

He stopped in front of me, all his features tight.

"Is he going to be okay?" I could barely get the words out through my labored breathing. "What happened? Did he kill the motherfucker who did this to him?" I listed off questions in my hysteria, but they didn't matter. There was only one question that needed an answer.

The same pained expression continued.

No.

"Melanie, I'm sorry... He's probably not going to make it."

It was an out-of-body experience. I could actually see myself from a different point of view, see the horror on my face, see the mess of tears that had washed off my makeup hours ago. The panic confused all the internal systems of my body. I was hot. Cold. Deaf. Weak. Full of adrenaline.

Paralyzed.

Once I grappled with the news, the sobs hit.

Hysteria.

Mania.

Misery. Fucking misery.

Raven came to me, and I didn't push her away.

I didn't care about anything right now.

All I could do was drown.

SOMETIMES, I paced in the waiting room. Sometimes, I took a walk through the hospital. Sometimes, I sat alone in a chair. It was a constant cycle, a constant rhythm of discomfort that I couldn't fix, no matter what I did.

Every hour that I wished would pass was an hour that he fought for his life.

A fight he would lose.

I stood at the window in a hallway, my head pressed to the glass, needing something cool against my forehead. My headache pounded in my temples because of all the crying, and I bought some painkillers from the gift shop. The cashier couldn't take her eyes off me because I was an emotional mess, but she didn't ask any questions. Now I stood there and looked at the sunshine outside the window, the buildings of Paris as the backdrop.

"Melanie?" Raven's gentle voice came from beside me.

With my hand pressed to the glass, I looked at her, feeling nothing for her right now. My ring was on my hand, and whether he lived or died, I couldn't imagine ever taking it off.

Her eyes showed her pain, how much my despair affected her. "I said that out of anger. I would never wish for this... wish for you to go through this."

I looked out the window again.

She stood there with me for a while.

"I just want to be by myself, Raven." My voice was lifeless, like it rose from a corpse.

"I understand. I just wanted you to know—" She cleared her throat.

I turned back to her.

"Magnus told me that the reason Fender is here is because...he saved Magnus's life."

My eyes watered for the millionth time.

"If Fender hadn't gotten there, Magnus wouldn't be here right now."

Tears dripped down my cheeks. "I asked him to stay for me. He wouldn't. He said he had to protect his brother..."

Raven's eyes watered too.

"He loves his brother so much..."

"I know he does," she whispered. "It's the way I love you."

I sniffled.

"Maybe Fender and I are more alike than I realized..."

MAGNUS FOUND me in the hallway. "Melanie?"

I turned to him quickly, hoping for news, good news.

"I just talked to the doctor—"

"Oh god..." I dug my fingers into my hair on either side of my skull and prepared for another mental breakdown.

"Melanie, he's stable."

"What...?" My hands lowered then moved to my mouth.

He gave a slight smile. "He pulled through."

My palms covered my face entirely, and a new round of sobs hit me. "Oh my god..." I cried for a bit before I dropped my hands.

Magnus held out a tissue.

I took it, touched by the gesture, and cleaned myself up.

"The doctor said we can see him." His eyes softened as he looked at me. "But I thought you should go first..." Every look he'd given me before had been a bit cold, like he didn't care for my existence. But now, he looked at me differently, the way he looked at Fender sometimes.

"Thank you." I darted around him and headed to reception.

"Melanie?"

I turned back around.

"It'll be nice to have a sister again."

***

I STEPPED into the private room with large windows along one side.

His big mass was in the bed, wires everywhere, wearing a blue gown rather than being shirtless like usual.

I slowly crept to the bed, unsure if he was awake, unsure if he was coherent at all. When I stood over him, I saw that his eyes were closed. The monitor beside him beeped. His blood pressure cuff squeezed his arm.

My hand went to his wrist, feeling that strong pulse.

My eyes closed, and the tears dripped.

"*Chérie.*" His voice was raspy and gruff, his throat dry from the breathing tube that had been placed there during surgery.

My eyes remained closed, and I broke into sobs, afraid I would never hear that deep voice again.

His voice became stronger, but also turned gentler. "*Chérie.*"

It was too much. I couldn't do it.

"*Chérie.* Look at me."

When my eyes opened, the tears that had been held back by my lids came spilling down. I locked my gaze with his, seeing dark eyes that were tired and a bit bloodshot, but still intense as always.

His hand gave me a tug. "Come here."

I got into bed beside him, cuddling with him just like I did at home, but keeping my arm over his chest rather than his stomach.

His arm circled me, and he pressed a kiss to my forehead.

Beside him, I cried.

"It's over, *chérie.* It's over."

TWENTY-EIGHT
RETIREMENT

FENDER

I stayed in the hospital for a week.

Melanie rarely left my side.

She would go back to the palace to shower and change, but then she would stay with me until the next morning. Visitors weren't allowed, but some cash was enough to change that policy.

Even days later, Melanie was still an emotional mess.

It didn't matter that I was still here, that the doctor said the wound was closing nicely—it wasn't enough to erase the trauma.

Gilbert brought us lunch, so she sat beside me in the chair and ate while I remained in the bed.

Having to stay in bed for a week was ludicrous, but I didn't try to get discharged early because that would get Melanie worked up. She was obviously more comfortable having medical help at the press of a button.

She hadn't asked me about the camp, the girls, anything. She just seemed to be content that I'd survived the ordeal. But now that it'd been a few days, she brought it up. "So... what happened?"

I gave her the G-rated version. "We underestimated Napoleon—again. But we got the best of him, so it doesn't matter. We lost a few of our men. Not many. Their men were all massacred, so that's over."

"The girls?"

"We had them brought to Paris with money and clothes. Told them they were free."

"I bet a lot of them went to the police..."

I took a few bites. "Doesn't matter. It won't amount to anything."

"And the camp itself? Is it just...vacant?"

"Yes."

"What will happen to it?"

"No idea." We'd taken the remaining coke and sold it off. The valuables in the cabins were removed. The horses were taken to my pasture. The camp was gutted, and the bones remained behind.

"What will happen to you?" She looked down at her food and pushed a few pieces around with her fork.

I watched her, seeing the apprehension. "I'll get married. Take my wife on a nice honeymoon. Greece is beautiful this time of year. Knock her up a couple times. Live happily ever after, or whatever that line is."

She raised her chin, a slight smile on her lips. "You got it right. But...is that enough for you?"

My eyes narrowed on her face. "Yes. Because you've always been enough for me."

Her eyes softened like the rose petals in the garden, like the fire that glowed red before it went out for good, like the wick of a candle as it slowly met its end.

A knock sounded on the door, and Magnus entered. "Still here? Fucking pussy."

I grinned. "Shut the fuck up."

He came around the bed on the opposite side of Melanie. "That doesn't look like hospital food."

"I'm not eating that shit."

Melanie smiled at the two of us before she rose to her feet. "I'll give you guys some privacy." She took her meal outside.

I watched her go before I took another bite.

Magnus watched me, his look turning serious. "How are you?"

"Never better." I took a few more bites before I set the container on the table beside me.

"How's the pain?"

Pretty fucking painful. "Insignificant."

Magnus knew I was lying but didn't call me out on it. "Melanie really loves you."

A half smile entered my lips. "Damn right she does."

He didn't mirror my look. "She was a mess the entire time you were in surgery."

I could only imagine.

"I've never cared for her. You know my reasons. But she really loves you...which is all that really matters."

"You're coming to the wedding, then?"

He nodded. "Wouldn't miss it."

"Will Raven be a problem?"

His eyes shifted away momentarily, as if I'd struck a chord. "I don't think so. Not anymore."

"I'll do my best to make amends with her, but I don't think I'll ever be successful."

"Probably not."

I looked out the window next, the energy in the room changing. The conversation neither one of us wanted to have was on the horizon, like the sun at dawn, almost on the crest of the earth.

"Thank you...for saving my life."

I didn't look at him.

He gave me all the time I needed to respond.

Which was a very long time. "Always, brother." I turned back to meet his gaze.

He was relaxed in the chair, one ankle resting on the opposite knee, hands in his lap. "I would do the same for you, brother."

I already knew that without his having to say it. "Looks like we won't have to worry about that again."

"Guess not." He rubbed his hands together. "I thought you were dead before I got you in the chopper. But the medic said there was still a pulse..."

I was alive when I shouldn't be—and I knew exactly why.

"I just can't believe you pulled through that. Looks like Melanie gave you the will to live..."

"It wasn't her."

He watched me, his eyes narrowed.

I looked out the window for a while, seeing the dust motes float in the air from the beam of golden light. "It was Mom."

All the features of his face softened. His hands stopped moving. He stared in silence, desperate to understand my meaning.

"She was there."

He didn't say a word, his eyes still on me.

"And she forgives me."

I SAT on the couch across from Magnus, in a tuxedo with shiny shoes, ready to pledge my undying love to the only woman I'd ever love. I had to vacate the room so she could get ready, and I'd been down here for hours, just waiting.

Just wanted to fucking marry her already.

I took a drink and regarded my brother, who looked visibly different than he used to. A couple weeks had passed, and while the changes to his face were subtle, they were noticeable. We spent more time together, did things that brothers did, like drinks at the bar, watching sports, doing something besides discussing work. "You gave it all away. I'll never understand that." Raven had given him an ultimatum because she considered his wealth to be blood money. I didn't agree with that. I didn't agree with her extreme views. But it wasn't my place to disagree with her anymore.

His expression didn't change, remained lighthearted. "We don't need it."

"Where do you live now?"

"In her old apartment. The tenant moved out, and we moved in." His mood didn't drop or change, like it was a simple decision.

"And you're okay with that?"

He nodded. "It feels right."

"Our goal was to retire. And you're working again." We'd worked to earn back the wealth that was stolen from us, so his actions made everything we'd done pointless. I would offer my money to him, but he would never take it.

He shrugged. "I like horses. As long as I don't deal with people, I'm fine."

"You could start the business again. Just do it the right way."

He was quiet for a long time before he shook his head. "I'm not interested in that anymore."

I nodded in understanding, wanting to accept his decision without judgment, but I needed to know something first. "Are you happy?"

His eyes shifted away, his mind elsewhere. "Yes."

That was all I needed to know. I raised my glass to him. "Cheers."

He smiled and did the same. "Cheers."

We both took a drink.

"What about you?" he asked. "Are you happy?"

"The love of my life is marrying me today. Fuck yes, I'm happy."

His eyes gave a smile. "I meant with retirement. You really think you can do that?"

I wasn't obsessed with crime. But I was the kind of person that always needed to be doing something. I needed to be working toward something. I couldn't just hit the gym all day and fuck my wife afterward. "Maybe I'll start some other kind of business. Or maybe when we have kids, that will be enough to keep me busy."

"What kind of business?"

I took a drink. "I've always admired art. Maybe an art gallery."

He nodded. "That'd be cool."

"So, when are you going to ask her to marry you?"

His eyes immediately flicked down the hallway to the stairs in the foyer, making sure the girls were still upstairs and nowhere nearby. "Soon."

"Yeah? How?"

"I have an idea."

"You going to tell me, or what?"

"You never told me how you proposed to Melanie?"

I grinned. "Because it was romantic as fuck, and I don't want you to copy me."

He rolled his eyes and laughed into his drink. "At the Eiffel Tower."

"Cliché."

"I'm going to put the ring inside the *Count of Monte Cristo.* It's one of her favorites, and I gave her a copy when she was a new prisoner at the camp. Meaningful to her for a lot of reasons. I thought she would open it, see the ring inside, and that would be it."

I grinned at my brother. "Okay, that's pretty romantic."

He grinned back.

"She'll say yes."

"She won't. Because I'm not going to ask."

I nodded in approval. "Melanie loves that book too."

"She does?" he asked in surprise.

I tried not to be offended because nothing would upset me on my wedding day. "She's a lot smarter than you realize. And you also fail to realize that if it weren't for her, none of this would have happened. She kept Raven alive. She reminded me who I was. Without her, we'd still be at the camp right now."

He absorbed what I said, his gaze turning serious. He gave a subtle nod in agreement. "Mom would have loved her."

"Yeah, she would have. And she would have loved Raven, too."

WITH HER ARM through her sister's, she glided toward me.

Like she had wings.

The gown was more expensive than my car, and she was the only woman who deserved to wear it. With her hair down, diamonds in her ears and around her neck, she was divine.

And she was mine.

Eyes locked on mine. Confidence in her spine. Love in her eyes. She walked slowly, but she was so eager to get to me.

Just as eager as I was to get to her.

They stopped in front of me, and Raven finally let her go.

Melanie was my responsibility now.

I took that responsibility seriously.

My arms circled her waist, and I pulled her into me, kissing her like no one was there. It was just the two of us, and she stepped into my office after she woke up. My lips took hers with a gentleness I'd never exhibited before, because my love had never been as deep as it was now. Deeper than the roots of the oldest tree.

She rested her forehead against mine, her hands on my arms, just a few inches shorter than me in those sky-high heels. A breeze moved through her hair, making it dance in the wind. Her eyes reflected the sunlight behind me, but they were brighter because they glowed entirely on their own.

The priest cleared his throat. "Shall we begin?"

I had been married to her the first time we were together in that cabin. My commitment was solidified for a lifetime. There was never another woman for me after that, even when she left me, because I was miserable without her. There was no hesitation or doubt. She was the woman for me—and I'd known it the moment I saw her. "Yes."

TWENTY-NINE
FORGIVENESS

Melanie

Nothing changed.

Marriage didn't change our lives whatsoever. Our honeymoon didn't feel like a honeymoon. We didn't feel like newlyweds.

Because every day was our honeymoon. Every day felt like we were newlyweds. Every day was experienced with the same commitment we'd always shared. My last name was different, and I was a countess, but I'd felt like royalty the moment he'd laid eyes on me.

Raven stood across from me at the kitchen island, where we used to eat together when we both lived in this apartment. We drank our coffee and picked at the muffins she'd bought at the bakery that morning.

It was strange to be there, because I was a different person than when I had first arrived.

Now I didn't even know that woman anymore.

"How was your honeymoon?" Raven's voice brought me back to reality.

I held the mug between my fingers, feeling the warmth against my skin. "It was amazing. Greece is...indescribable."

"What did you guys do?"

"Well...other than the obvious, we went shopping, had lots of lunches and dinners, lay by the pool. We stayed on the island of Santorini, in Opa, and it's this little village where you can walk everywhere. I thought Paris was beautiful..."

"I'm glad you had a good time." Raven had dropped her hostility toward Fender, but she wasn't warm toward him either. There was just calm acceptance, and that was all I wanted.

"How are things with you?"

"Magnus is liking his job at the stables. He trains horses, grooms them, takes care of them. He keeps Rose there."

"That's nice." When Raven told me she'd made Magnus give away his money, I'd thought it was harsh, but I accepted it without question or judgment. We were different people. She saw the world in black-and-white. I saw it in all the colors of the rainbow. "What about you?"

"It's nice to be back in school. I'm also working at the bar I used to go to."

"Is it weird...to be living a normal life?"

She looked down into her coffee for a long time as she considered the question, probably reflecting on her life in the camp, everything that had transpired. "It's weird that it happened so quickly. It feels like...it's always been this way. I feel like Magnus has always been a part of my life, when I've only known him for months. I guess our shared journey changes the measurement of time."

I understood exactly what she meant. "When do you think he'll ask you to marry him?" I brought the mug to my lips and took a drink.

A smile moved on to her lips. "He already has."

"What? Why are you asking me about my honeymoon, then?"

She laughed and held up her left hand, a simple band there.

I'd noticed it earlier, but since it didn't have diamonds, I'd just assumed it was a ring she'd decided to wear on that finger. It wasn't anything like mine, but it was perfect for her, perfect for them. "Aww, I'm so happy for you. How did he ask?"

We talked about it for a while, and it was a proposal that was ideal for her. Our coffees were depleted, and we picked at the muffins until nothing was left.

"Where do you want to get married?"

She looked out the window for a long time before she ripped off another piece of muffin and placed it in her mouth. "The chateau."

We had been deep in the snow, a blizzard blowing around us, and she'd claimed to hear that bell. I couldn't hear it—but maybe I wasn't meant to. I gave her a smile. "It's perfect."

She nodded, emotion moving into her eyes. "I think so too."

We sat together in silence for a long time, each of us reflecting on the events that led us here. I came to Paris looking for a trip over Christmas break, but in the end, I would never return to America.

Because it wasn't my home anymore.

Fender was my home.

Magnus was hers.

All we'd had was each other—but now our family had grown.

"Melanie." Her voice changed abruptly, dropping a few decibels, turning serious the way it did before she reprimanded me.

I'd thought her dislike of Fender was resolved, but perhaps it wasn't. Perhaps she wanted to request that he not be at her wedding. I braced for the impact.

"I'm sorry...for the way I've treated you."

My eyes didn't blink. My body was still. I stared at her because I had no idea what she meant by that.

"You didn't ask for Mom to die. You didn't ask me to take care of you. I've resented you for the burden, but it was never your fault...and I'm sorry for that." She dropped her gaze to her coffee, like she couldn't look at me as she said all this. "I moved to Paris because I was tired of being responsible for you. I was tired of cleaning up your messes. I'm ashamed of that now, because if I'd just taken the time to help you grow into your potential, I would have seen what Fender sees. I would have seen your kindness, your compassion, and your bravery. But I was too busy resenting you to do that." She lifted her gaze and looked at me, her eyes a bit watery. "I didn't realize how deeply my resentment affected you...until Fender told me."

I inhaled a deep breath, feeling my eyes water, because that man was always there for me—even when I wasn't in the room.

"You've always been loyal to me, Melanie. You've always been loyal to what we both believe in. But I was too lost in myself to see that. If it weren't for you, I would have died a long time ago. If it weren't for you, that camp would still be running this very moment. If it weren't for both of us, the future would be different for a lot of people. We both played our parts, and I think it was meant to happen. I think we were meant to come here, end that camp, fix those broken men, and together, heal. We've lost the same thing that they have—family. But together...we've become our own family."

Tears dripped down my cheeks for the first time since my wedding. I didn't realize how much I needed to hear that to forgive myself, to find the closure my soul desperately needed. "I'm still sorry that I got us wrapped up in the first place—"

"Don't be." She looked at me with her own watery eyes. "Because I wouldn't change anything. I had to go through hell to find Magnus—but he was worth it. There's no one else I could ever be with. He was made for me."

I nodded because I completely agreed. "I forgive you."

She inhaled a deep breath. "You do?"

She hadn't always been as compassionate toward me, but that didn't matter anymore. "Always."

THIRTY
THE CHATEAU

FENDER

An arch in front of the entrance was covered in white flowers, the only decoration they needed. The chateau showed its weathered age, the color of the walls faded, cracks in some places. It was ancient, hundreds of years old, but her bones were strong.

Magnus stood in his tuxedo, his hands in his pockets, looking out at the landscape as he waited for his bride.

"This place looks like shit."

His eyes shifted to me. "We're spending our honeymoon here."

I cocked an eyebrow. "Really?"

"Yes."

I gave it another scan before I looked at him again. "Does it have AC?"

He smiled. "No."

"Alright, then."

He chuckled. "We don't need it."

"Apparently..."

He looked forward again, waiting for her.

"She let you keep it."

"It was mine before the camp." He turned around and looked at the ancient building behind him. "We're going to restore it. It'll take a long time, but we'll get there. Maybe we'll move here eventually."

My brother was clearly happy, so I was happy. "That'll be nice."

He faced forward again, his eyes squinting slightly in the sun.

When Raven escaped the camp, this had been where she'd disappeared. This had been her escape plan. While my men had combed the countryside in search of her, she was here, hidden from sight, right under my nose.

I understood why it meant so much to him.

"Can you do me a favor?"

"Anything, brother."

He reached into his pocket and pulled out a remote. "I wired the bells to this. When the priest announces we're husband and wife, hit the button."

I grinned and took it from him then clapped him on the shoulder. "King of romance over here."

He grinned back.

The priest walked up the path and joined us, the same one who married me. "She's ready."

A harpist began the quiet music.

Melanie came first. In a green gown with flowers in her hair, my wife was stunning, smiling at me like she was walking down the aisle to me all over again.

I inhaled a slow breath, loving her from a distance.

Damn.

She stopped on the other side of Magnus, holding an arrangement of flowers. Her eyes were on me.

Mine were on her.

When Magnus inhaled a deep breath, I knew he'd seen her.

I turned to watch Raven.

She wasn't alone. She pulled her chestnut horse by the reins, wearing a simple white gown with her eyes on Magnus.

Magnus smiled and released a quiet chuckle because he'd had no idea about the horse. I'd arranged for her to be delivered without Magnus knowing—and it worked.

I'd never doubted Raven's love for my brother, but now I could really see it.

She loved him the way Melanie loved me.

She stopped in front of Magnus, and I took Rose by the reins, guiding her to the side so she wouldn't step on anyone.

Their hands came together. Eyes locked. And the priest began the ceremony.

Her eyes were wet. His were too.

It didn't seem like they were listening to anything the priest said, so focused on each other.

I remembered that was how I was on our day. Just wanted it to be over—so she would be my wife.

"You take this man to be your lawfully wedded husband, for richer, for poorer, in sickness and in health, as long as you both shall live?"

Raven smiled. "I do."

"Do you take—"

"I do."

She smiled wider.

"I now pronounce you husband and wife. You may kiss the bride."

I hit the button in my pocket.

The bells started to ring.

They were just overhead, so they were loud.

Powerful.

Echoing.

Raven's entire expression changed when she heard that sound. Eyes watered, her face scrunched together, and she cupped her mouth as the tears spilled over. She completely lost it, succumbing to her tears.

Magnus cupped her face and kissed her. "Ma petite amie..."

The bells continued to toll. Rose petals were thrown into the air. Melanie and I clapped. The harpist continued the beautiful music even though it was barely audible over the bells.

Lost as they were in each other, everything else faded away.

Except the sound of the bells.

Ring. Ring. Ring.

EPILOGUE

THE ONLY SOUND WAS THE WIND.

It howled in bursts before it turned quiet once again.

The winter air was so cold that every window was frosted in the corners. A broken door creaked as it swung on its hinges. Snow was piled high between the cabins. Untouched by humanity, white powder was everywhere.

Boots crunched against the snow.

Vapor emerged from his nostrils.

Eyes bluer than the sky took in the sight.

A slow smile stretched across his lips. It turned into a full grin.

Every tooth visible.

Maniacal joy. Reckless excitement. Insanity.

He looked over his shoulder to the men behind him. Then he raised his arms in the air and turned in a circle, his boots kicking the snow aside. He dropped his arms and marched in the lead, heading to the abandoned opening between the cabins. "Here it lies."

New York Times bestselling author Penelope Sky pens another dark and suspenseful masterpiece.

Fender and Magnus have moved on from the camp. But someone else has moved in.

The Cult.

I see his wicked smile in the theatre. I see it in the apartment across from mine.

I see it everywhere.

Before I can run, I'm taken.

And when I wake up...I'm in the middle of nowhere.

The man who's taken me claims to be a demon.

And claims I'm his angel.

What happens when he finds out I don't have wings?

I'm not the only prisoner in this forest. There's a little girl too. Her name is Claire. She's beautiful, happy, wonderful. It's my responsibility to protect her--and I will give my life to accomplish that.

She says her father will save us both.

She says he's powerful, formidable, that he'll burn this entire forest to get to her.

I hope she's right.

*** Claire is unharmed throughout this story. There is no violence against children of any kind. ***

<u>Order Now</u>